Oh No! We're Gonna Die

HUMOROUS TALES OF CLOSE CALLS IN THE ALASKA WILDERNESS

By Bob Bell

Todd Communications Anchorage, Alaska

Oh No! We're Gonna Die
HUMOROUS TALES OF CLOSE CALLS IN THE ALASKA WILDERNESS

Library of Congress Control Number: 2006902661

ISBN: 1-57833-341-5 (hardcover)
ISBN: 1-57833-340-7 (softcover)

First Printed May 2006
Second Printing May 2007
Third Printing December 2007
Fourth Printing May 2008
Fifth Printing June 2009
Sixth Printing September 2010

Printed by Everbest Printing Co., Ltd., Nansha, China.

Book design: Mike Larsen, Todd Communications

This book was typeset in 12 point Georgia typeface.

Published by
Todd Communications
611 E. 12th Ave., Suite 102
Anchorage, Alaska 99501-4603
Tel. (907) 274-TODD (8633)
Fax (907) 929-5550
e-mail: sales@toddcom.com
WWW.ALASKABOOKSANDCALENDARS.COM

with other offices in Ketchikan, Juneau, Fairbanks and Nome, Alaska

DEDICATION

This book is dedicated to my long-suffering wife, Candace Bell, who over the years has resisted the temptation to terminate me as I put myself, her and our kids at risk in the Alaska wilderness.

ACKNOWLEDGMENTS

This book would not have been possible without the encouragement and assistance of a lot of people. Billie and Rae typed, edited and wordsmithed the rough drafts and turned them into legible documents. Candace spent hours checking for spelling and grammar. I also have to thank my hunting, fishing and flying friends for just going out here with me. Writing this book was a lot of fun mainly because of all the people who worked with me to complete this task.

PROLOGUE

After more than 30 years of banging around Alaska's wilderness, I can recall instances when I was fairly certain I was done for, or, at the very least, someone with me was going to bite the big one. All of these situations were impromptu and usually totally unexpected. They also involved some form of IQ-challenged decision often resulting in the utterance of the name of this book. There were a few exceptions along the way when people would comment, "If you go out there equipped as you are, you will probably get killed!" We didn't get killed, but the truth is, we probably should have.

Alaska has a full arsenal of ways to do you in. She can get you with weather; she can get you with terrain; she can get you with water and her most exciting method is to sic her critters on you.

Besides the obvious bears, we have had people rubbed out by moose stomping, wolf mauling, caribou impalement and halibut beating, just to name a few. When it comes to reducing the number of Homo sapiens in Alaska, there is no end to the ways our part of the country can devise.

I have personally had brushes with many of the techniques noted here and have so far avoided Alaska's best shots. So why do I stay here? Well, the place is spectacularly beautiful and full of wildlife. I have flown through Lake Clark Pass more than 100 times and I am still awestruck each time I see it. I have hunted and fished throughout Alaska every year for more than 30 years and still find new things to do in the outdoors. I guess the place is as wild as I want to be and as peaceful as I can get without being dead.

The purpose of these tales is to share the experiences, mainly for entertainment purposes. Those inclined to put themselves in similar circumstances without taking heed of my misfortune are most likely IQ-challenged anyway, so there is little or no value to these stories in preventing similar incidents.

With this in mind, the yarns herein begin with the early years of putting myself and my friends at risk, due more to naive ignorance than just plain stupidity. As you travel with me through the misadventures in this book you will meet several unique people, most of whom are still friends of mine, and most of whom are still alive (!) Therefore, I would like to introduce them to you in advance so that you will not be encountering strangers as you read each story.

CAST OF CHARACTERS

Uncle Rod is someone everybody likes right away. He is several years older than most of the other folks in the book. Uncle Rod is a very trusting guy and it got him into some trouble when he didn't check out the pilot before he stepped into the airplane.

Randy is Uncle Rod's son. He is a big burly guy with a heart of gold, just like his dad. He is also much too trusting to survive in Alaska.

Daring Don was one of those people who never should have been issued a pilot's license. He didn't understand that a good flight is an uneventful flight. He was always pushing the envelope. It finally got him and his two passengers killed.

Mellow Mel never quite got out of the 1960s. He is a great camp cook and an interesting conversationalist, but not much of an outdoorsman.

Alaska Les is the quintessential Alaskan. Raised in the small town of Hope, Alaska, he had eaten wild game all of his life and was very skilled in the Alaska back country.

Mad Man Murphy is the typical Alaskan pilot. He doesn't get into his Super Cub; he puts it on. The guy can make his airplane do things it was not designed to do.

Laid Back Deke was a walking definition of the term from which his nickname was derived. I don't think I ever saw him get excited. (I did see him quite scared at times, but not excited.)

Bad Burt is a very worldly and personable guy which is somewhat rare for a person born and raised in a remote Alaska village.

Good Ole John is a typical engineer. He loves detail and is blessed with considerable common sense. He approaches the outdoors with caution and respect, unlike the rest of us.

Crazy Carl was the manager of a huge food warehouse operation. His outdoor skills were minimal or non-existent.

Jittery John was a draftsman. He was new to Alaska and had an unnatural fear of bears.

Captain Gary was a U.S. Air Force officer stationed at Elmendorf Air Force Base in Anchorage. This guy can have fun in almost any circumstance.

My brother John is a totally free sprit. He has traveled through life with little worry or stress and very little economic success. He goes hunting and fishing whenever he feels like it. I often envy his freedom.

Fritz was a fellow Cessna 185 pilot. He described himself as Wasilla's oldest teenager. It was a very accurate description.

The Italian Stallion is a fraternity brother from college. He is a good friend, but somewhat excitable at times.

Deadeye Dick served on the Anchorage Municipal Assembly with me. He is a gun nut and owns hundreds of guns from .22-caliber pistols to machine guns. Filling the air with lead is his passion.

Bear was the president of the laborers' union local 341 for more than 25 years. He played hockey for many years and now owns a lodge on the Yentna River. He is a big strong guy, hence the name Bear. He is a good friend and would be a very frightening enemy.

Delusional Dave is an engineer who has worked for me for many years. He is also a hunting and fishing companion. Delusional keeps coming along on outdoor adventures, even though he was sure he was going to die on several occasions. He just keeps thinking it will go better next time.

The Caretakers are the various guys our acquaintance, Rocky, recruits to watch his lodge over the winter. They work for room and board only. These are not the first guys you would hire if you had a choice.

Ed and I grew up together and have been close friends for more than 50 years. He loves to hunt and fish. He is also a very good pilot. When it comes to bad luck he seems to corner the market sometimes. His wife Linda is one of his few occasions of good luck.

Pete worked for me as a manager and surveyor. He was an excellent jack of all trades. You could always count on Pete to get things done.

Billy is one of my best friends. He hunts, fishes, and flies whenever he can. Billy retired from the FBI after 25 years as a special agent. He is a long-time Alaskan and is quite comfortable in stressful situations in the wild.

Sam is a guy who loves the outdoors, but not the hardships associated with hunting and fishing. If he can find a way to participate in either activity with no effort or discomfort, he will go to great lengths to do so.

Raymond is a retired Alaska guide. He worked for Sam's construction company for many years. Raymond is a very accomplished outdoorsman. He is invaluable in camp and knows how to call or stalk any Alaska game.

Zoe owns and operates the Shell Lake Lodge. She is the quintessential Alaska woman- very self reliant, personable and a tremendous cook.

Scooter is the Shell Lake "ranger." He and his wife, Champagne Ann, are delightful people who always seem to be having a good time.

Kenny is the Shell Lake "marshal." He lives on this remote lake full time. If you need any kind of favor, Kenny will do it for you.

Dave the Torch is the Shell Lake "fire marshal." He got this title after over-imbibing one Saturday night and burning up the supply of firewood we had spent two days gathering for an Iditarod sled dog race bonfire.

Gordy grew up at Shell Lake. He is one of Zoe's kids. He has run the Iditarod a few times. A typical Alaskan.

Captain Curt is Kenny, the marshal's, nephew. He is a very physically strong guy who wrestled in the NCAA championships.

Vic is a third-generation Cordova commercial fisherman. He is a big, powerful man who loves to hunt Sitka blacktail deer on the rugged islands of Prince William Sound.

John was my surveying manager for awhile. He is an enigmatic person, so you never quite know what he is thinking.

Joe is a taxidermist who goes on hunting trips around the world.

Merrill is the son of Noel Wein, who built Wein Airlines, which evolved into the largest Alaska-based airline. Merrill is a top-notch pilot in his own right.

Craig worked for me as a surveyor for many years. He was not particularly safety-oriented, and therefore had more adventures than most of my employees.

Bernie and Vinco are both emigrants from Yugoslavia. They are very hard working and professional surveyors.

Fred is a long time Alaskan. He was a student at the University of Alaska, Anchorage, in addition to holding down a full time job. Fred flew a very small Taylorcraft.

Mark lived across the street from us. At the time he was an enlisted man in the U.S. Air Force. He enjoys the outdoors, but does tend to get lost a lot.

Scary Gary worked for me as an engineer. He was always coming up with plans that had high potential for injury.

Plano John worked as a contract engineer on the (U.S. Petroleum Reserve) Pet-4 project. He reluctantly got included in some of our activities.

Peter was a DEA special agent. He is a buddy of Billy's, but I am his idol.

Macho Jim is another long-time Alaskan. He has a cabin on Shit Lake near Mount Yenlo north of Anchorage.

Dandy Danny owns a popular bar in Anchorage. He has a very dry sense of humor. Dandy Danny does the best he can to live the good life and is successful in that endeavor.

Bob was a very good friend until his passing. He could tell jokes for hours and keep everyone laughing. He was also great at practical jokes. We all miss him.

Raunchy Rick is a radio talk show host who makes Rush Limbaugh look like a liberal. He also works construction and is quite an outdoorsman.

And finally, there's my family, who are not IQ-challenged like the rest of us. Candace (*aka* Ma Bell) is my wife and best friend. She has the good sense to have me heavily insured. She is also a pilot and hunted and fished with me for many years. Several years ago, she wised up and cut back considerably on the trips into the wilds with me.

Candace and I have wonderful kids. They are all intelligent, good looking, and personable. Christopher (Babu) is a medical doctor; Jennifer (JJ) is the mother of our 4 grandkids; Gretchen (Sissy) is the manager of a bar and restaurant in Girdwood; Frank (FT) is a sophomore at Alaska Pacific University; and Elizabeth (Betsy) is in high school and an actress.

TABLE OF CONTENTS

CHAPTER 1:
The Early Years—Combining Stupidity and Inexperience

NEVER FLY WITH A PRIVATE PILOT YOU DON'T KNOW

Uncle Rod is a good ol' boy who moved to Alaska from Oregon in 1974 or thereabouts. He is the kind of guy who will do anything for you. At the time of this adventure he was in his late 50s, a bit overweight and disinclined to get involved in strenuous physical activity.

He made his living as a sheetmetal worker, but had lots of hobbies, mainly having to do with home improvements. It seemed Uncle Rod was always building a wall, painting a floor or doing something of that sort. He was born and raised in Oregon and moved to Alaska much later in life than most who immigrate to the state. He is very easy to like and has a multitude of friends throughout Alaska.

Randy is Uncle Rod's son. Randy has always been a jack of all trades and was quite good at several trades having to do with construction. He manages to earn a good living at various jobs. Randy, like his dad, is easy to get along with in most every circumstance. He is a big strong guy, but at the time, had limited experience in the Alaska wilderness. Like his dad, he is a little too trusting at times.

It was moose season. Uncle Rod and Randy had made a deal with a fellow who worked with them whom we called Daring Don. They were going to go moose hunting in the Iliamna area at Kulik Lake. Daring owned a Cessna 180 floatplane. This is a four-seat, high-wing craft with a 260-horsepower engine. The payload is about 800 pounds. Daring Don was in his 30s and had been flying for two or three years. He fell into that category of Alaska pilots who had enough flight hours to convince himself that he was a much better pilot than he really was. This type of pilot accounts for a large percentage of the small plane crashes in Alaska. If this information had been available when I first arrived at the airplane, this story would have been very different and far more uneventful.

Rod and Randy's plan was that they would pay Daring to take them to the hunt area in his Cessna 180 floatplane and then he would stay and hunt with them. He was also supposed to bring them home, but that became a moot point. They were not aware of his piloting skills. They just figured if he owned a plane and had a pilot's license then he must have known what he was doing. They were soon to find out how wrong they were.

The flight down was uneventful, proceeding southwest along Cook Inlet to the Alaska Range. Upper Cook Inlet, where Anchorage is located, has slate gray water with some very fast tides. Several glacial rivers empty into the inlet with their waters full of rock flour from the grinding action of the glaciers. This is what gives the inlet its unique color. The water clears up as you travel down the inlet until it's the sparkling clear blue you expect from the ocean. The north side of the lower inlet is bordered by the Alaska Range. Both sides of the upper inlet are low rolling hills mostly covered in spruce and birch with some alder and willows in the clearings. It was early fall and the leaves hadn't changed color yet, so it was a sea of green everywhere you looked.

The Alaska Range near Cook Inlet is composed of several very formidable mountains reaching up to almost 10,000 feet. The glistening snow-capped peaks form a spectacular picket fence that thrusts out of the sea into the blue sky so dramatically that it just leaves you in awe of God's work. In this area there are vertical cliffs of pure granite rising over 1,000 feet.

The tops of the mountains are covered in snow and the flanks are bare rock or covered in brush and grass. In geological terms, this is a very young mountain range, so the valleys are steep and narrow. There are spectacular waterfalls, some of which drop 1,000 feet, turning small streams into a cloud of mist before they reach the bottom.

Kuluk Lake lies just on the other side of this tremendous barrier. Uncle Rod, Randy, and Daring Don had a pleasant trip in good weather. They were able to enjoy the view while they planned their hunt. After landing, the guys set up their camp in a spot about half way up the shoreline from the outlet of the lake. There was a stream nearby with both rainbow trout and salmon resting in the eddies. The campsite was in a small clearing surrounded by birch and willows. There were a couple of flat spots just big enough for the tents, but the rest of the site sloped down to the lake. The trees were somewhat sparse, so the campsite was not well protected from the wind. They were about 20 feet from the shore of the lake. The shore was a 3-foot-wide beach made up mostly of gravel and sand. The topography sloped up quite steeply from the edge of the camp to the top of the mountain. Therefore, the hunting area was a long narrow strip running along the lakeshore.

The next morning they got up before dawn, cooked breakfast and started their hunt at first light. They were working along the shoreline of the lake glassing the steep hillsides rising above them. The area was forested with some birch trees, but mostly alders and willows. It was a nice clear morning with blue skies and little or no wind. When the weather is nice, Alaska wilderness can be very pleasant. These were almost ideal hunting conditions. The view across the lake was spectacular, with the Alaska Range rising above the foothills that thrust up from the shore. Trout were rising to catch bugs on the surface of the lake and all was well with the world. Within an hour they had a bull spotted. He was standing on a steep slope not 100 feet from the lake. Randy dropped him with one well-placed shot.

He was not a huge trophy bull, but was certainly a good meat bull. He had a 40-inch rack with medium palms. They made short work of butchering him out and packing the 500 pounds of meat to the shore of the lake so Daring could taxi the plane right up to the meat. The pack was not bad. They had to work their way through some alders and a few willows, but the ground was hard and easy walking.

Things were going great so far!

Moose at Kulik Lake before Jimmy Carter made it off limits.. This is the lake we crashed on two year's earlier.

The plan was for Daring to fly the meat back to Anchorage and return to help them get a second bull. The fly in the ointment was that the weather was deteriorating quickly, so the plane left early in the morning to avoid getting caught in the approaching storm.

Daring told us later that he had a touch-and-go flight all the way back to Anchorage. The weather had continued to deteriorate. The ceiling was dropping and the wind was picking up quite a bit. Several times, he had to "run scud," the practice of flying around low-lying fog banks that can be quite exciting at times. Most pilots try to avoid this practice by better route planning, an unfamiliar process to Daring. In spite of himself, he arrived in Anchorage in one piece, more through luck than skill.

Good ol' Uncle Rod, being the nice guy he is, asked Daring to phone me when he got to town and invite me to accompany him back on the return trip so I, too, could share in the superb hunting. In the meantime, it began to rain like crazy at the campsite and the weather on the return route was getting progressively worse. Daring failed to inform me of any of this, but being the trusting guy I was at the time, I readily agreed to the flight. This was the beginning of a very short but stressful relationship between Daring and me.

Unbeknownst to me, Alaska was beginning to gather her resources to try and get us; she now had bad weather, difficult terrain, water and, of course, a pilot with the IQ of a tulip. The plot was thickening!

When I arrived at the plane I was perplexed that Daring Don had a Lake Hood tie-down. The Lake Hood-Lake Spenard complex is the largest floatplane facility in the United States. In the summer there can be hundreds of takeoffs and landings every day. Every inch of the shoreline is used for floatplane tie-downs. The average wait for a tie-down was about 18 years, hence my surprise that someone as young as Daring had one. He advised me he had figured out how to beat the system and was using a tie-down that belonged to someone who didn't fly anymore. This is totally illegal and should have given me pause, but not being up to speed on Lake Hood etiquette, I just blew it off. I did remark to Daring that the weather looked a little bad. He replied that he had just flown in from the camp a few hours earlier and it was no problem. (At least, none that he was willing to tell me about.) Like Uncle Rod, I assumed he knew what he was talking about and got into the plane.

First mistake.

We took off and began flying down the middle of Cook Inlet. This was a little unusual because flying in the middle of the inlet puts you right in the flight pattern of Anchorage International Airport (AIA), which can result in your playing *Frogger* for keeps with a significant number of very large and very fast airplanes. AIA is the busiest cargo airport in America. It also has numerous passenger flights of all sizes. There is a steady stream of planes from huge cargo planes to small Cessnas approaching this airport. These flights are vectored in by the tower mostly to the east/west runway. This puts the majority of air traffic right down the middle of Cook Inlet as they approach the airport. Daring's flight plan put us, in essence, going the wrong way on an airborne one-way street.

Another problem with Daring's flight plan was that if you have an engine failure, you are downed right out in the middle of some very treacherous water. Upper Cook Inlet has 15-knot tides that swirl past sandbars and rocks. This creates some exceptionally strong currents and rip tides that can tear an airplane apart in a matter of minutes. Competent pilots (a group Daring had not bothered to join) will avoid the inlet and fly along the shoreline for just these reasons. Again, I assumed he knew what he was doing.

Second mistake.

As we bumped along in the rain and low visibility, I couldn't help but notice the large number of other aircraft streaking over, under, and around us. I did notice one of the 747 pilots had a mole on his nose with two small hairs growing out of it. I also noticed he tended to spit on the window while screaming at us. After about 30 minutes of observing airplanes up close and personal we staggered out of the AIA flight pattern and headed toward the mountains. I was beginning to have some second thoughts about Daring's piloting skills, but decided to give him the benefit of the doubt. By the time we approached the Alaska Range we were flying in marginal weather. We had about one mile of visibility and a ceiling of less than 2,000 feet. Unfortunately, the mountains varied from 3,000 to 9,000 feet in this area. As noted earlier, these were mountains with shear cliffs that even a mountain goat couldn't navigate with any prospect of a long life.

Daring informed me he intended to fly up a small valley and through a pass he had found to get us to the lake. I could see the valley and noted that the top part of it was completely lost in the fog. It was flat gray in every direction due to the rain and the route he was proposing was almost black except for the fog. He said that was no problem; he had done this before... and lived to fly again. (There is an old saying - "there are old pilots and bold pilots, but no old bold pilots.")

My survival instincts were instantly wide-awake! Just how

much did I want to trust this clown? My experience, so far, was not inspiring. He was making life and death decisions here and doing so with limited data and suspicious intelligence. The hair on the back of my neck resembled one of those nail beds the guys from India lay around on.

I informed Daring that I was not in agreement and had no wish to accompany him on his "final" flight. I suggested that there were three options open to him: He could find another, safer route. He could drop me off at the nearest lake. I could beat him senseless and try to figure out how to fly a plane myself. He chose option one, the first good decision he had made to date.

After consulting the maps and some in-depth discussions about mortality, we decided to fly through a nice wide pass called Bruin Bay. This pass is more than five miles wide, with an elevation of only a few hundred feet above sea level. The area is low rolling hills covered in spruce and birch trees with numerous lakes and streams. The Native village of Kakhonak (population less than 100) is located on the Iliamna Lake side of the pass. Other than that, there are no people in the area, so if we crashed it would be awhile before anyone found us. With the low ceiling and limited visibility it was difficult to keep track of where we were (this was before the advent of GPS), but at least we were not dodging mountains in the fog.

In the next 45 minutes, Daring managed to get lost twice, which required that I study the maps and figure out how to get back on course. The only way I could do that was to look for a terrain feature such as a lake or a river bend and then try to find it on the map. This was made more difficult by Daring's constant whining about being lost. My confidence in Daring Don was dropping at an exponential rate. After several false trails and some very spirited conversations we finally arrived at our destination. The wind was blowing across the lake at 30 or 40 knots and the fog had the visibility reduced to a half mile or less. It was also raining like crazy, hardly ideal conditions for landing.

Now keep in mind this lake is in a narrow valley with very steep slopes raising on both sides from the lakeshore to more than 4,000 feet. The brisk wind blowing across the valley results in very turbulent air, which is not good when landing an airplane. Because of the terrain it was necessary to land crosswind in the very turbulent air and, to add interest, into two to three-foot waves.

Being a Vietnam combat veteran, I have had occasion to be frightened. This landing was one of the top two most frightening events of my life. I am sure I used a least a quart of adrenaline in the one minute it took us to land. Alaska could have easily done us in right then, but decided to wait and get us all at once. We had already demonstrated our ability to put ourselves at risk, so Alaska knew she would have ample opportunity to pick us all off in one fell swoop.

We found Uncle Rod and Randy in a sorry state, having endured 24 hours of driving rain and winds of up to 50 knots. They were soaked to the bone, their sleeping bags were wet, their tents were half torn apart, the temperature was 40 degrees (the ideal temperature for hypothermia), and they couldn't keep the fire lit. The camp looked like one of those Midwest trailer parks after a tornado. Other than that, things were just fine.

They strongly suggested we immediately get out of there. Daring noted that there was a cabin at the other end of the lake and perhaps we should fly down there to dry out. I reminded him that the wind was blowing like a hurricane, that I could spit farther than I could see in the dense fog and that the lake looked like the north beach of Oahu when the surf is up.

Daring said he flew in this kind of weather all the time (my respect for his opinion had long since dropped to zero.) We spent the next hour arguing over whether it was better to stay there and die slowly of hypothermia, die quickly in a plane crash or try to beat the odds and make it to the cabin. I am sure Las Vegas would have put the odds at 50:1 against us. In the end, stupidity overcame caution and I was outvoted. It was decided we would load up and take off for the cabin. We would return for the camp when the weather improved. It was a simple plan conceived by simple minds.

Mistake number three.

Alaska now had everything in place for a clean kill: weather, terrain, water, and stupidity. Since there was no back seat in this plane (Daring had forgotten it back in Anchorage) Randy was in the co-pilot seat while Uncle Rod and I sat on the floor in the back. I am sure the Federal Aviation Administration would have had a short but pointed comment on this arrangement, but they were not in the loop in our planning program.

The takeoff went fine... until we hit a big wave. There were several to choose from. The left wing tip went into the water. Daring responded by over-reacting and managed to then put the right wing in the water--enough to rip off about half of it. Following that, we went nose first into the lake. None of this was in the plan we had agreed upon. Something about mice and men came to mind. This was a bad thing, not only for the plane but also for us. Alaska was chuckling to herself. Now she only had to administer the *coup de grace*.

Randy and Daring both immediately jumped out of the plane. Uncle Rod was knocked goofy and didn't know which end was up, so he couldn't figure out how to get out. I stumbled out and went into the icy water up to my waist before my feet reached the floats. This was not a good situation. It was not even a bad situation. It was a catastrophic situation!

We were about a half mile or so from either shoreline, in some very cold water, and even though there was a small chance we might make it to shore by swimming, there was no way Uncle Rod would be able to make it. For all practical purposes he was a dead man. If not dead, at least Alaska could count coup on him at that point.

I recall thinking that if someone had to kick the bucket on this trip, it should be the idiot pilot. Alaska had knocked us to the mat and the referee was up to an eight count. The life insurance people were getting ready to type out the checks.

Then I remembered there was an air mattress in the plane: maybe we could float Uncle Rod to shore. I crawled back into the plane to retrieve it. By the time I got back out, the floats had popped back to the surface. That was the first good thing that had happened since Randy had bagged the moose the day before. We were now bobbing along in three-foot waves and 30-knot winds, with a broken airplane in the middle of the Alaskan wilderness. Things could get worse, but it was hard to imagine how! Randy commented that the pleasant day of hunting yesterday was becoming a dim memory.

We were soon blown by the wind to the opposite shore from our camp. Being on shore was good; no access to our camp was not. We set up a temporary camp in the alder bushes, using part of the wing and the air mattress as a roof. We got a fire started and warmed up at least a little. Daring sat in the airplane and sent out mayday calls each hour on the hour on the radio. We settled into a routine of manageable misery.

Toward morning a commercial flight crew finally made contact and said they would send help. Alaska had a good power-play going, but it appeared she had failed to score. That morning the wind changed direction and we managed to get the plane back across the lake to our camp.

Over the next four days there were several rescue attempts, but no one could get to us. The weather was just too bad, but not nearly as bad as the weather Daring had tried to take off in earlier. We enjoyed our camp of wet sleeping bags and torn tents. It is interesting how your values change with your situation. If Alaska wasn't going to win, she was at least going to make us pay.

On the fourth day the Kulik Lake Lodge people finally got to us by boat and transported us back to the lodge at the other end of the lake. We had an opportunity to dry out and get a good meal. It was the end of their season, so we helped them winterize the lodge. The next day we got a ride on a supply plane to King Salmon and a commercial flight back to Anchorage.

The following week I started flying lessons. If I were going to get killed in a plane wreck, I would do it to myself.

Fate finally caught up with our esteemed pilot a few years later; he took off from Lake Hood in icing conditions in spite of the tower warning him not to fly. Icing on the leading edges of the wings causes the airflow to become turbulent and the wing loses its lift, so the plane can no longer fly. Daring's plane iced up and went into Cook Inlet. They never found him, his passengers, or his plane.

Uncle Rod and Randy are still alive and well. But they are far more cautious in choosing a pilot. I have my own floatplane now, but fly only in good weather. The only good thing that came out of this experience with Daring Don was a healthy respect for Alaska weather when flying an airplane.

LOOK, A CARIBOU!

Caribou are funny critters. You find them in groups of one to as many as ten thousand. They never quit migrating and, therefore, tend to show up in odd places at odd times. They also tend to do odd things. I guess they just are odd.

I have come to this conclusion after 30 years of matching wits with these critters. They can find all kinds of ways to trip you up. Sometimes they can outsmart you by doing nothing. This is such a case.

I was hunting moose up in the Denali country with two friends, Mellow Mel and Alaska Les. Mellow was a sixties-type hippie and a deep thinker. He was on this trip to "experience the primordial feelings of the hunt." Mellow sold real estate, put business deals together and generally did what he could to make a buck.

Alaska Les was born and raised in Hope, Alaska (population 65). He was a civil engineer who worked with me and didn't consider moose hunting as a recreational pursuit. He considered it shopping for a winter's supply of meat. This difference in perspective made for interesting talks around the campfire.

We were camped on a small lake where we had been dropped off by an air taxi outfit. Our pilot was Mad Man Murphy. Mad Man had a theory that a Super Cub would fly with anything you put in it no matter how much it weighed. This made for some very exciting takeoffs. He scared us half to death every year, but I know of no occasion where he actually crashed a plane. There is nothing like a shot of adrenaline to start off a hunt.

Denali country is mostly open tundra with a few small patches of spruce and alder thickets. There are some small rolling hills, but it is generally very flat. As we settled in for the hunt, it was full fall colors with lots of reds, greens, and yellows--the typical Alaska postcard scene. We had encountered several bull moose in the first two days and had two hung up on the shore of the lake. We had collected these two bulls in the afternoon of the second day.

I was sitting on a small hill about two miles from the camp watching for moose. It was getting late, so I decided that after I had killed a hundred more mosquitoes I would head back to camp. Having accomplished my goal, I stood up to leave and noticed a movement in the willows a hundred yards away. I put my scope on the spot and saw it was a set of moose horns. He was lying down in the willows so all I could see was the top of his rack.

I was contemplating what to do as I peered through the scope when another bull walked into the scope picture. I could see all of this guy, so I just put the crosshair on his shoulder and fired. The recoil caused me to lose sight of the moose for a second, but I soon saw him running through the willows so I gave him another round and down he went. A few seconds later I heard Alaska yelling at me. He had been on a stand 100 yards away. I told him I had one down and he needed to come give me a hand. I had marked the moose down near a lone spruce tree among the willows.

I stayed put and began directing him toward the moose. He was about 50 yards from where the bull went down when he yelled he had found him. I said, "No, he is over by that spruce tree." Alaska replied that he was standing next to a dead moose that was still bleeding. I then began to wonder where the other bull had gone. I told Alaska to stay put and wandered over to the spruce tree where I promptly found number two. It appeared that I had shot the first moose and when he dropped the other moose jumped up and took off. Thinking it was the same moose, I shot him.

We now had two bulls down, it was getting dark, and we were nearly two miles from camp. It was one of those mixed-emotions situations. We were delighted we had meat down but not so happy we had so much meat on the ground this late in the day. We opted to get both moose gutted and propped open so they could cool and then make our way back to camp. We were concerned the grizzly bears would find the kills, but we were out of viable options.

As we approached camp in the dark of the night we noted Mellow Mel sitting next to a very large fire with his .44-caliber Magnum pistol sitting on the rocks next to the fire. We immediately deduced that Mellow was spooked by being alone in the wilderness at night and that we should make sure hc knew it was us approaching through the brush, lest we find ourselves on the wrong end of that pistol.

Bob with one of the two Denali moose.

We began yelling, "Hey Mel! We are coming in, don't shoot." We thought this would reassure Mellow. Instead it startled him and he grabbed the Magnum. Since it had been sitting next to the fire it was quite hot, so Mellow immediately let go of the gun, causing the barrel to fall into the fire.

Even when you are tired, it is amazing how a little adrenaline can speed up your reactions. I shot out of that brush like a cat with its tail on fire and kicked thc gun out of the fire. It landed in the tall grass so that none of us could see where it was pointed. The three of us then scattered like a covey of quail. We spent the next ten minutes wondering if the damn thing was going to go off or not. Alaska finally found the gun. We then had a short but intense discussion on gun safety with Mellow Mel, who was not all that mellow at that moment in time.

After a good night's sleep Alaska and I spent the next day packing moose meat down to the lake. It was a difficult pack because it was mostly through two-foot-high hummocks.

Mellow had made a deal with us before the hunt that he would not pack meat, and therefore he would not take any of the meat. Alaska and I had agreed to this, but as the day wore on Alaska became less and less sure that was a good deal. I spent the last few meat-packing trips talking Alaska out of taking vengeance on Mellow. We hung the meat on a pole at the opposite end of the lake from the camp, but no sweat: Mad Man could just taxi down in the float plane and load it up when he came to retrieve us. This would save us packing it another mile.

Things were now going quite well and we had settled in to a got-it-made frame of mind. We didn't really need any more meat, but we weren't due to be picked up for three more days, so we were satisfied to be just sort of hunting for a giant trophy--or nothing.

One morning Alaska and I had hiked to the opposite side of the lake from our camp. About mid-morning, we saw some animals a mile or so away. They were coming our way, so we just sat down and waited. It was a nice sunny day and we were in no hurry.

We soon realized that it was a small herd of caribou with one very nice bull in the bunch. We didn't have any caribou meat, so after a quick consultation we decided to take the bull once he walked within range. This was obviously a no-sweat deal: two moose on the meat pole and now a nice caribou walking right to us. We were on a perfect hunt. The sun was shining, the birds were singing, the fish were jumping in the lake. Life was good.

When the caribou were about a quarter mile from us they changed direction and started to move away. This necessitated a new plan.

There was a large swamp between them and us, and to go around the swamp would take too long. We assumed the caribou would be miles away by then. After an abbreviated planning session, we made a strategic decision: if they wouldn't come to us, we would go to them. We opted to cross the swamp and try to get close enough for a shot. (One trick in stalking caribou in open country is to walk directly at them with your arms above your head to imitate antlers. They think you are another caribou and don't spook.)

In the excitement of the moment we didn't wonder why the caribou had chosen not to cross the swamp. One reason could have been that they were smarter than we were, or at least more experienced with swamp crossings. We were soon to be much more informed on this subject.

At first things went well. We were making good time and the caribou didn't seem concerned with our approach. In fact, they seemed to be encouraging us. They had stopped moving and were just standing there chewing their cuds. I did notice that as we got closer to the middle of the swamp it was beginning to be more and more like walking on a waterbed. Soon everything within 30 feet of us was moving like waves on a pond, but we had a plan and pushed on without a second thought--in fact, with no thought at all. We had discovered long ago that we were not good at thinking and therefore tried to avoid it whenever possible.

What we didn't realize was that the "waves on a pond" were exactly that. We were walking on a thin mat of vegetation that was floating on water--dirty, deep water.

This became abundantly clear when I suddenly broke through the mat and went in up to my armpits. My feet were not touching bottom and I could not swim because I was wearing hip boots and had a rifle strap, with rifle, around my neck. I was grabbing at the vegetation trying to pull myself out, but it just broke off when I pulled on it. Panic had not set in yet, but I was becoming very concerned. I tried screaming and cussing to no avail. I was running out of options and ideas at the same time. Alaska was 30 feet away frozen in midstep with his arms still over his head and afraid to come any closer. I am not sure if he was afraid of me, or falling through the tundra. This was not a good deal except that I am quite sure the caribou were getting a good chuckle out of it. They just stood there and stared with bemused looks on their cud-chewing faces.

Alaska suggested he go back to camp and get Mellow Mel and a rope. I immediately vetoed that idea. I was sure he would end up falling through also, and then we would both be a great find for some archeologist 1,000 years from now. Also, I was becoming wetter and heavier by the minute. Swimming in this configuration is tiring. I was convinced that even if Alaska made it back to camp he and Mellow would come back and only find bemused caribou and my hat floating in a hole in the tundra.

After some discussion--and a few threats of physical violence (I still had my rifle), it was decided that Alaska would tie his shirt and pants together, then crawl on his belly close enough so that he could pull me out with his clothes. I can imagine how baffled anyone would have been if they had happened to fly over us - one guy in his long johns lying on the tundra while throwing clothes at another guy up to his armpits in the ground. Indeed, a strange sight.

Anyway, it worked, and after several minutes of struggling and cussing, Alaska pulled my muddy and water-logged body out of the hole. My clothes and my hide were now the color of peat moss from my neck down. My hip boots were full of muddy water and my disposition had soured considerably. Our perfect hunt was developing some flaws. We managed to slog back to the edge of the swamp without further incident.

The caribou, by the way, had watched this whole ordeal with much idle curiosity and had not moved more than a few feet the entire time. It was probably the best show they had seen in years.

No longer interested in caribou meat, we conceded the area to them and headed back to camp with me making squishy sounds with each step. There was very little conversation. In the course of our travels, we had ended up closer to the opposite end of the lake, so we decided to return to camp by the new route. We didn't realize that this end of the lake had a 10-foot deep, 50-foot wide stream running out of it. Upon arriving at the stream and assessing the situation we concluded we had two choices: walk the five miles around the other end of the lake or figure a way across the stream. Due to the fact that I was soaked to the bone, we went with the second choice. Once again we came up with a plan.

We yelled to Mellow who was still in the nearby camp contemplating the state of world events or wondering what a chair would look like if your knees bent the other way. We asked him to bring a rope and an air mattress. I'm sure you can tell the situation was most likely going to deteriorate rapidly; we had a dubious track record so far. Once again I refer you to our being thinking challenged.

The plan was for Mellow to throw one end of the rope across the stream and then pull us across on the air mattress. A simple plan for simple guys. This worked like a charm for the guns and the packs. I was next. Because I was already soaked, I just lay down on my stomach with both arms and legs hanging over the side for stability. The trip across was uneventful. In fact, I arrived at the other bank slightly cleaner from the elbows and knees down.

Alaska, on the other hand, was nice and dry and preferred to stay that way. He plopped face down on the air mattress, with his knees bent 90 degrees and both hands clutching the front of the mattress. Alaska and I are both engineers, so some stability calculations probably would have been in order, but we were in a hurry. He made it about 10 feet before the air mattress flipped over. We now had the air mattress riding Alaska across the next 40 feet of stream. By the time we got him on the bank he had built up a tremendous repertoire of cuss words. Mellow and I were both impressed! (even though Mellow wanted to know how Alaska really felt deep down.)

Having crossed the stream safely, we detailed our caribou adventure to Mel. He expressed his concern and sympathy by laughing until he was crying. I have to say that Alaska and I were a sorry sight as we slogged our way back to camp with Mellow bringing up the rear howling with laughter.

Mad Man showed up a few days later in his Cessna 206. He advised us that he didn't want to taxi down to the other end of the lake to pick up the meat because there were too many rocks in the water down there. He was worried that he would knock a hole in his floats. He suggested we pack the meat the mile or so up to this end of the lake while he took a nap. We noted that he was better off taking a chance on knocking a hole in his floats with the rocks than the sure bet that my 30-06 would put a big hole in his floats.

After amicable discussions involving several threats on both sides, it was decided he would taxi down the lake, but would not come to within 50 feet of the shore. We would carry the meat out to him. This involved going into the water up to our armpits to deliver the meat to the plane. It was still better than packing it a mile, and besides, we needed the bath. Mad Man then delivered us and our meat back to our trucks.

This took two trips. First the meat and then us. When we arrived back at the lodge Mad Man told us that our meat was in the smaller meat shed. He advised us that only our meat was there so we could just load it all up and be on our way.

We loaded the meat into both trucks and headed down the Denali Highway. After a short distance, we came across a Department of Fish and Game check station. We stopped and the game warden came out and looked in both trucks noting that we had two racks and lots of meat. He checked us off, took our names and other vital statistics, and sent us on our way.

We delivered the meat to the butcher. A few days later Mad Man called and asked what we had done with the meat. I advised him it was at the butcher's locker. He then asked me to call the butcher and inquire as to how many moose we had delivered. Upon making the call I was advised we had, in fact, delivered three moose.

It turns out there had actually been more than just our meat in the shed. We made sure the third moose went to the right guy, but I have often wondered how the conversation would have gone with the Fish and Game guy if he had bothered to count quarters.

It was more than a week before I could get all of the dissolved peat out of the pores in my hide. Mellow wandered out of the state to "find himself" the next year. We never saw him again. Alaska and I went on many more hunts. He ended up in California a few years ago. I can't imagine how that is working out.

DANCING WITH BEARS

There are a lot of bear stories in Alaska. Unfortunately, I have been an involuntary participant in several of them. I made a deal with the bears when I first got to Alaska back in the sixties: if they would leave me alone, I would leave them alone. The pact worked for five or six years. This story is about the deal-breaker.

I was hunting with Deke, a fellow pilot and a laid-back fellow. He owned an airplane that would be the ideal plane for a soccer mom who happened to live in a cabin in the middle of the Alaska wilderness.

The plane was an Aeronca Station Wagon, the SUV of the Alaska bush. Deke called her "Bertha." If you defined a Learjet as sleek and thin or even svelte, then Bertha would be short and thick, maybe even portly.

Deke was one of those detail guys. He had bought Bertha from an insurance company that had declared her a total wreck and paid off the previous owner. He spent two years in his garage totally rebuilding her from the airframe up. Several of his friends helped him in this endeavor and we were all subjected to Deke's almost fanatical attention to detail. Every little thing on that airplane was studied, tested, and inspected several times before he would move on to the next task. That is why it took two years to do a six-month job.

I was there with a crowd of his friends on a warm spring day when Deke took her up for the first time. To say he was nervous would be an understatement. It took him three hours to get up enough nerve to take off. We all breathed a sigh of relief when Bertha flew like a bird. Deke and Bertha spent many adventure-filled years exploring Alaska.

The other participant was Bad Burt, who claimed his ethnic background to be half Aleut and half Coast Guard. Bad was born and raised in a remote Aleut Native village named Pilot Point, located on the Alaska Peninsula.

Brown bears were no mystery to Bad. He grew up with bears. He was also imbued with a low tolerance for them due to a lifetime of bad experiences.

Deke, Bad, and I had flown down in Bertha from Anchorage to the west end of Becharof Lake to hunt caribou. Located on the Alaska Peninsula about 75 miles south of the city of King Salmon. Becharof is a large lake 30 miles long and half as wide. The trip from Anchorage to the lake took about three and a half hours. (Bertha is not only short and fat, she is also slow; my Cessna 185 cruises at 140 miles per hour; we were chugging along at about 90 miles per hour.)

Bertha on her maiden flight.

I have always enjoyed this trip. You go from urban Anchorage across Cook Inlet to a thick forest of spruce and birch trees on low rolling hills. There are huge expanses of open areas that look like giant lawns from the air. The fall colors are everywhere with yellow birch, green alders, red berry bushes, brown grass and multicolored wolf willows. It's amazing; 10 miles from Anchorage and you are already in a roadless wilderness. The most prominent feature of this area is Mount Susitna, also known as the Sleeping Lady, a small mountain that looks like a woman lying down with her arms across her chest. (The Native legend of this mountain says that a young woman from a clan of peaceful giants falls in love with a young man who is sent away to battle. He tells her to wait for him in their favorite spot. She falls asleep while she is waiting. None of the other giants wake her once they realize the young man was killed at war. The legend has it that she will awaken when peace returns to the land. Until then, people can gaze across Cook Inlet at Mount Susitna, the legendary Sleeping Lady and see her waiting for her lover's return.)

Once past the Sleeping Lady, the land begins to rise up to the Alaska Range. This is a spectacular mountain range dominated by several volcanoes. Mount Iliamna is one of the tallest and always seems to have a steam cloud in its crater--just to let you know it is still active.

As you continue west, you enter Lake Clark Pass, which is one of the most beautiful flights in all of Alaska. This pass has very steep sides with several large glaciers cascading down the slopes. Most of these rivers of ice break open as they come down the steep slopes. This exposes the turquoise-colored ice inside the ice column. When the sun hits this ice, it is just spectacular. The colors become almost fluorescent. This unique pass takes you through the Alaska Range to Lake Clark, a 50-mile-long lake, surrounded by mountains, located in the Lake Clark National Park. This has to be some of the most awe-inspiring scenery in the world. The snow-capped mountains thrust up into the clouds with Dall sheep perched on the rockslides and cliffs. The mountain flanks are covered in spruce and birch trees in their fall colors. Moose and brown bear inhabit the valleys. Caribou roam the low hills to the west of the lake. It is quintessential Alaska wilderness.

Once past Lake Clark you come to Lake Iliamna, which is an even bigger body of water. This is where the terrain begins to level out from snow-capped mountains to low-lying tundra. In the 50-mile flight along the shore of Iliamna Lake, you go from 8,000 foot, snow-capped mountains to almost totally flat tundra that stretches to the horizon. It's as if you have been transported to a different part of the world. (Back in the 1930s my father paid the villagers in this area the five-cent bounty the federal fisheries department had on trout. The theory was trout eat salmon eggs so if you thin out the trout you will have more salmon. I remember dad talking about using a 10-foot pole with a spoon tied to the end to count the fish heads that had been piled up all summer. A very smelly job, indeed.)

After another 30 minutes of flying time, you arrive at the Alaska Peninsula. This area is also generally very flat terrain covered by tundra. There are thousands of small lakes scattered across the area like freckles on a red-headed five-year-old. A few small rivers meander through the tundra with heavy brush along the banks. You can see salmon resting in the eddies as they make their spawning beds. Other than that, it is mostly just open country with visibility to both horizons.

As you travel south from King Salmon to Becharof Lake, the terrain develops more into small, tundra-covered round hills and valleys. Becharof Lake is where the foothills to the Aleutian Range begins. On the south side of the lake, the land rises up quickly while on the north side it is still quite flat. The higher terrain is both moose and caribou habitat, while the flat country is mostly just caribou habitat.

It was September, so the tundra was brown grass with patches of red berry bushes. Along the rivers the willows were yellow and the alders were green, with the snow-covered mountains in the background. It was quite a view.

While flying around looking for a campsite, we were surprised to spot two large bull moose where the Kejulik River flows into the south side of the lake. Since moose season was open, it was decided to postpone the caribou hunt. We would set up camp on the river delta and see if we could get the moose the next morning. This would be a big bonus for a caribou hunt. There are not a lot of moose in the area, so this was a very fortunate find.

It seemed like a good plan; pick up a couple of moose, ship them to town and then go caribou hunting. In hindsight we probably should have just stuck with the caribou.

Things started out great. We found a dry and level campsite on the river delta within easy walking distance of the moose. The immediate terrain was mostly round, basketball-sized and smaller boulders interspersed with sand, almost a moonscape without the golf flags. There were small patches of alder bushes along the river that emptied into the lake. The countryside generally sloped up on both sides of the river and was covered with low brush such as willows and blueberry bushes. The river was quite shallow and full of salmon swimming upstream to spawn. They were packed in like proverbial sardines in a can. It looked like a red tide except it was going up stream.

The spot seemed like a suitable campsite. Not a great campsite, but OK. We set up our tent next to an alder patch so if the wind came up it would act as a windbreak. (The wisdom of that decision would be called into question later.) We cooked a nice dinner and hit the sack. We didn't go after the moose right then because there is a law in Alaska that says you can't hunt until the day after you are airborne.

It was an uneventful night, and we woke up to a beautiful clear morning. The temperature was about 40 degrees, and a light breeze was blowing--ideal hunting conditions. We had a leisurely breakfast and then hiked up on a nearby hill and immediately spotted the two bulls. They were browsing in willows about a half-mile behind the camp on our side of the river. It was an easy stalk along the river using the willows and the riverbank as a screen. With relative ease we got to within 75 yards of the bulls without them having any idea we were there.

Deke and I each picked a moose, settled into a good rest, and Bad counted to three. Neither bull knew what hit him. When you're good, you're good. It was an ideal stalk, excellent shots and close to camp.

They were both nice bulls, with racks of 57 and 55 inches. They had not started the rut yet so they still had their summer fat. They both had wide palms with long thick brow tines and lots of points on each palm.

We took pictures, congratulated each other and then went into skinning and butchering mode. They say the fun part of moose hunting ends when you pull the trigger. With two big bulls down that is more than twice as true. We had 1,200 to 1,400 pounds of meat to deal with. It was a short pack with good footing so we had them butchered and packed back to camp by the time it was getting dark. With no trees in the area, we laid the meat on the alder bushes near our camp to cool. We then cooked dinner and retired to our tent.

We'd had a successful day and we were quite smug and content with our prowess as outdoorsmen. Most Alaskan hunting trips involve wind and/or rain, climbing mountains covered in tangled alders and the nasty spikes of devil's club and then packing the meat out through the brush and swamps. Of course, mosquitoes would be sucking you dry the whole time. This trip had none of that stuff. We concluded it doesn't get any better than this. At least it seemed that way. All we had to do was get up in the morning and ferry the meat and horns into King Salmon and then get on with our caribou hunt.

Anyone who is familiar with the Becharof area knows there is an abundance of brown bear in that vicinity. Brown bear make their living by smelling stuff. Their sense of smell is 10 times better than a dog, allowing them to smell moose meat from two or three miles away. Also, there were thousands of salmon swimming past our camp enroute to their spawning grounds, carcasses of which had been scattered along the banks of the river, due to previous foraging visits by bears. That odor was difficult to miss and another great bear bait.

The odds of us having a restful night's sleep were not very good. The good ol' Alaska elements were lining up on us. Of course, we were oblivious to the impending drama about to unfold.

We were just crawling into our sleeping bags when we heard something big outside the tent. It is amazing how alert your senses become in situations like this. After the first noise it went very quiet. Inside the tent all you could hear was both ends of our alimentary canals tightening up. Bad was breathing through his nose, which indicated he was not only scared, but also getting irritated. Deke was frozen in an odd pose with one leg in his sleeping bag and the other leg suspended in air. I was kneeling at the front of the tent about to zip it shut. It seemed like the whole world had stopped. I swear I heard someone cough in King Salmon 75 miles to the north.

The next noise we heard was when a bear bumped our tent while enroute to the moose meat. This caused Bad to become quite agitated. Bad doesn't think well when he is agitated. So he didn't think the situation through before he acted. He let his disdain for brown bears override his limited reasoning capacity. He stuck his rifle out the tent door and touched off a round. This caused Deke and me, who were not informed of the plan, to hit the top of the tent.

We had now gone from frozen in place to hyperactive. I was frantically digging out my rifle and chambering a round while giving instructions to the other two who were not listening to me. Deke was also digging around in his stuff looking for his rifle with his sleeping bag still wrapped around one leg. Bad was chambering another round fully intending to shoot the first bear he saw.

This was all taking place in a very confined space. The excitement inside the tent was minor compared to outside the tent, where the resulting chaos was breathtaking. The large boar that bumped into our tent took off, but so did several other bears that, unbeknownst to us, were in the camp. Two of them ran into each other and proceeded to duke it out.

Brown bear fights are very violent and awesome, but much more so when they occur within 10 feet of your tent in the twilight. The possibility of your involvement increases your focus and anxiety several-fold. In the meantime, two large cubs had gotten separated from their mom and were running around bawling like they were about to be dinner, which was a distinct possibility with some adult boars involved in the brouhaha.

This, of course, upset mom who promptly charged back into the camp to save her kids. She was striking out at everything that moved. We had bears running in every direction, fighting, bawling and generally panicking. In a flash, the situation had gone from uncomfortable to extremely precarious.

All of this was taking place just as it was getting too dark to see. The three of us sat in our tent back to back with rifles in hand watching in awe. An experience like this gives you a good look as to where you really stand in the grand scheme of things. In this case, it was obvious that we were quite low in the pecking order. Things settled down in a few minutes even though it seemed several hours, and all the bears retreated to the alders, which were just behind our tent. The tent location decision was now coming home to haunt us.

It was now dark, very dark. Once we had time to re-engage our brains, we deduced that we had several problems. The first and by far the most important was that the bears would soon be back and they probably would not be in a good mood.

They also would be focused on eating something. Seeing as how God had made us out of meat, we were probably on the menu along·with the moose meat. This was not good unless you're a bear.

The other problems in descending order of priority were as follows: 1) We had moose blood all over our clothes which were still on our backs or inside the tent with us; 2) We had put the backstraps and tenderloins in Bertha which, by the way, was made of fabric and now smelled of moose meat and 3) The rest of the moose meat was still stacked outside of our tent.

For all practical purposes, we were a smorgasbord for bears. All we needed was a sneeze shield. Another small problem was how to get Deke's sleeping bag unwound from his leg.

As noted earlier, bears have an excellent sense of smell, so we were sure they would make short work of locating everything that smelled of moose and immediately rip into it. Based on these deductions we realized we needed to come up with a plan fairly quickly or our situation would continue to deteriorate. Wrestling with a 1,000-pound brown bear or two for moose meat or our own flesh was not a viable option. We did consider just feeding Bad to them, but he still had his gun, so we set that option aside. It was now a battle of wits between us and the bears. Considering the circumstances, the bears had the advantage.

We didn't have time for a detailed planning program, so we went with the first thing that came to mind. Our plan was to build a large fire between the tent and the moose meat. We then put Deke in Bertha with instructions to turn on the landing light if he saw or heard a gun go off.

Poor ol' Deke was trying to maintain his laid-back composure, but I did notice his eyes were much bigger than normal, and he seemed to be sweating quite a bit. It is interesting to note that he had not expressed concern for the possibility of Bertha being damaged. Two years of nitpicking over her construction, and it never came to mind. He was obviously more focused on his hide than his plane. He went along with the plan, but in hindsight, I think it was because he was still in shock from the gun blast and the resulting chaos. This left Bad and me in charge, which had to be a step backward.

The new plan was for Bad and me to get our guns and flashlights and position ourselves between the tent and the lake. The only sound was the crackling of the fire and our pounding hearts. The rancid odor of dead fish, the musky odor of moose, the unique smell of bear and, of course, the smell of fear hung in the air like a thick fog. Every olfactory nerve in our bodies was working overtime. This was not a great plan, but we were dealing with limited brainpower.

It is difficult to doze off when you are pumping a quart of adrenaline a minute, so we were all pretty well awake when the first bear moved in on us. He didn't like the fire but he wanted that meat so he moved around to where the meat was between him and the fire and went for the brass ring. The games had resumed.

I fired a round and Deke turned on the landing light. Once again, there were seven or eight bears in the camp, all of which took off into the alders and stopped, maybe 100 feet away. It was hard to tell where they all were. The fire provided some light, but really just made everything look spooky. We could see them moving around in the alders, scheming. They were obviously planning a counter-attack.

We noted that they didn't panic like they did the first time Bad fired a shot. This was not a good sign. It seems they concluded that guns make noise, but don't hurt. Brown bears don't work in packs, but these bears must have had some wolf relatives. They sure seemed to be working together.

We were now beginning to realize there might be some serious holes in our plan. It dawned on us that, after the first inning, the bears now had our campsite and we were sitting on a couple of boulders on the lakeshore. Now I know how the British troops felt at Dunkirk. It was not a good time to be revising a plan, but we had to make some changes. The battery would keep the landing lights going for 30 minutes or so, and then the advantage would go back to the bears; besides, the light only covered a narrow part of the camp.

We didn't know what their plan was, but it was becoming obvious that it was probably better than ours. We could start the plane to charge the battery, but by morning we wouldn't have enough gas to get to the nearest fueling station. Also, the bears would still be there in the morning with enough light to hunt each of us down if we ran out of bullets. The bears were one move away from checkmate on us.

It was the old fight-or-flight situation. Do we jump in the plane and flee, leaving everything to the bears, or do we start shooting bears? Wounded bears in the dark are not a good combination for a pleasant evening or a reasonable life expectancy. We decided neither option was very attractive. We reluctantly went back into planning mode. Deke continued to defer to Bad and me. I think he figured we were already destined to be bear scat, so why fight it.

We came up with Plan B. We decided to put as much meat on the floats of Bertha as we could and Deke would taxi the 15 miles across the lake using his landing light. He would then unload the meat on the beach and return for another load. In the meantime, Bad and I would stand guard.

Sunset on Becharof Lake with Bertha & Deke.

This was a better deal for Deke than for Bad and me. Guarding moose meat in the dark with several bears in the area is stressful, and we were just about out of adrenaline and whatever it is that counters stress. It was only about 11 p.m. and it had already been a very long night. Another problem with this plan was that Becharof Lake happens to have several rocks that stick out of the water in this area. Deke would be playing pong for keeps with Bertha's floats. Knocking a hole in the floats in the dark could have a very negative result. His landing light gave him some help, but it was far from adequate. To say Deke was overwhelmed with dread as he climbed into Bertha would be an understatement.

It took three trips and four hours to ferry all the meat across the lake. I think Deke only aged two or three years in that time. Now, we needed to get our camp taken down and loaded up. This was a little tricky. We assumed the bears were mostly in the alders right behind the tent. Deke positioned Bertha so the landing light was on the tent, then Bad and I simply picked up the whole tent and all its contents and staggered back to the beach and Bertha. Deke stood by with rifle at the ready. We then disassembled the tent and took the camp across, leaving behind a bunch of unhappy bears.

We didn't set up the camp but just sat there the rest of the night, well away from the alders, listening to the bears raising hell on the other side of the lake. I think Deke still had that sleeping bag wrapped around his leg. Apparently the bears didn't like the idea of the meat being gone and were taking it out on each other. It made for a tense night, but Plan B actually worked. They say even a broken clock is right twice a day.

The next morning we ferried the meat into King Salmon and shipped it to Anchorage by commercial jet. On our final trip, we flew over the first campsite and could see the remains of a bear scattered all around the area.

Because there was no meat, they must have drawn straws and someone got to be dinner. We were glad it wasn't us. As we flew home, I reflected that this was a dance I never wanted to attend again.

ELEANOR CAN BE A MEAN WOMAN

When I first came to Alaska, I was employed as a civil engineer by a local consulting engineering firm. One of my fellow employees we called Good Ole John owned a 17-foot cabin cruiser that he kept in the quaint Alaska village of Whittier, a gateway to Prince William Sound.

Ole John was a very thin guy and somewhat prone to illness, but loved the outdoors even if it took him a few days to recover when he got home. He was, therefore, quite careful when he was in the woods, avoiding exposure to too much weather. Ole John was a typical engineer, very practical and analytical. He had lived and hunted in Alaska for many years.

This adventure was planned before the quaint Alaska village of Whittier had a small boat harbor, so Ole John's boat was stored in a warehouse. There was a guy who would trailer it to the water and take it out again for $25. Things were simpler in those days. No mooring waiting list, no slip number, no harbormaster. This adventure came about when Ole John, my next-door neighbor, Crazy Carl, and I decided to go deer hunting in Prince William Sound on a three-day weekend.

Crazy was the warehouse manager for the largest food broker in Alaska. He was a macho-type guy with a short stocky build and spent very little time in the outdoors. This was Crazy Carl's and my first Alaska deer trip and our first trip to Prince William Sound. Therefore, the survival knowledge pool on this trip was somewhat shallow. In fact, in Crazy's and my case it was pretty much dry. If there were such a thing as an Alaska outdoors IQ with 100 being normal, I would guess the combined IQ of the three of us would have been 102.5 with Ole John having 100 of those points.

It was 1972, prior to the Marine Mammal Protection Act, so there was a bounty on seals. You could get a $10 bounty and $15 for the hide. Our plan was to shoot 10 seals, which would pay for the trip and then some. As we embarked on this adventure we had both a financial and a hunting plan. What we lacked was a safety or survival plan. Alaska was looking at a gimmee on this one: two "cheechako" newcomers and a sickly guy venturing into some of the most remote land in the state.

Alaska had several weapons available in this case: seas that can go from calm to 15 feet in a matter of minutes; absolutely no infrastructure or shelter available; very unpredictable weather and a small boat with two dumb guys and Ole John aboard. I am sure she was counting coup on us as we confidently motored out of the quaint Alaskan village of Whittier.

Our destination was Eleanor Island at the northeast end of Knight Island, about 40 miles from the harbor. Prince William Sound is a spectacular part of Alaska. The sound has numerous islands, some over 100 miles long and 10 miles wide. It is a rainforest with heavy spruce stands and underbrush covering almost every square foot of ground. These waters are somewhat protected by the islands, but it can still get rough at times.

The trip out was enjoyable. It was a nice August day, the sun was shining, and the seas were calm. We stopped and caught some salmon in Long Bay and dug some clams along the beach. We were lulled into the mindset of a pleasant and uncomplicated three-day vacation. Why not? With the exception of Ole John, none of us had a clue about Alaska weather or for that matter much of anything else about Prince William Sound.

Anchored off Eleanor Island on a nice day.

Eleanor Island is a figure-8 shaped island with very steep topography and thick vegetation. It is about 4 miles long and 1.5 miles wide. The peaks go up to about 1,500 feet. When we arrived at Eleanor, we found a decent anchorage for the night. We noticed that there was a large rock sticking out of the water with several seals hauled out. They watched us with idle curiosity as we anchored up. They were not aware of our intentions to include them in our financial plan. Things couldn't get much better. We had fresh salmon and clams for dinner, the crab pots were set and, of course, the seals were close by to pay for the trip. We slept contentedly that night knowing all was well with the world. Ignorance is bliss, and we had an ample supply of both.

We woke to a beautiful 45-degree day with a light breeze and a few clouds in the sky. The seals were still in their languid mode on the rock. We considered them money in the bank. We had breakfast and went ashore in the skiff to begin the hunt. Ole John decided to walk along the beach so he would have easy access to the boat in case of inclement weather. His outdoor IQ was fully engaged. After a short conference in which we applied all 2.5 points of our outdoor IQ, Crazy and I opted to follow a trail up one of the many steep ridges on the island. This, in effect, separated the main source of outdoor IQ from the two wholly lacking in it.

We followed the very faint trail through heavy forest and thick underbrush about one mile to the top of the ridge, where we had a good view of several valleys and some clearings. This was an excellent stand so we just sat down and started to glass the area with our binoculars. It would only be a matter of time until a deer would step out into one of the clearings and we would shoot it. That was pretty much our plan.

After an hour or so, I noted a fog bank coming our way. Crazy and I both commented that if it got to us, our lookout would become inoperative and that we would go back to the boat for lunch and wait for it to pass. No big deal. We were only a mile or so from the boat. What's a little fog, anyhow? This is where the outdoor IQ would normally kick in, but we had already used up the little supply we had.

There is a rule about Alaska weather; never, ever trust it to do what you think it should do. If you trust the weather in Alaska, your life expectancy drops significantly. There is a reason for all the weather reporting stations throughout the state. We were about to get a very dramatic lesson in this rule.

Crazy Carl and I, both being somewhat new to Alaska, hadn't been briefed on this truism. Rather than return to the boat, we waited until the fog got to us and our visibility went from miles, to yards, to feet, to inches. Once we were fully engulfed, we decided to head for the boat. Remember, it was just down the trail a mile or so, through heavy forest and brush.

I suspect we retraced our steps for a few feet; there was really no way to know in the heavy fog. But after walking for much more than a mile, we still had not reached the boat or the shore. Realizing that we were not where we thought we were, and not knowing how to get to where we wanted to be, we decided to make a bad situation worse. We chose to go back to the lookout and start over. Nothing like following up a bad decision with a worse one. Then, to make it more interesting, it started to rain.

Now we were climbing through thick brush back up the mountain in heavy fog and rain. Of course, we never found our lookout or anything else that looked familiar. After a short discussion we came up with another marginal plan. We would just head downhill until we reached the shore. It would then just be a matter of walking the beach until we came upon the boat. Unfortunately, we wound up on the shore on the other side of the island from the boat. We figured this out after walking the beach both ways to discover vertical cliffs blocking passage at both ends of the beach. We now realized that, not only were we lost, but also we had no food or rain gear and we were, to put it mildly, screwed.

My first impulse was to run up and down the beach with my arms over my head screaming incoherently. Instead, I opted to stand in one place and chant, "man this is bad, real bad" over and over until Crazy slapped me a couple of times. Our relaxing, quiet vacation was now a major survival exercise, with the odds in favor of Alaska and her evil friend Eleanor.

By this time, we were both quite wet from crawling through the wet brush and the rain. We were tired and hungry and somewhat apprehensive. Standing in a downpour on the beach of a remote Alaska island soaking wet and lost is a bad feeling to say the least. It was getting dark and we didn't even have any matches to start a fire. The temperature was about 40 degrees--perfect conditions for hypothermia. Eleanor had us right in the crosshairs and was squeezing the trigger with Alaska coaching her. (One big lesson learned here was to always take survival gear with you no matter how short the hike.) We had no choice but to huddle under a tree and gut it out. Ole John would find us in the morning, or we would find our way back when the weather cleared.

Meanwhile, Ole John was wondering where we went. It was getting dark and he had no idea of where to look for us. The waters around Eleanor have lots of rocks sticking out of them, so cruising the shoreline in the dark was not an option. Ole John assumed we would build a shelter and he would find us in the morning, or that we had fallen off a cliff and he would recover the bodies in the morning. Either way there was nothing he could do that night. He didn't take into account our inexperience or that we were both thinking-challenged.

Ole John spent a comfortable night in the boat not all that concerned. At that time in my life, I was a skinny guy; Crazy had quite a bit more insulation under his skin. Both of us were wearing blue jeans, wool shirts, and light coats. Not much help when you are soaking wet. I soon became hypothermic and was shaking so badly I was bruising myself on the rocks we were lying on. Also, every time I moved I would throw up. Crazy told me later that he was sure I would not make it through the night. If he had told me that at the time, I would have agreed. Somehow, I did survive until morning. I was feeling so bad by that time, I was not sure survival was the best option. Only two years earlier I had been an Army officer in Vietnam standing in the 100-degree-plus heat fantasizing about what it would be like to freeze to death. Now that 100-degree heat sounded real good.

After a night that seemed to last at least 20 hours, dawn finally arrived. We saw that the fog had lifted to several hundred feet but the top half of the island was still covered. Of course, it was still raining. We were both too weak to start climbing again and were at a loss as to what to do. It seemed the only difference the daylight made was that now we could see the area we were going to die in much better. Spending the night cold, wet, and hungry had not made us any smarter. The term dead meat popped into my mind frequently.

To our great relief, we heard a gunshot on the ridge above us. It was Ole John. After a comfortable night on the boat, he had been looking for us for several hours that morning. We fired off rounds to let him know where we were. Ole John went back to the boat and motored around to pick us up. Boy, that boat sure looked good coming around the point. Crazy and I would have done a happy dance, but we were just too pooped. When Ole John motored up to the beach in the skiff his first question was, "did you get any deer?" We had used up all of our ammo firing signal shots, so instead of shooting him, we just said no.

Eleanor had missed her shot. She had us dead to rights and either lost interest or took mercy on the pitiful. Maybe she just wanted us to come back again and entertain her some more with our outdoor skills.

Once I had on dry clothes and had a warm drink I felt better, but it was more than a week before I fully recovered. We pulled anchor and steamed out of the bay with the seals watching impassively not knowing they had avoided being part of our financial plan. We just beat feet back to the quaint Alaska village of Whittier and caught the train to Portage and drove home. When I walked into the house my wife asked, "How did the hunt go?"

"Eleanor almost bagged us," I replied.

TOUGH GOING ON TUSTUMENA

Tustumena Lake is a large body of fresh water on the Kenai Peninsula in Southcentral Alaska. It has a well-deserved reputation for sudden changes in weather and big waves. From all the stories I have heard about this lake, I am sure the bottom of the lake is covered with the bones of unlucky and careless Alaskans. One of the problems with this 26-mile-long aquatic wonder is that the road only goes to one end of the lake; therefore, the only access to the rest of the lake is by boat, floatplane or shank's mare.

I planned to hunt moose at a place called Bear Creek, which is near the end of Tustumena farthest from the road. Jittery John, a draftsman who worked with me and was a cheechako, reluctantly agreed to come along. He was not well versed in the outdoors and he was very skittish about bears. Being a long-time Alaskan (almost two years) I assured him there were no bear problems where we were going. The dummy actually believed I knew what I was talking about.

First day at Bear Creek when things were still calm & pleasant.

I owned a flat-bottomed Smokercraft riverboat with a very old 55 HP Mercury outboard that ran on occasion. Jittery and I towed the boat to the end of the road where we loaded up the camping gear and headed out on the lake. It took us about three hours to get to Bear Creek due to the motor quitting several times, but it was nice weather, so no big deal. Even though to most people it would have been a warning, to us it was just an inconvenience. As they say, ignorance is bliss, so we were quite happy. Tustumena was being nice. Of course, she was just setting us up.

We made camp at the mouth of Bear Creek that evening and caught some salmon for dinner. Again a warning. If it is easy for you to catch salmon where you are camped, it is also easy for bears to catch salmon there. In other words, not a good place to camp. Also the name of the creek should have been a clue. So we weren't clueless, we just didn't know how to recognize a clue. We neglected to heed this warning or even know that it was a warning.

That night we had several very large visitors who not only kept us awake and alert but also helped themselves to our food, bit a hole in our gas can and tipped over our boat. We were left with some freeze-dried food, half a can of gas, permanent finger imprints in the pistol grips of our guns and a new appreciation for the science of picking campsites. This was an unfortunate turn of events, but in retrospect, it was to be a minor bump in this trip's odyssey.

Undeterred and still relatively stupid, we rose at first light and promptly went moose hunting. The easiest walking was to just follow along the creek bank as it meandered up into the mountains. The problem was that the creek bank was mostly grass, which was shoulder to head high. We considered this a problem because it was difficult to see very far, so it would be hard to spot the moose. We also wondered about all the salmon carcasses that were strewn along the bank--how did those fish get so far from the water? There was a nice, well-worn trail through the grass, so we pushed on occasionally wondering what made this nice trail. We were still in the ignorant and blissful mode.

The fish and trail questions were suddenly and dramatically answered when two grizzly bears stood up just 20 feet in front of us, causing all bliss to immediately disperse. With the high grass we could see them when they stood on their hind feet, but could not see them when they were on all fours. We were playing a high stakes game of hide-and-seek in the tall grass with us having much higher stakes than the bears. In fact, the bears may have considered us steaks. As I saw it, the bears could win or we could not lose. There was no way we could win.

Each time the bears stood up, we would duck and when they were on all fours we would retreat further down the creek. Problem was they were going the same way we were going, so we were not getting the separation we wanted. In fact, they were gaining on us. The bears also seemed to be getting more and more agitated with the game and with us. Grizzlies are not known for their tolerance. We finally came to a large birch tree and we set a new world record in tree-climbing. By the time we reached the top of the tree, there was a smoldering pile of birch bark shavings at the bottom, near where we had left our guns.

The bears arrived shortly thereafter, and in perfunctory manner tore our backpacks all to hell and moved on. Our situation had now improved to being up a tree with the bears between us and camp, somewhere in the tall grass. Not a big improvement, but a temporary respite from playing hide and seek for keeps. Logic suggested we not follow down the creek but go up the hillside and make our way back to camp with a much better view. Never having tried logic, we figured, why not? Jittery seemed a little distracted but still responded when spoken to.

This meant fighting our way through 200 yards of alder and devil's club, which was no fun but better than bear wrestling. Once we got through the brush it opened up into a birch forest with good visibility, so we began side-hilling our way back to camp. Other than bears tearing up our camp and chasing us up a tree, things seemed to be going well so far!!

Partway back we spotted a bull moose on the other side of the creek. Our situation now having improved from very precarious to just risky, we opted to go back to very precarious. We immediately charged down the hill, back through the alders and devil's club, across the creek and promptly shot the moose. We now had 1,000 pounds of bear bait on our hands. We skinned and butchered the bull and took turns packing meat to the boat and guarding the kill. The packing was relatively easy due to the ample supply of adrenaline. The bears didn't make an appearance. I am sure they were just waiting for darkness. They also needed time to digest all of our food.

Now we were at our campsite, with salmon flopping all over

the place, 600 pounds of moose meat stacked in the boat, and at least two grizzlies in the grass nearby biding their time. Everything we had--except our sleeping bags and the tent--had been torn up by the bears and we were out of food, the last of which was in the backpacks. Jittery kept looking at me like a bomb disposal technician wondering if he should cut the red wire or the blue wire. He knew something bad was probably going to happen. He just didn't know what it would be or what to do about it.

We reflected on our situation for awhile (30 seconds) and figured it was time to go home. Now this is where the story gets exciting. Our trials and tribulations to date were about to be relegated to humorous footnotes to the truly perilous part of this story.

We loaded all the torn-up camping gear into the boat. With the moose meat, the gear and us, we had about six or eight inches of freeboard. No sweat! It was a nice day with very little wind. If the motor kept quitting, we could just paddle to shore, fix it, and move on. Anything was better than having to duke it out with the bears. Jittery was beginning to fidget a little and seemed more distracted. I am sure Tustumena was rubbing her hands together. "I got em' now," she muttered.

Once we got going, it dawned on us that we probably didn't have enough gas to travel around the shoreline due to the bear bite in the gas can. It was much shorter to just run across the middle of the lake. Tustumena is five miles wide at this point, but the lake was almost dead calm, so why not? We had already survived hide-and-seek with the bears. What could be worse than that? With the total confidence that comes with complete ignorance, we changed course and set sail across the lake.

The bliss was back as we neared the middle of the lake. Then the motor quit. I tried to start it for some time to no avail. I pulled off the cowling and began to tinker with stuff. Jittery was starting to make small high-pitched noises. Other than that, he seemed to be taking it all quite well. I noticed a hole in the fuel line and, in true Alaska tradition, duct-taped it. The engine started right up. Got it made now!

Jittery pointed to a rainsquall that was coming down the lake toward us. Well, bummer. We might get rained on. No big deal. See what I mean about complete ignorance?

We were probably between one and two miles off shore when the wind and rain slammed into us. The lake went from calm to three-foot waves in less than a minute. We had no choice but to turn into the wind and head to shore. We were in a flat-bottomed boat with six inches of freeboard and an unreliable motor, slamming into three-foot waves two miles offshore. Suddenly, we were back to very precarious on a whole different plane. Once again, the bliss evaporated. The bear wrestling was beginning to look like a safer activity. Jittery was now the color of new snow and was sweating profusely. I was beginning to be concerned for his mental state.

I was trying to keep control of the boat; Jittery was bailing like crazy because some of the waves were breaking over the bow and the rain was coming down in buckets. With the flat bottom, each wave we hit felt like we had been dropped from 10 feet on to concrete. Jittery was losing the battle with the water and was starting to hyperventilate. I pulled the plug in the back of the boat and water was going out as long as I could keep the speed up. Of course, that increased the shock of each wave. I also noticed a piece of duct tape fall out of the engine. On the "concern for your well-being scale"--with crossing the street being at one and having Hannibal Lector as your roommate at 10--we were definitely at 9 or more!

Jittery was losing the bailing battle, so he opted to throw out all the camping gear and the moose horns. The camping gear had little value in its bear-eaten state, but that was a nice set of horns.

I was also trying to figure out what we would do when the motor quit, as it most assuredly would. We spent the next year or two (seemed like) in this state of frenzied activity, with the threat of motor failure looming over us the whole time. That piece of duct tape kept swirling around in the little whirlpool behind the motor shaft, almost as if reminding me that it was no longer on the fuel line. I noticed that Jittery had gone from nervous to just short of total panic. I was calm but had to yell a lot to reassure Jittery.

For some reason the motor gods were asleep and the old Mercury kept running. As we approached the shore, the boat had about a foot of water in it, the freeboard was down to half, and Jittery was about used up physically and emotionally, but it appeared we were going to make it. Nice try Tustumena!

That is when the motor god woke up. Just as we reached where the waves were breaking, the motor quit. The boat immediately turned sideways to the waves and the next wave flipped us over. I landed in about two feet of water and was rolled up in a ball by the next wave and deposited on the beach.

Jittery's experience was just as delightful. He did some sort of inverted body surf thing. It was quite impressive. Once we reoriented ourselves, we managed to get the boat turned right side up, but the waves breaking over the stern soon filled it with water. We were already soaked, so we just waded in to retrieve the guns and the moose meat. We were not dead, so things were looking up! We were a wet, sorry looking mess sitting on the beach in the rain.

The day had gone from scary to a real pain in the butt. The storm blew over in an hour and the lake calmed back down, its work having been completed. Even with new duct tape we could not get the motor restarted, probably due to its being under water for so long. So we bailed out the boat and loaded up the wet, sand-covered meat and pushed the boat along the shoreline the three or four miles back to the road. We arrived in the dark, soaking wet and exhausted. Moose hunting in Alaska can sure be an adventure. I could tell by Jittery's body language that he probably would not accept another invitation to go hunting for anything in the near future. In fact, I found him to be somewhat uncommunicative on the ride back to Anchorage.

That moose meat was the toughest eating of any moose I've ever had. Seems appropriate.

WHITEOUT CONDITIONS IN AUGUST-- NAW, CAN'T HAPPEN

Captain Gary and I were putting together our first sheep hunt, which would take place on a slab of ice called Eureka

Glacier. Captain Gary was a supply officer at Elmendorf Air Force Base in Anchorage. He was a big, boisterous fellow, but was somewhat new to the outdoors and quite new to Alaska. Nothing scared him, not even all of Alaska's weapons. Captain Gary was a guy who knew how to enjoy himself.

An example of Captain Gary's ability to have fun took place the year before this adventure. The State of Alaska had decided to open Ship Creek in downtown Anchorage to king salmon fishing after many years of being off-limits to fishing. The season was to open at exactly midnight on a Friday night. Captain Gary, a fraternity brother of mine named Rich, AKA The Italian Stallion, and I elected to participate. We arrived at Ship Creek about 11:30 p.m. after consuming an appropriate amount of beer for an occasion of this import. There was a huge crowd of anglers lining both banks of the creek, shoulder to shoulder, waiting for midnight.

After a somewhat incoherent conversation, we concluded we didn't want to participate in this exercise in combat fishing after all. Besides, there was no room left along the bank. Captain Gary then crawled up on a 10-foot-high rock on the edge of the stream to observe the scene. We didn't see how he could cause any trouble up there. He had a six-pack of beer and a bag of corn chips, so he was well supplied. The Stallion and I retired to the rest of the beer.

At about 5 minutes to midnight, we observed Captain Gary rise to his feet and put his hand to his mouth as if to make an announcement. Then from his perch on the rock we heard him yell, " FISHERMEN, WET YOUR LINES!!!!!" A thousand fishing lines hit the water five minutes early. The fish and game guys unsuccessfully pursued Captain Gary through the crowd by following a trail of corn chips until it ran out. They finally decided to cut their losses and gave up on him. Shortly thereafter, The Stallion and I ran out of beer so we gathered up Capt. Gary and went home. Now, back to our sheep hunt.

We had hired a bush pilot to fly us to the foot of the glacier in his Super Cub, and then we planned to climb up the ice for 10 miles and shoot some sheep. Seemed like a simple and straightforward plan. Most of our plans start out that way.

The pilot's landing strip at the glacier was about 2.5 inches longer than he needed to land and take off. He explained that, once he left, we needed to roll a large rock onto the strip so other pilots couldn't land. He also suggested we roll it back off before he came to pick us up. Needless to say, the landing used up quite a bit of adrenaline before we even started up the glacier.

Eureka Glacier is a chunk of ice 12 miles long and four miles wide nestled in the Chugach Mountains 80 miles north of Anchorage. The area around the glacier is steep country with sheer rock faces and scree slides. It is very difficult country to hunt or just stroll around.

Eureka Glacier without the storm.

The view is fantastic and the silence is so pure you can hear a kind of ringing sound in your ears. You sit up on the top of that glacier for a few hours and realize how big the world is and how small you are. The trip up was exhausting because we had to keep climbing down off the ice to get around crevasses in the glacier. There were only a few places you could do this because in most places it was impossible to get off the glacier and still be alive.

When we did find a way off the ice, we found ourselves walking on a thin layer of ground-up rock spread over ice. In most places this combination of rock and ice was on 30-to 40-degree slopes. To say the footing was extremely difficult would be an understatement. It was the old scramble up three feet and slide back two. With the added convenience of a pack on your back this exercise can grow old after a few hours. It soon became clear my army combat boots were an unfortunate choice. You need to keep in mind we were both fairly new to Alaska and this was the first sheep hunt for both of us.

To give you some idea of how prepared we were, you only have to consider my gear. I had a wood and canvas military backpack with an army duffle bag tied to it. As noted earlier I was wearing my old combat boots from Vietnam. Now top that off with blue jeans, cotton shirt, army field jacket and a baseball cap. Captain Gary was not outfitted nearly as well as I was. Mister L.L. Bean would have cast a disapproving eye on us.

After considerable trial and tribulation we did arrive at our campsite in the late afternoon of August 9, the day before the opening of sheep season. We chose to camp at the mouth of a valley a few hundred yards off the glacier. There was a small stream for water and some big rocks for shelter from the wind. We had a good view of two large drainages on the other side of the ice. This would allow us to glass for sheep at our leisure. We made camp and then went scouting.

It was a nice sunny day and we had several hours of daylight left. We weren't more than 100 yards from camp when we spotted a very large mountain goat on the rocks above us. I swear he was big enough to saddle up and ride. It would have been impossible to get to him if we shot him, and if he fell, he would have had a 200-foot freefall. We opted to pass on him. It is very unusual to see a goat in this country. We were sure this was an omen of good things to come.

We crawled back up on the glacier and headed to the top. Most glaciers have a streak of rocks that generally run down the middle and either side. We got on the middle strip of rock and it was like walking on a sidewalk. We had a leisurely stroll up the glacier.

A mile or so above camp, we spotted two very large rams on a hillside. The rams were halfway down the steep hillside that terminated at the edge of the ice. There was no way we could cross the glacier without the sheep seeing us. We concluded that we needed to come back the next day before daylight and cross the ice to the hillside and then wait for the sheep to come down for breakfast. It would then just be a matter of shooting them and heading for home.

Off we went, back to camp full of confidence and thinking there is not much to this sheep hunting. Our friends who had advised us of the rigors of sheep hunting obviously were wimps. We were going to come home with two 40-inch rams and no pain or strain. We did note that it was beginning to cloud up a bit.

The next morning we awoke to a very heavy snowfall. (Remember, it was August 10.) It hadn't snowed on the arctic coast yet, let alone Southcentral Alaska. The visibility was about 10 feet, so we just stayed put in the very small tent. There was no way we could spot sheep in that weather. It snowed all that day and that night, and the next day and night. There was now more than a foot of snow on the ground.

On the third day, the wind came up and it went to whiteout conditions. We came to the conclusion that we needed to get the hell out of there. We were not outfitted for winter camping and we were 10 miles away from, and about 4,000 feet above, the airstrip. This far above the vegetation line there was nothing to burn and we had used most of our stove fuel.

It was becoming more and more difficult to keep from getting chilled. Hypothermia was a real concern. With the heavy fog and snowfall we couldn't see more than a few inches. This was not a good situation.

With 20/20 hindsight we should have just waited it out and been late for the bush pilot pick-up. Unfortunately, all we had was legally blind foresight. And, of course, we were invincible. Besides, we had spent about as much time as possible cooped up in that tent without a death being involved. Captain Gary also noted it would be easier going downhill. Boy, was he wrong.

We realized it would be a tedious trip so we left most of our stuff behind. We just took the tent, sleeping bags, guns, two meals of freeze-dried food, one pack board and a pot. We tied ourselves together, in case one of us fell in a hole or down a crevasse. I guess we figured if one of us had to freeze to death at the bottom a crevasse he might as well have some company.

There was an ominous feeling as we started on our journey. Due to the total lack of visibility, the going was very slow. You would take a step, make sure your foot was on something solid, and then take another step. All we could do was make sure we were headed downhill. We also needed to stay on the rock strip that was now under the snow, which required some guesswork as to its location. Other than that, we had no idea of where we were or where we were going. We were about five feet apart, but could not see each other. In fact, we couldn't see our own feet. We were really having fun. Captain Gary was uncharacteristically quiet.

It was a surreal experience, walking along with no depth perception--for all practical purposes, blind--knowing there were crevasses in our path. We also had to be concerned about tripping over rocks and ice chunks, falling off the glacier, and just slipping on the ice.

Captain Gary was in front of me when he stepped into a deep crack and wedged his foot tightly in place. He yelled for me to stop. I stopped, got down on all fours, and crawled over to him. It took us a few minutes to get his foot free. We were cold, tired, confused and lost. We had only been going for about 2 hours at this point. Things could have been worse, but I am not sure how. As we rested there, we realized that the crack he had been stuck in was a piece of ice that had cracked away from the wall of a crevasse that was six feet wide and probably several hundred feet deep. One more step and Gary would have been down the tube with me tied to him.

We hyperventilated for a few minutes and then set about figuring how to get around the crevasse. We determined it was six feet wide by throwing the rope until it hit the other side. We couldn't see that far so we knew it was six feet, but had no idea what was on the other side. Climbing off the glacier was not an option because of the steepness and vertical walls. Therefore, our plan was to tie the rope to me, tie the other end to Captain Gary who would dig in as best he could, and I would jump across. Jumping six feet is no big deal unless you are doing it blind and your life depends on getting to the other side.

If I didn't jump soon enough, I would step off into space and if I jumped too soon, I wouldn't reach the other side. The situation's potential for disaster was far greater than its potential for success. We considered turning back, but the chances of our finding the camp were between slim and none and Slim had left town.

I had Captain Gary stand up right next to the edge, hoping

I would be able to see him just before I jumped. I paced off 15 feet, said a short prayer, and took off running. I never saw Captain Gary but after 5 strides I jumped---.

It seemed I was airborne for 2 or 3 minutes. I landed on the other side, on my face. I have never experienced such reassuring pain. Now, it was Captain Gary's turn. He went through the same process, with far less fanfare, and we were across. It was probably 15 degrees Fahrenheit, but we were both sweating profusely. We were beginning to see why our friends had warned us that sheep hunting can be hard on you. Maybe they weren't wimps.

From our trip up, we knew the next crevasse was too wide to jump across, so when we came to it, a few hours later, we opted to camp for the night. Climbing off the glacier would not be fun, or conducive to a long life, in these conditions. We were betting on better conditions tomorrow.

Spending the night lying on ice with no ground cloth or air mattress is not recommended. At the beginning of the night, the hard cold ice under you makes it quite uncomfortable. By the middle of the night, your body heat is melting the ice under you and renders your sleeping bag wet and of little use for staying warm. You then go from uncomfortable to just plain miserable. This makes the night last 20 or 30 hours, at least. I can't say I woke up refreshed.

The next morning we got our first break. The fog lifted, giving us a 100-foot ceiling and good visibility. Captain Gary was used up by this time. He decided that we should just stay where we were until somebody came to rescue us. I simply grabbed the end of his sleeping bag and shook him out of the conglomeration of goose down, nylon, and water. We shared a package of cold freeze-dried pork and beans with water and started down the trail. We managed to get down off the side of the glacier and around the crevasse without killing ourselves. I am not sure how. The point at which we were forced to get back up on the ice was problematic and resulted in a couple of falls, but no serious injury. Once back on the ice, we took full advantage of the visibility and made it to within a half mile of the landing strip before it got dark.

We camped again on the ice, with all of its comforts, and woke up to a clear sky. If we had just waited one more day... The last half mile was uneventful.

The pilot arrived about an hour after we got to the abbreviated landing strip where we had removed the rock. He found a sorry looking pair, wet, tired, banged up, hungry and totally OJT'd on sheep hunting. He said he had never seen such a storm so early in the year and that they had been worried about us. (We had only paid half down for the flight.) He then suggested that the weather was so nice now that we should go back up and see if we could get a sheep; he'd come back and get us in a week. We declined. We did let him know, however, that his next hunters would have quite a bit of camping gear available to them that they would not have to pack in.

I didn't even mind the takeoff on the super short runway. Neither Captain Gary nor I went sheep hunting again for several years.

NELCHINA CARIBOU NUTCASES

Years ago, several Anchorage radio stations would announce the Nelchina caribou herd crossing at the Lake Louise Road. At the time of this adventure, the Nelchina herd population was about 30,000 animals. They migrated from the Canadian boarder to the Lake Louise area and back each year. This usually put them crossing the road in mid-winter.

When we heard these announcements, we would make the three-hour drive from Anchorage to the road and shoot a winter's supply of caribou and then drive home again. It made for a long day, but with the five caribou limit per person, it was always productive. This time of the year big bulls had dropped their antlers, so this was mainly a meat hunt.

It was mid-January when Rich, the Italian Stallion, and I set out for Lake Louise in my pick-up truck. The Italian Stallion was a fraternity brother from our college days. At the time of this hunt, he was a captain in the U.S. Air Force stationed at Elmendorf Air Force Base in Anchorage. He was a good guy but tended not to think things through. That is probably why he was in the Air Force.

The Stallion had grown up in Chelan, Washington, where his father was a police officer. He went to Washington State University and majored in Air Force ROTC and general studies. He had been hunting and fishing since he was a little kid. Therefore, The Stallion and I hit it off right away when I showed up at WSU. After we graduated, I lost contact with The Stallion until I ran into him at the Kit Kat Club strip joint in Anchorage 10 years later. We renewed our friendship and over several years shared many fishing and hunting trips.

The Italian Stallion on Alexander Creek.

The word was out that the caribou were crossing and everyone was getting their limit. The Stallion and I had agreed that we would only take five caribou instead of the full limit of 10 allowed us. We both had small families then and didn't need a lot of meat. It was to be our contribution to game management and the environment.

The drive from Anchorage takes you from sea level to an elevation of 3,000 feet. The route is through spruce and birch forests from Anchorage to the Knik Glacier. Then you begin a climb up to Eureka. The spruce and birch give way to much more open tundra with patches of forest. Upon emerging from the Knik River drainage you find yourself in a grand valley that is 50 or 60 miles wide with mountain ranges on both sides. Everything is covered in snow and it is quite spectacular. It really brings home how vast Alaska can be. Twenty miles north is the beginning of the Lake Louise Road.

We arrived at the road just about daylight and started the 22-mile drive to where the road ends. This area is mostly swamp spruce with an abundance of small clearings. There is not much topography, so the road is flat with very few hills. There had been quite a bit of snow, so there were steep berms along both sides of the roadway placed there by snowplows, leaving only about a lane and a half of traveled way. We, therefore, had a little problem getting around cars that were haphazardly parked along the road. Some of these cars were left with all four doors open, indicating the passenger's rapid exit to chase caribou. This was road hunting at its finest! Due to the flat terrain it is difficult to spot any animals more than 100 yards of so from the road, but that didn't seem to be hindering the hunting.

By 10 a.m. The Stallion and I had driven to the end of the road and back--and had not seen a single live caribou. We were complaining about the lousy hunting when I spotted a small herd standing 50 feet off the side of the road. We slid to a halt and jumped out of the truck and blasted four of them before the rest made it to the woods. The snow was about 2 1/2 feet deep, which required the animals to plow through it, making for relatively easy targets. One animal made it about 150 yards away from the road, but the other three were within 30 yards. From a road hunter's point of view, things could not get much better. It was just a matter of gutting the animals and dragging them across the snow to the truck. We didn't even break a sweat. We were 80% of the way to our goal and back on the road in less than an hour looking for number five. We quit complaining. The words "fair chase" kept nagging at me, but I managed to ignore it with relative ease.

We had gone another five miles when we came upon two guys in a station wagon parked next to the snow berm, facing toward us. We noted two caribou standing on the road 50 feet behind their vehicle. They obviously were totally unaware of the two animals, but did take note of us as we slid to a halt and piled out of the truck loading our guns. The thought that we might be planning to shoot them probably flashed through their minds when The Stallion and I went to one knee and started aiming in their general direction.

Early season Nelchina caribou.

Both guys jumped out of the station wagon with their guns just as we opened up on the caribou. We hit both of them with our first shots. One dropped in his tracks; the other staggered across the road with both of the station wagon guys firing at him. I doubt if they hit him, but it was a 50-foot shot and they only fired nine or 10 times. The second animal finally lay down and died next to the berm. We now had one more caribou than we wanted.

It turned out that the two guys were Air Force sergeants who were from Los Angeles and also had been assigned to El-mendorf. They were on the first hunting trip of their lives. They had heard the radio announcements, borrowed some guns and driven up to give it a try. In order to forego the extra caribou, we convinced them that they had shot the second caribou, not us. We told them that caribou always stagger when crossing roads because they are not accustomed to walking on hard surfaces. It was a logical fabrication. These guys didn't have a clue, so they bought the story. They were extremely happy to take their first caribou. We dressed out our animal while they watched and asked questions. When we were loaded up, we asked if they wanted help with their animal. They said they had it under control, so we were on our way.

We just had to drive about three miles to find a turn-around and we would be headed for home. Within two miles we came to six or seven cars and trucks stopped on both sides of the road. We thought there had been an accident. They flagged us down and informed us there was a large herd of caribou just ahead and they didn't want us to spook them. The Stallion and I got out and went over to where everyone was standing around.

The caribou were about 200 yards off the road in a herd of maybe 500. The boys were all trying to come up with a plan on how to stalk them. Once again we were not dealing with experienced outdoorsmen, or for that matter, very smart guys. I pointed out that the caribou were all looking at us, so any attempt to approach them would result in a whole bunch of caribou tracks leading away into the woods and no meat on the ground.

The second thing I pointed out was that the caribou were only 200 yards away and were in easy range of their guns where they stood. This immediately resulted in a reenactment of the British army battle tactics from the Revolutionary War. There were 15 or 20 guns all in a line blazing away, caribou dropping like flies, and general chaos reigned. When the shooting stopped and the smoke cleared, they all ran over to the dead critters and started trying to figure out who had shot what. In typical Alaska style they finally decided to just split up the animals evenly and call it a day. The Stallion and I continued on our way... our work being done there.

We soon came to our two Air Force friends who were standing next to their caribou with their chins in their hands, looking puzzled. We stopped and went over to see what was up. I couldn't believe what I saw. The two guys who said they had it under control had cut the caribou in half crosswise at the middle of the rib cage and then pulled the two halves apart. There they were with the front half three feet from the back half, with all the guts strung out in between. The Stallion and I were on our knees laughing. The Air Force guys didn't see the humor, but then they were new to this hunting thing.

Once we composed ourselves, we helped them square away the critter. We quartered the animal and put it in game bags, cut up the ribs, and stripped the meat off all the other parts. We helped them load it in the station wagon and advised them to take an experienced friend with them on their next hunt. They thanked us profusely. We shook hands and headed for home. As we drove off it began to snow.

We were five miles from the main highway; it was now snowing like crazy and visibility was down to 50 feet. We were only going 15 mph due to the conditions. All of a sudden, a large heard of caribou began crossing the road. By the time we got stopped we were only 15 feet away from them. Caribou hood ornaments usually are quite expensive so we were relieved to be stopped short of the herd. We decided to just sit there and watch the critters go by. It was kind of neat watching them coast past in the snow. At least it was neat until we saw the outline of a car on the other side of the herd. It was very difficult to see through the snow, but it was obvious what was about to happen when all four doors popped open! These guys were going to start blasting caribou and probably could not see us on the other side of the herd.

I started flashing the headlights and blowing the horn. Rich jumped out and started shooting in the air--but the caribou just kept coming. When the shooting started we both hit the deck and crawled into the ditch alongside the road. I had snow up my nose, in my ears, and gravel embedded in my hide. It seemed like those guys were shooting for at least an hour, but it was probably only a few minutes. Anyway, when it was over the caribou herd had all crossed and our friends had dropped 15 or 20 of them. There were dead caribou on both sides of the road as far as you could see in the snow storm. They had no idea we were there and were, in fact, somewhat surprised to see us.

As luck would have it, they had agreed to not shoot any animals on the road because in the low visibility they were concerned that someone might come along and run over them. Of course, they would have hit our dead bodies first, thereby saving the valuable caribou meat. Also, it is illegal to shoot off of or along a road in Alaska, but I don't think that fact entered into their planning. They had heard The Stallion's shots, but had assumed it was someone shooting at the caribou. We discussed hunter safety with them in words we had learned in the third grade. They showed appropriate remorse, so we departed.

The rest of the trip to Anchorage was uneventful. When we got to the edge of town, The Stallion suggested we take the caribou to the Elmendorf Air Force Base processing facility because it would be cheaper. I agreed, but it was late in the day and there was no one on duty to take our cutting order. So I left it up to The Stallion to return the next day and let them know how we wanted the meat cut up. My recent experience with Air Force personnel should have caused me to question the advisability of leaving another Air Force guy in charge, but I was tired. It seems most of my bad decisions are made when I am tired. The Stallion's habit of not thinking things through should also have sprung to mind.

It was two weeks later that The Stallion called to say our meat was ready and that he would meet me at the facility right after work. We backed our two pick-ups up to the ramp and these two butcher-types started hauling out boxes of Polish sausage. I was waiting for the steaks and roasts, but they didn't come--just more sausage and more sausage. When the last box came out, I asked where the cut meat was. He said there wasn't any. The Stallion had told them to make it all into Polish sausage!!! We now had 900 pounds of Polish sausage and a bill for $300.

The Stallion was standing there with his mouth hanging open. He had no idea that five caribou would make that much sausage, once again confirming why he was in the Air Force. If you add 200 pounds of other meat to 700 pounds of caribou, you get 900 pounds of polish sausage.

I didn't have my gun with me, so I couldn't shoot him. I just walked over and told him I would kill him at a later date and drove away with my humongous share of sausage. Absolutely everybody I knew ended up with all the sausage I could pawn off on them, and I still had a freezer-full.

It's been 20 years, and I'm still not fond of the stuff.

IF YOU KILL BOTH OF US, MOM WILL BE PISSED

I have two younger brothers and an older sister, all of whom have had adventures with me in Alaska and survived. The older of my two brothers, John, traveled to Alaska shortly after I got my float rating and acquired a Cessna 185 floatplane.

Since he was a little kid, John has always been very excitable. This was especially true when it came to hunting and fishing. I recall when I shot my first deer. John was about 12 at the time. He and I had been hunting for deer in northeastern Washington all day. We had only seen a few grouse but no deer.

Late in the day, we headed back to the campsite where our parents were waiting for us. We broke into the clearing 200 yards from where the camp was located when a spike whitetail buck burst out of a clump of trees and started running across the clearing. I was shooting a 30-30 saddle rifle. I snapped off a shot and the deer hit the ground. The whole thing took less than 2 seconds. The round hit the deer at the base of the ear and traveled around the back of the skull and came out the other side. It knocked him out, but didn't kill him. Of course, we had no idea he wasn't dead. John wasn't sure what had happened. He turned to me and said, "What was that, a coyote?"

I said, "No, it's a deer."

He asked where it had gone. I told him I had shot it and it was down right in front of us. He became overly excited and immediately ran over to the deer and for some strange reason grabbed it by the two hind feet. At this point, the deer came to and proceeded to kick the crap out of John. I was yelling at him to let go, but he just hung in there accumulating bruises. Dad had witnessed this whole drama and was running over to help. I finally took the butt of the gun and hit the deer on the top of the head as hard as I could. That stunned the animal, so I was able to get John unwrapped from the deer and administer the *coup de grace*. Dad arrived on the scene a few seconds later. After making sure neither of us was seriously injured, he commented that that was the most exciting deer kill he had ever seen, but advised us there are better ways to get the job done. He said it is always good to make sure the animal is dead before grabbing it. Since that day I have always made sure.

John flew from Seattle to Alaska on a commercial flight in a Boeing 727. It was the first time he had ever been in an airplane. The second time he was in an airplane, it was my floatplane, with me doing the flying.

John had never really trusted me since we were very young. All of his serious injuries as a kid had been at my hand (as in the aforementioned deer hunt). I never intended to injure him; it just seemed like he was always the one who got hurt. I suppose that is why he had some misgivings about flying with me. But we were going caribou hunting; this was his first trip to Alaska, and he had never seen a real live caribou. He loves to hunt, so he ignored his better judgment and decided it was worth the risk. He would come to regret this decision.

The hunting party was comprised of John and me in my plane and Gary and Fritz in Fritz's plane. Gary was a friend of John's who had moved to Alaska a few years earlier. He was a short burly guy who loved the outdoors. Fritz was my friend. We had bachelored together for several years. Chasing girls, drinking, hunting and fishing. By the time of this adventure we had both settled down and were raising families. Fritz, who hailed from Wasilla, a small town north of Anchorage, referred to himself as "Wasilla's oldest teenager." It was a good description.

We planned to fly to a lake on the Alaska Peninsula near Egegik. It was a clear day, so we went over the top. This involves climbing to 8,000 feet and flying over the Chigmit Mountains. You fly over a great expanse of glaciers and snowfields nestled in rugged rock ridges and mountaintops.

Other than the great view, it was an uneventful flight, but John was still not at ease with flying. He just kept looking down at all that snow and rock and stressing. He was uncomfortable with the size of the airplane, he still didn't trust me, and he particularly didn't like the takeoff at Lake Hood, which had been normal and uneventful except for the screaming coming from the co-pilot seat that John occupied.

Regardless of John's misgivings, it was a good flight. After crossing the Chigmit Mountains, we flew down Lake Iliamna to the Alaska Peninsula in smooth air and clear skies. As we approached the lake where we planned to camp, we saw several caribou herds nearby. There were bunches of 10 to 150 with some very nice bulls in several of the herds. We landed and set up camp with caribou watching us as we worked.

We were all pumped when we got up the next morning, knowing there would be plenty of animals to choose from. We had something to eat and split up into two parties. Gary and Fritz headed north and John and I went south. John and I had only gone a short distance before we came upon a small herd of 5 or 6 cows and two nice bulls.

The country we were hunting in was treeless tundra with small rolling hills. This time of year it is mostly brown tundra with green and yellow alder and willows along the lakeshores and creeks. It made it easy to stalk the animals by using terrain to hide our approach. We managed to get within 100 yards without much difficulty. We had to get downwind and then crawl up a small creek bed for a few hundred feet, but it put us in an ideal shooting position on a small hill looking down on the caribou.

These were the first caribou John had ever seen, so I gave him the shot. True to form, he was a little too excited, so he missed the first shot, but did manage to hit a bull with one of several more shots. It humped up and staggered over a small ridge and out of sight.

We waited 30 minutes to let him lie down and then followed. When we topped the ridge, we were surprised to find two brown bears had also found our animal. With all the shooting you would think they would have been long gone, but not these two. They were only about 150 yards from where we stood. In fact, just as I spotted them, one of the bears grabbed the caribou with his mouth and threw it 10 feet in the air. Now, remember we are out on the tundra where there are no trees to climb. It is just you and the bears *mano a mano.*

I suggested to John that we let them have that caribou. Problem was, I was talking to myself. John was already half a mile away with a rooster tail of tundra flying out behind him. He didn't shut down until he was all the way back at the camp.

Within minutes the bears had divvied up the caribou, so I gave up on it and wandered back to camp. I found John hyperventilating in the tent with his gun clutched to his chest. It took several minutes to get him out of the tent and pried loose from his gun. I explained that the bears would be busy with the caribou for a few days and we were in no danger. From the look on his face I think the trust thing was an issue again.

After he settled down and started breathing again, we went back to hunting. Just to be safe, we went north this time, away from the bears. Within an hour we spotted a nice bunch of animals with several good bulls in the herd. They were coming right at us. The wind was right and we had a small clump of brush to hide in, so we just waited until they walked to within 50 yards. I had John pick out the bull he wanted and I selected another bull.

John with the caribou the bears didn't get.

This time things went better and we dropped both animals with one shot each. John was very excited with his first caribou and I had to take a million pictures of him and his bull. By the time we had them butchered, he was beginning to settle down. We stashed the antlers and meat about a mile from a marginally landable lake about five miles from camp.

When we got back, Fritz and Gary were back with two more caribou. That was enough meat, so Fritz and I agreed it was time to load up and head back to Anchorage. John quickly concurred. I doubt that he wanted to spend another night in the tent with the bears so close.

The plan was for John and Gary to walk over and pick up our two caribou and pack them to the lake. Fritz and I would load the camp and the two caribou in the planes and then fly over to the other lake and pick up John and Gary and the rest of the meat. I took off first.

As I approached the lake I saw John packing meat about a half mile from the lake. I also noticed a brown bear following along about 100 yards behind him. The bear was obviously tracking the meat smell left by John.

My first thought was that the bear would get our meat, probably tear up my pack, which was quite expensive, and scare the hell out of John. Based on these concerns, I decided to buzz the bear with the airplane and scare him off. It worked. The bear ran into some brush and stayed there. Of course, John had no clue what was going on.

When I landed, he said he had one more load to bring out and then we could be on our way. I said, "okay" and that I would come along with a gun just in case we saw another big bull. I didn't plan to tell him about the bear until it showed itself or we were back in the plane. No sense having him worry. Fritz had elected to land on a larger lake nearby. Gary had already packed two loads, so he opted to walk over to the lake where Fritz was waiting.

John and I headed out to get the last of the meat. When we got to the kill site, the meat was gone, so I didn't have to say anything. John spun around and shifted into high gear again and beat me back to the airplane by 10 minutes. At this point, I think he had run over more tundra than he had walked over. I am sure his adrenaline meter was on low.

Taking off from this lake was a little hairy. The lake was almost perfectly round and a little short for a heavy plane. It required that I get the plane on the step and then do a step-turn at the end of the lake to get up enough speed to take off. This technique has you running in a circle around the edge of the lake building up speed. We had one and one half caribou, camping gear, guns, and us. The plane was full. All of these factors resulted in an exciting takeoff. At this point John was over the bears and was once again stressing on the flying thing. We hooked up with Fritz, climbed to 8,000 feet and set off for Anchorage. Nothing to sweat now. John was even breathing normally again.

John with his caribou and packing bear bait.

Between Egegik and Anchorage there is a tall mountain called Iliamna. This is a dormant volcano that rises more than 10,000 feet. It usually has a small cloud of steam coming out of its crater, just to let you know it is not dead.

We were coming up on the mountain when Fritz called and said we were going into a 35-knot head wind. He had a DME, which is a device for determining ground speed, and I didn't, so I'd had no idea we were fighting that much wind. This brought my fuel management into question. I had to get out of that head wind or I wouldn't have enough gas to get us home. We were on top of the clouds, but I could see the edge of the clouds to my right. I radioed Fritz and said I was going to turn right and descend to 2,000 feet to try and get out of the head wind.

We're going to have a physics lesson now. When you have a 35-knot wind hitting a mountain, it tends to roll up and over the mountain and down the backside. This can cause a downdraft on the backside of the mountain with a velocity approximately equal to the speed of the wind. It was, therefore, an unfortunate decision to cut across the backside of Iliamna that day. I realized that when I noted that my vertical speed indicator was pegged at 2,000 feet-per-minute down, which is the highest the gauge would go. It would not take us long to descend to 2,000 feet. Another quick physics lesson: When the downdraft gets to the bottom of the mountain it gets very turbulent. Think of water running over a dam. As the water runs down the face of the dam it is smooth and fast. When it hits the bottom it becomes very turbulent. Air flowing over a mountain acts the same way. I knew it was going to get real rough.

I turned to John, who was now experiencing the third airplane ride of his life, and said, "You might want to tighten your seat belt." He gave me a worried look, but did as he was told. I would soon be testing what little faith he had in his big brother.

The turbulence went from moderate to severe to extreme in about 10 seconds. Even I had not expected such a violent encounter. For short periods of time I lost control due to the pitching and yaw of the plane. We were bouncing up and down as well as sideways. Some of the bumps were so hard that the dirt on the floor of the airplane hit the ceiling. The caribou meat and camp gear were flying all over the plane with some of it landing in our laps. It was not fun.

In the middle of all this I looked over at John. He was grasping the dash so hard his fingers were white; his jaw muscles were sticking out two inches and his eyes were the size of softballs. He looked back at me and said through clenched teeth, " If you kill both of us, mom will really be pissed." I believe he was totally sincere in that statement. He probably thought it was a dying remark. I know I did!

After half a lifetime, we came out from behind the mountain and left the worst of the turbulence behind us. As we bumped our way down Cook Inlet toward Anchorage reveling in the fact that we were still alive, John ate two pounds of cookies and smoked a pack a cigarettes in the 45 minutes it took us to get to Lake Hood. Unfortunately, his ordeal was not over.

I called Lake Hood for landing clearance. They said the wind was blowing 25 knots, with gusts to 35. The wind was also switching from west to north unpredictably. We were in for a nasty landing.

Fritz was ahead of us because he had the good sense to forgo the turbulent route. He had crossed upwind of the mountain. We discussed the best way to deal with the wind situation in landing. It was a tough call. If you chose to land one direction and the wind switched, it could get exciting, and we had had enough of that this day. Fritz said he would go first and elected to land north. A north landing on Lake Hood is shorter than a west, but with such high winds the length of the landing is not your main concern. Just as he was about to touch down the wind switched and he did an unscheduled crosswind landing with a big bounce. He came within inches of putting a wing in the water, which usually results in the plane cart-wheeling down the lake and then settling to the bottom with the bodies of the occupants wrapped up in the wreckage. This did not build my confidence. John was too scared to talk. I was not sure he was even breathing.

I chose a west landing and went for it. The wind held, but it was so strong that I dropped my flaps just as I touched down and the wind still put us back in the air when we hit the first wave. For you non-pilots, this is a big deal. I found myself 15 feet in the air without enough airspeed to keep flying. The only thing you can do is hit the power and try to soften the hit when you come down. We came down hard, but stayed upright. Now, we were on the water facing into the wind with my tie-down behind us. There was no way I could turn downwind without the plane flipping over.

I taxied to an empty tie-down that was directly in front of us, left a note on the windscreen explaining why we were there, and called it a day. I had to help John out of the plane. Once out of the plane, John said he would never fly with me again. I said I didn't blame him. I left him sitting on the ground next to the airplane and hiked down the lake to retrieve the truck. We loaded up and drove to the house. John went right to his room and didn't come out for hours. He finally joined us for dinner, but couldn't stop talking about how dangerous it is to fly in Alaska.

A week later I flew over to Coal Creek and caught a bunch of silvers. John took one look at those fish and decided maybe a few local trips would be OK. Over the years John has flown with me on occasion, but he always checks the weather first. He has never asked to go back to Egegik.

CHAPTER 2:
Got Experience and an Airplane—
Still Stupid

WELL, MR. CHAIRMAN,
ARE YOU HAVING FUN YET?

Several years ago I planned a caribou hunt in the Mulchatna area with one of my high school buddies named Rick. He was a Washington state trooper and a fellow Vietnam veteran. We had both attended Washington State University and had kept in touch over the years.

For a cop, Rick has a very friendly and outgoing personality. This was his first Alaska hunt, so he was not sure what he was getting into with this trip. We had hunted together in high school and college, so he was comfortable going out in the wilderness with his old friend. I doubt he thought his training as a U.S. Marine in Vietnam and as a state trooper would be brought into play on a caribou hunt.

I served on the Anchorage Municipal Assembly (our local city council) for six years. I represented South Anchorage, a district of about 35,000 people. The chairman of the assembly at that time was a guy named Dick. He was also invited to come along.

Dick is a gun nut and owns more guns than most gun shops.

Therefore, I was not surprised when he showed up at the airplane with some kind of semi-automatic 30-06 with a clip that held about 40 pounds of ammo. Based on this, we dubbed him "Deadeye Dick." Deadeye is a stocky guy with a very macho personality. I had spent a lot of time with him doing city business, but had never been hunting with him. Among the three of us, it was an interesting dynamic.

We took off from Lake Hood mid-morning and headed down Cook Inlet toward the Chigmit Mountains. It was a beautiful day with clear skies and smooth air. Our route took us past Big River Lake where we observed several brown bears fishing for silver salmon. Rick got a real kick out of watching those bears. We went through Lake Clark Pass with its spectacular views to Lake Clark. Then it was just a short hop over to the Mulchatna.

The Mulchatna River is a slow meandering river that flows just north of Lake Clark in a southwest direction toward Dillingham. The lower part of the river is well forested on both banks, with open tundra when you are less than a mile from the river. In the fall, it is an interesting contrast from the vivid fall colors of yellow, green and red of the forest and the dull brown of the tundra. Moose inhabits the forested areas along the river, but you seldom see any moose on the tundra. You see caribou everywhere. They are in the forested areas and on the tundra. We also saw a pack of four wolves trotting along the riverbank.

I had hunted here for years, but it was the first trip to this area for my companions. They were very impressed by the amount of game we were seeing and the vastness of the area. After flying around for a while to determine where the caribou were located, we landed on a lake I had hunted on for several years. We saw a few caribou around the lake, so things looked good for the next day. This lake is kidney shaped and a little over a mile long and three-quarters of a mile wide. It is full of grayling, many of which volunteered to join us for breakfast. There is a hill next to the lake that rises up about 300 feet. From the top of this hill you can see several miles in all directions. It is an ideal lookout for caribou.

The campsite is almost perfect. There is a large flat area covered in gravel, which makes a good dry area for the tents. There are stunted alders along the lake to help break the wind and provide firewood. With the grayling, the lookout and the great campsite, this is a place we return to almost every year. We set up camp and settled in for the night. The weather was great, we caught some fish, and life was good.

4448R flying over the Mulchatna River in route to the camp.

We were up bright and early the next morning. As we were eating breakfast, I noticed four young bulls bedded down across the lake. We talked it over and decided to take two of them for meat and then spend the next two days looking for trophies. There was a limit of five caribou per person, so we had plenty of tags. Since a light wind was blowing across the lake, we pushed the plane off the beach and stood on the floats as it drifted across the lake. The caribou paid little attention to us as we cruised toward them. We tied up on the opposite shore and began our stalk.

There was excellent cover from the alders growing along the shore. It was simply a matter of walking down the beach until we were adjacent to the bulls. The alder were only 10 feet wide at this point, so we just stepped through the brush. The animals were just behind a 15-foot-high bump, so we started walking toward them. We were soon within 50 yards of them. The four bulls were laying in a row in front of us. I suggested that each guy shoot the outside bull on their side. I would be the back up. They agreed that this was a good plan.

I would like to point out, once again, that I had not been hunting with Deadeye before this trip. We began walking toward the caribou so that they would stand up and we could put two of them down. We were within 25 yards when they finally got up. They were young bulls and didn't have any idea of what was going on, so they just stared at us with no alarm. This was a gimmee.

The fusillade of gunfire that erupted was breathtaking. When the dust had settled I swear Deadeye was knee-deep in spent cartridges. All four caribou were dead several times over, and everything within 500 yards of us had a bullet hole in it. Rick and I peered through the smoke at Deadeye for several minutes as he searched for something else to shoot. I commented that it appeared we had plenty of meat and that maybe we should stop shooting and start cutting up caribou. When we walked up to the corpses I observed that each animal had been shot several times. Rick noted he had fired one shot. He was not sure he had hit anything.

Even with the parts that were blown away, we still ended up with more caribou than I wanted to carry in the plane, so we boned the meat to reduce weight. We packed it to the shore and loaded it on the floats then taxied back across the lake and hung the meat in the only tree within 10 miles. Other than the carnage, we were off to a good start. With all of this meat we opted to take only one more animal. Since we only had two days left we decided to look for a trophy for Rick and head home. Anyway, Deadeye's gun needed some time to cool off.

One of the things you have to keep in mind when hunting in the Mulchatna area is that the weather can get bad very quickly. It is usually a good idea to get your meat and depart as soon as possible. Our decision to stay one more day was a gamble, but the weather was holding fine so we stuck around. This would prove to be an unfortunate decision.

Around 2 p.m. the next day we spotted a nice bull walking along the opposite shore of the lake. If he continued along the shoreline he would end up about 300 yards from the camp.

There was good cover for us to move to where we could ambush him and set up so Rick could get a good shot. Deadeye was the backup. I left my gun in the camp so I could help Deadeye carry his ammo. We scurried over to a small ridge where Rick had a perfect view of where the caribou was headed. The bull walked right into the trap. Rick made a good clean shot right behind the shoulder. The bull staggered and began to lie down. At that point Deadeye shot him four more times. I think his gun jammed or he would have kept shooting. Again we didn't have quite as much meat to pack as normal. Rick and I were both giving Deadeye quizzical looks, but he didn't notice because he was busy reloading.

Bob with a nice Mulchatna bull.

Arriving back at camp with the last caribou, we noted that the wind had increased quite a bit. It was too late in the day to start back to town so we settled in for another night. By early evening the wind had increased to 40 or 50 knots. The airplane was tied up in the path of the wind. It was hitting right on the tail of the plane. This is hard on the control surfaces and can result in damage.

I knew I had to get the plane turned into the wind, but I was also concerned about its location and determined that we needed to move it down the shoreline to get it behind some terrain so it would be out of the direct path of the wind. The plan was to untie the plane and move it down the beach to the safer location by pulling the mooring ropes attached to the floats. The wind was blowing straight offshore when we untied the plane.

You would think a registered professional engineer (yours truly) and a former Marine Corps helicopter pilot would have thought this plan through. The fact was that it was blowing hard, it was getting dark, and our transportation out of this remote place was getting battered. We didn't think. We just bulled ahead like we knew what we were doing, having not properly considered the physics of this situation. The airplane is a big sail with 50 knots of wind hitting it broadside. The chances of three guys in hip boots holding it against the shore were equivalent to the chances of a snowball in hell. Of course, when we untied it, the plane immediately sailed across the lake, dragging us with it.

Just before I went in over my hip boots I jumped on one float and Rick jumped on the other. Deadeye was left back on shore. We were now out in the middle of the lake in three or four foot waves with a multitude of options running through our minds, none of which seemed good or safe. After considering several bad to marginal options, I chose to start the engine and see if I could get the plane in the air. Big mistake. When I hit the throttle the plane surged forward, hit a wave, and almost turned over. By the time I had the engine shut down Rick was already out of the plane and on the float ready to swim for it. I talked him back into the plane.

The next plan was to fire up the engine and apply just enough power to keep the waves from turning us sideways and rolling us over. It was very exciting being bounced around out in that lake not knowing if the plane would stay right-side-up or not. But this worked and we drifted backward until we reached the shore. We were now on the far shore of the lake from the camp, with the wind right on the nose of the airplane. My airspeed indicator was reading between 35 and 55 knots, and we weren't moving. In fact the engine was not even running.

Rick and I jumped out of the plane and pulled the back of the floats as far up on the beach as we could. The waves were breaking over the front of the floats, but at least we were on solid ground. The only good thing was that now the plane was facing the wind. I did not feel that I could leave the airplane for fear the wind would flip it over. I sat there with the yoke pushed full forward to keep the nose down. Rick sat in the co-pilot seat and just stared straight ahead. It was obvious we were not going anywhere soon.

Deadeye walked around the lake and joined us in the plane. He advised us that the camp had pretty much blown away, but he had saved the guns and some of the food. Everything else was wrapped around the alders along the lake or on its way to Russia. It is amazing how quickly things can go from great to real lousy in remote Alaska.

Camp as the wind was picking up.

We sat in the plane from 8 p.m. until 10 a.m.; it was not a fun night. The mood in the plane was somber and the conversation was sparse. Our enjoyable hunt had turned to crap and it didn't seem to be getting better. I had been in spots like this before, but my companions had not and were not taking it well. I am sure both of them were concerned about our survival odds. I was just waiting out the wind and hoping the plane didn't get damaged.

When the wind finally let up the plane had blown clear up on the beach--the floats were not even touching the water. Luckily, the beach was rounded pea gravel so I was able to power the plane back into the water. We taxied across the lake and salvaged what we could of the camp and burned the rest.

My next problem was that I had five caribou, two guys who each weighed more than 225 pounds, and the remnants of our camp to fit into the plane and then take off. This was pushing the carrying capacity of Triple four-eight Romeo (N4448R). Luckily, Deadeye had shot up 200 or 300 pounds of ammo. I had a 20-knot wind to take off into, so I decided to give it a try. We used the whole lake and several years off each of our lives, but we got into the air, clearing the alders at the end of the lake by inches. Good old 4448 Romeo flew, but she didn't like it.

Next problem. With the headwind, there was no way I had enough gas to get all the way to Anchorage. This meant stopping for fuel and another overloaded take-off at Port Alsworth, a small community of 75 hardy souls on Lake Clark. There are two landing strips there and a protected harbor for floatplanes to land and take off, if you are light enough. Otherwise, you take off in a channel located between the mainland and a small island. The landing and fueling went without incident. I did note some alder twigs wrapped around the front of the left float from the take-off. I guess it was a little closer than I thought when we left the lake. Because we were heavy I opted to use the channel for the take-off.

The take-off channel at Port Alsworth is protected from the wind coming off Lake Clark by the small island. If you are not off the water by the time you clear the island, it can get rough--we didn't and it did. I think it was the third or fourth wave that bounced us high enough to get us flying, but I am sure we incurred several thousand dollars worth of dental liability prior to getting airborne.

The rest of the trip was routine. We went back through Lake Clark Pass with some turbulence, but nothing to write home about. When we got home we took care of the meat. Both guys complimented me on both my flying skills and survival instincts, and they went home.

Neither has asked to go hunting with me since.

CONFERENCE ROOM BEAR

One fall I was at the moose camp with three friends: Billy, who had been on several adventures with me and was somehow still alive (Billy was still working as a special agent for the FBI - they hadn't caught on to him yet even though he had been with them for 25 years); Peter, who was a very soft spoken DEA agent (I was his mentor and idol. He didn't get out much so he didn't know very many people) and Floyd who was also an FBI agent and several years younger than the rest of us. Floyd wasn't his real name, but we called him that because that was the name of the head of the FBI and we were all sure Floyd would some day become a federal bureaucrat in charge of the FBI.

We had been hunting for a couple of days when Peter shot a nice 60-inch bull about four miles north of the camp. Camp Creek runs through this area and has stretches where it meanders quite a bit. This creates ox bows and allows for numerous beaver dams and ponds. These ponds are surrounded by thick willows, alders and swamp spruce.

Compared to the open areas farther from the creek, this area is a virtual jungle of brush. It makes for very short sight distances and up-close and personal hunting. Not a good place to be dealing with anything that bites.

Peter spotted the bull when we saw his horns sticking up from the willows. The bull was near the end of a 100-foot long beaver dam on a small flat piece of ground, which then sloped to the edge of the beaver pond five feet away. It was an easy stalk through high grass and willows.

Peter ended up on the other end of the dam with a clear view of the moose across the pond. It was a nice clean kill. When he got to the animal, he noted another large bull standing 50 feet away watching him. Billy arrived on the scene and they discussed whether they wanted to have two bulls down. It was decided to let the second bull go. He still hung around for another 10 minutes and then wandered off into the alders. In retrospect it was a good decision to let him go. We quartered the moose and packed it across the dam to where the trail to camp began.

It was getting dark and camp was about four miles away, so we decided to put the meat up a tree and go back to camp. It was a simple plan. We always seem to do better with simple plans, but in this case even a simple plan goes bad.

We selected a nearby spruce tree that was about 30 feet tall with a 6-inch butt. Using a rope and a lot of muscle we got the meat about 20 feet off the ground so it would be safe from the bears. At least, that was the idea. The plan was to return in the morning with the three-wheeler and haul the meat to camp. We took the tenderloins and back strap with us. It was a pleasant walk back to camp. We had a moose down, the weather was good, and we were in good company. Mount McKinley's snow-covered flanks were pink with the setting sun, the willows were yellow, green spruce surrounded the clearing, and the red blueberry bushes were everywhere. It was a beautiful scene and a great finish to the day. To celebrate the moose we had a nice steak dinner and a few beers and went to bed. All was good with the world.

The next morning we returned to the meat cache with the three-wheeler, prepared to haul meat. We were flabbergasted to find the spruce tree had been uprooted and all of the meat except one front quarter was gone. There were pieces of meat strewn around the area, the bone from a hindquarter lay on the ground, and moose scraps trailed off through the tall grass toward the beaver pond.

All of us simultaneously chambered a round.

Keep in mind, now, I had with me some of the best-trained investigators in the country, so it only took them a short time to figure out that we had a bear problem. It took them another minute or two to figure out where the meat went. We walked into the beaver pond and looked across the dam and could see a large mound of dirt where the moose guts and horns used to be and a telltale trail of moose pieces leading up to the mound. Their highly trained minds immediately figured out that the bear had torn down the tree and hauled the meat across the dam and buried it with the guts and horns. Man, those feds are really something; that's why I don't rob banks...

We crossed the dam and while one guy kept watch with his gun at the ready (we knew that bear was close by watching us and not liking what he saw), the other two dug up the meat.

The bear had eaten one whole hindquarter and the rest had been shredded, then urinated on and ruined (bear do this to mark their cache and warn scavengers to stay away.) All we could salvage were the horns and the one front quarter the bear had left behind.

We went back to camp in a surly mood. Clouds had moved in so McKinley was nowhere to be seen and all the fall colors seemed muted now and then it started to rain. We ate beans and hot dogs that night and went to bed mad at the world --and particularly that bear!

The next morning after breakfast we were getting ready to go find another moose when we noticed the meat rack was down and the front quarter and back straps were gone. After another investigation by the feds, it was determined that the damned bear had come into camp that night and stolen the rest of the meat. (We knew it was the same bear because he was missing a claw on his right front foot, so he had a distinctive footprint.) That did it!!

We returned to the tent and held a short trial. There were three prosecutors, no defense counsel, and I was the judge. The bear was found guilty and sentenced to be shot as soon as possible. Peter and I were the only ones with bear tags so we had to carry out the execution while the other two went hunting for another moose. Armed to the teeth, the posse mounted up and rode out of town with our white hats.

It seems like every time one of these deals comes up, I always end up dealing with the critters with teeth and claws! I am either the bravest or the dumbest guy in the bunch. I prefer to think I am the bravest, but everyone says that probably isn't the case.

Peter and I returned to the scene of the crime. The end of the trail was about 100 feet from the pond. The 100 feet was covered with head-high grass with a bear trail running through it to the beaver dam.

I explained to Peter that the bear would most likely be on his cache on the other side of the beaver dam and we would not be able to see him until we reached the edge of the pond. This would mean the bear would be just across the beaver dam from us, maybe 75-feet away--or about 1.5 seconds if he charged us. I suggested he be *alert* as we went toward the pond. The suggestion was not really necessary. Peter was already very alert.

After some discussion, a fistfight, and threats of IRS investigations, it was determined that I should go in first. Peter would follow close behind. I took a deep breath, said a short prayer, flipped Peter off and started in. Upon reaching the edge of the pond, a small clump of willows blocked my view of the other end of the beaver dam. I was staring straight ahead as I stepped sideways. This caused me to trip on a root and lose my balance. I ended up staggering five feet down the bank and out from behind the willow clump. This attracted the bear's attention as he sat on his cache.

All of a sudden I was eyeball to eyeball with an eight and a half-foot grizzly that was guarding his stash. All indications were that he was not happy about this turn of events, nor was he inclined to leave his treasure to us. I could see him start to tense up as he prepared to charge. I figured I had about one second to do something.

I threw the good ol' .300 Winchester Mag to my shoulder and put the crosshairs right on his forehead. The thought that went through my mind was, "*You didn't sight this gun in this year. I sure hope it shoots where you're pointing.*" Thank goodness it did.

The first shot hit him under the left eye and ended up hitting the spine right at the head. The second shot went under his chin and hit the spine a little lower. He was dead when he hit the ground. My gun is a Model 77 Ruger bolt-action. Peter swears he only heard one shot. I'm sure there wasn't even enough time between the two shots to notice, so it only sounded like one shot. If there is enough adrenaline involved, a bolt action can function as an automatic.

We stood on the bank for several minutes to make sure he was done for and to get our legs working again and then very cautiously crossed the dam. The bear was lying with his back toward the water and his legs uphill. He probably weighted 1,000 pounds or more. We had a major skinning job ahead of us. It took two hours to skin the top half of the bear. We now had to roll him over to skin the other half. This presented a real problem because he was too heavy to roll uphill, particularly with his feet pointed in that direction, and if we rolled him downhill he would be in the water.

It only took us a few minutes to make a dumb decision. We rolled him downhill and into the water on the defective theory that he would float and we could get the skin off easily as he bobbed around the pond. He sank like a stone. I still haven't forgiven Peter for letting me make that dumb choice.

We spent the next four hours skinning a half-submerged bear with Billy circling overhead in his Super Cub watching us work. I appreciated his being our lookout for any other bears, but we could have used some help on the ground.

Once we got the skin off the bear I opened up his stomach. There were pieces of moose meat as big as a cantaloupe in there. He must have really wolfed down that hindquarter. We now had a very wet bear hide. This created another problem. A normal green bearskin weighs about 100 to 150 pounds; a wet one weighs three times that. We towed the skin across the pond to the bank on the other side. There was no way we could get it up the bank by ourselves, so we got the three-wheeler and pulled it up the bank and out to the trail. We now had a very wet, dirty and heavy bear hide to load onto the very small Honda 110 ATV three-wheeler (which weights about 150 pounds). We also had the problem of lifting a very wet, slippery and heavy hide onto the three-wheeler. There was no way for two guys to just lift it.

Once again, we combined our intellectual powers and came up with the idea of rolling up the hide in a ball and then rolling it up two poles onto the back rack of the vehicle. This worked like a charm except that the front wheel of the three-wheeler was now two feet off the ground! Not to be deterred, I jumped on the seat, forcing the front wheel to almost touch the ground. By loading some of our gear onto the front rack, we had the wheel down on the ground, but just barely. It was with this precarious steering situation that I began the trip back to the camp, grossly overloaded with minimal control. Peter followed on foot.

I made it about half way before I got stuck in a small creek. With considerable pushing, pulling, cussing, and some very sound engineering principles, I finally got it out of the creek with a very large pry pole. The engine had quit, and I managed to break the starter rope trying to start the damned thing.

I was now stuck with a 400-pound bear hide two miles from the camp, with no way to move it. I could just see this hide being ruined because we couldn't get it dried out. Peter wandered up and said we would have to take the three-wheeler engine apart and repair the starter rope. All we had with us was a

Leatherman. It is amazing what you can do with one of those things if you have no other choice. We had her going in an hour. No matter what, this bear was not going to win!

The rest of the trip to camp was without incident. I tipped the three-wheeler over a couple of times, but Peter came along and helped me get it back up on its wheels. This is all very flat country and I was traveling along the edge of a large clearing, otherwise we would have had many more problems with this precarious load. Once at camp it was another big deal getting the hide into the airplane. (The one-hour trip to Anchorage with a wet bear hide in the plane was not exactly an olfactory delight.)

Bob with the Conference Room Bear in his final resting place.

I got the hide back to town without further incident. He is now a full body mount in my office conference room. The (three) wheels of justice had turned and the long arm of the law had done him in. That's what he gets for messing with the FBI and the DEA.

He also messed with an engineer. That was probably his biggest mistake.

KILUDA BAY AND DIE?

A friend of mine named Rocky owned a lodge located in Kiluda Bay on Kodiak Island. The bay is located on the east side of the island facing directly into the North Pacific Ocean. It is therefore subject to some extreme weather. The bay is 20 miles long with very steep topography on all sides.

This part of Kodiak has few trees and is mostly open grassland. There are large alder patches and some cottonwood trees along the streams. The shoreline is almost all rock with very few beaches. There are limited places where you can climb up from the water to the hunting areas; hunting this area requires climbing a lot of hills and crawling over rocks. It is not a place for out-of-shape hunters. The lodge is located near the head of the bay on a small spit of gravel.

We had a deal with Rocky to use his lodge for a week each year to hunt deer. The deal required that we use the lodge at the end of the season--the last week in November or the first week in December. The upside is that the deer are usually lower on the mountains at that time of the year, due to the snow, and the bears are sleeping. The downside is that the weather is worse.

One of my partners on this hunt was a guy we call Bear. He is a bull of a man who was the president of the laborer's union local 341 for 26 years. Bear owns a remote fishing lodge on the Yentna River north of Anchorage called the Kingbear Lodge. He has lived in Alaska for 30 years and is a very competent outboard mechanic and outdoorsman. Bear is a good guy to have for a friend and a nightmare to have for an enemy.

The rest of the party included Charlie, who was one of my mechanical engineers. He was a very easy-going guy. He had limited experience in the woods, but was very willing to follow our lead and try to stay out of trouble. Troy was our computer geek. He was one of those new-age-thinking conservatives. He had hair down to his waist and he loved Rush Limbaugh. Dave was the manager of our mechanical engineering department. We call him Delusional Dave because he keeps going out in the wilds with me, each time thinking things will go smoothly, even when he is proven wrong time after time. Delusional had lots of experience in the outdoors, and in fact, this was his third or fourth trip to Kiluda Bay with me. He is a wiry guy so he doesn't tolerate the cold very well, but he is virtually unflappable in most any circumstance, which is a talent that has served him well on his adventures with me.

The Bear with a Kiluda buck.

In Kodiak if it is raining and the wind is blowing only 25 knots, that would be a nice enough day to take the family for a picnic on the beach. So when I say the weather is worse late in the season, I am talking about some serious wind, rain or snow.

Kiluda Bay never let us forget that fact. I believe it was at Kiluda Bay that we first noticed that we used the phrase, "Oh no! We're gonna die!" far more frequently than good taste would dictate or basic survival would require. Kodiak is an unforgiving place when it comes to making mistakes in the wilderness.

Rocky closes his lodge in October, so by the time we get there it is usually being maintained by caretakers. The lodge is 70 miles from the nearest road and 30 miles from the nearest village, so Rocky needs someone to maintain things and prevent theft during the winter. I am not sure how he recruited these caretakers, but they stayed at the lodge from October until May for room and board only. (The "board" being mostly what they can catch or shoot.)

Every year the caretakers are quite pleased to see us show up with lots of food and conversation. I suspect Rocky was recruiting from the shallow end of the labor pool or the deep end of the "people-on-the-run-from-the-law" pool. In all the years I have gone to the lodge, I can only recall one caretaker who could count to 20 without taking off his shoes.

This particular year Rocky had recruited two caretakers. I suspect that these guys were from the shallow end of both pools. They were about as sharp as a bowling ball, but far denser. Upon deplaning from the Beaver floatplane, the first thing we noticed was that there was only one boat. Rocky had two boats. When we inquired as to the location of the missing boat and motor they advised us that it was about 200 feet offshore under about 150 feet of water. They were reluctant to tell us how it got there and implored us not to advise Rocky of the situation because they intended to retrieve the boat and the motor. When we asked them how they planned to do that they said they didn't yet have a plan. They had been thinking about it for two weeks, but had not come up with anything. They invited us to give it some thought and get back to them.

Our esteem and confidence in these guys shot right up after that conversation. That night they announced that we would not be able to take the remaining boat with us when we went hunting. They would have to take us where we wanted to go and then come pick us up. Their reason for this new policy was that they couldn't trust just anybody with the boat. There were five of us on that trip. Bear, who owns his own fishing lodge with six boats and motors which he maintains himself; me, who owns two boats and outboards; Delusional, who has been running boats around Kiluda Bay for years; and two engineers. None of us had ever sunk a boat. So I guess the caretakers were more experienced in that regard.

We pointed this out to these two clowns, who couldn't see our point. They just kept saying it was the new policy. They were vague about whose policy it was, but it was in effect at that time. We finally agreed to be dropped off rather than endure the conversation any longer. We were soon to regret this capitulation to ignorance.

That evening we repaired and tuned-up the second outboard because we had been advised that the one on the boat was running rough. The next morning we were delivered two miles across the bay and dropped off. The last thing we said to our boat driver was that when he got back to the lodge he needed to put the tuned-up motor in the boat as a back-up. The motor that was on the boat had quit twice on the way over. Both times Bear got it going again while our driver stared off into space. We told him it would be a long row back to the lodge if the motor quit. Unfortunately, that was far too complicated of an instruction for this guy.

We had a successful day of hunting. The ground was well frozen, which allowed us to drag the deer behind us on a short rope. They slid across the ice and snow with very little effort. We made a practice of generally hunting uphill so we would be dragging the deer downhill at the end of the day. This made for less work when you were the most tired. The day was overcast, but no snow or rain. Looking to the west we could see a large storm coming, but it appeared it wouldn't get to us until we were safely back in the lodge.

We arrived back at the beach at the prearranged pick-up time with several deer in tow. There was no boat in sight but, with an hour of daylight remaining, we weren't too concerned. It is only a 10-minute run from the lodge.

Bob with a Kiluda buck that is much bigger than Bear's buck.

We assumed the dynamic duo had simply not noticed it was getting late and one of them would soon be on his way to get us. What we didn't know was there was a contest going on at the lodge to see who could make the dumbest decision that would have the most catastrophic results. It turned out to be a tie. They combined their anti-talents to make the prize-winning dumb decision.

Let me set the scene for you: The wind was picking up and was blowing straight offshore from the lodge. There was only one boat and it had a suspect motor on it. The good motor was still in the shed and there were only two or three operating brain cells in the vicinity.

Now the decision: One guy got into the boat without the good motor and the other guy launched the boat--BEFORE THEY STARTED THE MOTOR!

The wind immediately blew the boat out into the bay. Number one genius couldn't get the motor started and number two genius realized he was standing on shore with the oars. Our hero is now beginning a trip of two miles across the bay in two to three foot waves, in the dark, with no motor, no oars and no life jacket. Darwin's ghost was working overtime. Genius number one did have a short-range radio and called number two, who was still standing on the beach with the oars, to say he thought the boat was going to turn over and he would drown. I am not sure that would have been a bad thing except for losing the boat and motor.

Number two raced back to the lodge and called the Coast Guard in Kodiak for help. They said they couldn't come because they were experiencing 80-knot winds and couldn't leave the harbor. They also advised him it was coming our way. The Coast Guard proceeded to send out a message to all fishing boats in the area that there were five hunters stranded onshore and one idiot adrift in a boat.

We were sitting on the beach totally screwed, but we didn't know it at the time. A fishing boat named the *Sweet Pea* responded to the Coast Guard that he was in Kiluda Bay and would try to pick us up.

It was now dark and we were beginning to become concerned about the weather. We were also wondering what happened to our ride. The wind was doing about 20 knots and the waves were building. We found a sheltered spot on the beach, built a large fire and settled in to wait.

Now, here is the really weird part of this story. Genius number one floated past us in the dark 50 yards offshore and beached a mile down the shore from us. He saw the fire and knew Bear was a master outboard mechanic and could have gotten the motor running, but chose not to make his presence known. Also, when he beached the boat it was low tide. He took the motor off the boat and laid it on the rocks beside the boat. He never could explain why he did that. The tide came in and that was it for the motor. Unfortunately, he was still alive...

The wind was getting stronger and we were considering moving off the beach when we saw a light coming our way. We signaled back with flashlights, thinking it was our ride. We were somewhat surprised to see a 65-foot fishing boat. When the boat stopped several hundred yards before it got to us, we wondered what he was doing. It turns out he was picking up our boat person and the boat, sans the motor. He then came ashore in his skiff and picked us up and delivered us to the lodge.

Enroute, we learned what had happened, which resulted in a terse discussion with idiot number one about safety and following instructions. We left our deer on the beach because there was not enough room in the skiff. Once we got to the lodge we asked the guys on the fishing boat what we owed them for coming to get us. The only thing they asked was that we return the favor if the situation ever arose—a typical Alaska response. They then headed for Shearwater Cove to take shelter from the approaching storm.

Once we were in the lodge we talked Bear out of beating both of the idiots senseless and settled in for a big storm. Within one hour the wind was blowing 100 knots. It blew the windows out of the bunkhouse and took part of the roof off the lodge. It was so strong that it was blowing the tops off the waves resulting in a spray 20 feet off the surface of the water all across the bay. There is a picture of a guy hanging onto a pole in front of the lodge. He is parallel with the ground and his pants are down around his ankles. The wind is holding him up. He is wearing long johns so the picture is "G" rated. We could have taken a similar picture that day.

If that wind had hit two hours earlier I am sure Darwin's theory would have applied to the doofus in the boat. We would have spent a very windy night in the bushes and two more days walking around the bay to get back to the lodge. We, also, would have had to kill the surviving idiot to make sure he didn't reproduce. As it was, we spent most of the next day watching the wind blow and the day after repairing damage to the facilities.

During this time genius number one decided to make a buck on the situation and informed us he had paid the boat crew $300 for rescuing us. First of all it is unlikely he had $300 in his whole life, and second, we had discussed this with the crew. We advised him that if he persisted along these lines his life expectancy would decline substantially. He dropped the subject.

The next morning we took the boat and the good motor and retrieved our deer from across the bay. The caretakers chose to stay at the lodge. Later that day the floatplane arrived to take us back to Kodiak.

When we arrived back in Kodiak we called Rocky and filled him in on the situation. Somehow he was not surprised. In the spring when the two caretakers left the lodge there were several knives and a pistol missing. When Rocky confronted them with this fact, they told him that Bear must have taken them. Bear was not happy when advised of this conversation. Therefore, a few months later when one of these clowns walked into the laborer's union and asked Bear to use his position with the union to get him a job, it didn't go well for him. He did survive, but only because he could outrun Bear.

US TWO, MOOSE NOTHING... ALMOST

Every year we fly into our moose camp just south of Denali Park. The camp is located on a small pristine lake in the foothills of the Alaska Range. It is more than 50 miles to the nearest road, so we have it pretty much to ourselves.

Over the years we have developed a nice little camp. There is a raised wood floor for the 14 x 16 wall tent. We have a heater, cots, propane stove, camp chairs and a Honda 110 three-wheeler. The tent is located so we have a great view of the lake as well as a large clearing just south of the camp. We frequently spot bulls right from the tent.

This year the group was comprised of me and three friends: Ed, Reinhart and Pete.

Ed and I have been friends since fourth grade. He moved to Alaska three years after I got here. Ed is an outgoing guy and very easy to get along with. He has extensive experience hunting and fishing and is also a private pilot.

One bad thing about Ed is that he does seem to have the worst luck of anyone I know. A good example would be his house on Big Beaver Lake. There was a fire several years ago in the Mat-Su Valley called the Miller's Reach Fire. It burned thousands of acres and hundreds of homes. As this fire burned, Ed and his wife Linda, took a trip into Wasilla with their two dogs.

When they got to town they were informed that the fire had begun to spread and that it was headed toward Big Beaver Lake. They immediately turned around and raced for home to get their things, but found the road blocked by police who refused to let them pass. Everything they had in the world was burned up TWO DAYS LATER! Ed and I have been sharing outdoor adventures for more than 40 years and, in spite of the odds, are still alive.

Reinhold was a good friend of Ed's. I had met him a few times and he seemed like a good guy. He was born and raised in Alaska and was also a very good woodsman and pilot. Reinhold celebrated his 60th birthday on this trip. The last participant was Pete, one of my employees. Pete was a jack of all trades, but mostly a surveyor. He was a handy guy to have around because he could fix most anything.

It was opening day of moose season, and we were sitting at the lake without much expectation. We were very seldom successful on the opening day of the season; in fact the first two weeks generally have limited success. This is due to two factors. One is that the leaves are not off the brush, thereby limiting visibility; two is that the elusive bulls have not yet gone into the rut and are still thinking with their brains. During the afternoon of the first day, Reinhold took off to go get some items from my cabin. On his way back, he spotted four bulls in a bachelor herd near the camp!

We were, therefore, delighted to have four bulls just a short distance from our camp. The problem was that they were across a large creek that ran through a steep canyon with slopes covered by 20 to 30 foot alders. The alders were 100 yards thick on our side of the stream. (The other side also was thick with alders, but had some openings where you could get through without much effort.)

These alder barriers did not deter us because there was a small lake on the other side where Reinhold said he could land his Cub and ferry the meat back to our lake. This lake was about 1,000 feet in length and 150 foot wide, about one third the size of our base-camp lake.

We spent the rest of the evening planning the hunt. This included logistics, provisions, possible stalk scenarios and the consumption of several beers. The next morning we launched our expedition to collect one of the bulls. It was an overcast day with temperatures in the mid-40s. We left the camp at daybreak and began the one-mile hike to the creek.

It took us two hours through open tundra to reach the

creek and cross the canyon. We searched around for the best way through the alders, but ended up just busting through the brush down the hill to the creek. This was a 45-degree slope with large rocks interspersed in the alders. It made for some dicey footing. We were focused on getting to the moose, so we didn't give a lot of thought to how we planned to get back through this jungle.

The other side of the creek was not so bad. It was a flatter slope and far less brush. We located a path out of the creek with no alders or brush. Once out of the alders, we were in open tundra surrounded by spruce and birch trees. We could see for a couple of miles in all directions. Reinhold's lake was only a few hundred yards from where we came out of the bushes.

During the night the bulls had relocated to a spot about one and a half miles from the small lake, so, it took us another couple of hours to locate them. We followed their tracks a few hundred yards and then sat and glassed. We repeated this process several times. I spotted them first. All four bulls were in a small island of trees in the middle of a large clearing. There was one bull with a rack in excess of 60 inches, but he was in bad shape. He had patches of hide with no hair and you could see his ribs. I determined he would not be very good to eat. The other bulls were all in the 40 to 50 inch range and appeared to be in good health. It was simply a matter of slipping into the woods, concealing ourselves in the trees and moving up on them. The wind was right so I only needed to be quiet. Reinhold saw what I was doing and held back so he wouldn't spook the animals. Ed and Pete had gone in another direction and were a few hundred yards off to our right.

Within minutes I was within 75 yards of the bulls, all standing at the edge of the trees. I picked out a nice bull and dropped him with one shot. The other three ran back into the island of trees.

I had already determined that we only wanted one bull because of the long pack back to the little lake, so I intended to let the other bulls go on their way. As I got closer to the trees, I noticed that my bull was back on his feet so I shot him again.

At that point Reinhold started yelling, "Don't shoot anymore of them damn moose!"

I was perplexed by this admonition. I continued over to the

moose with Reinhold still yelling at me. The surviving bulls had exited the area. I found the bull quite dead and prepared to start skinning him when Reinhold arrived. He proceeded to berate me on how much work it would be to pack all this meat. I pointed out that there were four of us, so two trips a piece was not that bad.

Bob with one of the moose camp bulls.

That is when Reinhold pointed out the second bull I had shot which was lying 15 feet away. Oops, now we had a problem. Instead of 500 to 600 pounds of meat we now had 1,000 to 1,200 pounds one and a half miles from the lake.

Ed and Pete soon arrived and took turns slapping me and making references to my heritage. Once we had completed this ritual, we carefully analyzed our problem. Our combined intellect decided that the best plan was for Reinhold and Ed to start skinning while Pete and I would return to camp for the three-wheeler.

The trip back was no big deal. In fact it was a pleasant walk in beautiful country, other than crawling through the alders along the creek. We didn't know it at the time, but it was also our last pleasant experience for the day. It was on the return trip that we realized the extent of our undertaking. We found ourselves with the three-wheeler at the top of the steep alder-covered slope leading down to the creek.

Alder growth tends to angle down a slope. Thus, when you take a three-wheeler down the slope it tends to run on top of the alders. Even with this advantage, it took us more than an hour to go the 100 yards to the creek. We continued through an alder-free opening on the other side and that allowed us to get up out of the canyon with relative ease.

We headed for the lake and the moose meat with Pete riding on the rear rack of the Honda. Ahead of us was a small stream with heavy brush, trees, and large rocks along its banks. We walked up and down stream for a half mile before we found a crossing that was, at best, possible, but certainly difficult. This hairy crossing with an unloaded three-wheeler caused me some concern about crossing with a loaded vehicle. We were somewhat cavalier about this and concluded we would cross that bridge when we came to it.

When we arrived at the kill site we found that Ed and Reinhold had completed butchering one bull and had just started on the second. Pete took over Reinhold's duties so Reinhold could return to camp for the Cub and fly it to the small lake.

Meanwhile, we loaded the three-wheeler with about 300 pounds of meat, and I set out for the small lake. In order to haul that much meat, it is necessary to tie a hindquarter on the seat and then sit atop that hindquarter. The rear rack will take another hindquarter and the front rack will take a front quarter. This makes the whole contraption very unstable with a tendency to tip over at the slightest provocation. Once the small Honda 110 three-wheeler is loaded in this manner it looks like a pile of meat moving down the trail--with me astride the whole mess looking quite regal.

Reinhold had reached the creek crossing when I caught up with him. We took the hindquarter off the seat and Reinhold packed it across the creek. With great difficulty, we got the rest of the meat across while still tied to the 3-wheeler. We did this with Reinhold walking on one side of the contraption while I took the other side. I manipulated the throttle and we both did our best to keep the thing from falling over as it traversed the rough terrain. Once across, we reloaded the hindquarter and traveled to the small lake without incident. We left the meat on the shore of the lake. Reinhold continued on to our camp to get his plane and I returned to the kill site for another load. (It would take four more loads to get all the meat and horns out.)

The second load was also about 300 pounds and just as unstable. When I arrived at the creek crossing, I was getting very tired and, therefore, let stupidity and bad judgment overrule good sense. I figured I had crossed the creek with most of a load last time; why not cross with a whole load this time and save all the work of unloading, packing, and reloading the meat? I am a hotshot three-wheel driver! No problem!

Needless to say, it didn't turn out as planned. I was less than half way across the creek when one tire hit a rock and the whole thing rolled over on its side. I found myself flat on my back in mud and rocks with the three-wheeler and the moose meat on top of me. This was a predicament, but I wasn't hurt and the other guys would eventually wonder where I went and come find me. I settled in for an hour of being uncomfortable, but not really at risk, while I waited to be rescued.

My level of comfort changed dramatically when I noticed a disquieting sound. It was the sound of liquid dripping on a hot surface. I looked around as best I could and soon realized that the gas line had pulled loose from the gas tank and gas was dripping on the exhaust pipe and evaporating. It was only a matter of time until the exhaust cooled off or the whole mess, including me, went up in flames. I could imagine the guys trying to sort out roast moose from roast Bob. Basic survival instincts demanded that I not wait to see which option would prevail.

I go to the gym three days a week and lift weights. I never thought it would pay off in terms of saving my life. The three-wheeler was on my legs and hips and the hindquarter was on my stomach and lower chest. My arms were free so I could untie the hindquarter and get it off my chest. Then I managed to wiggle my elbows down to my waist so that I could push up on the seat of the three-wheeler. The idea was to push the contraption up and over so it would be back on its wheels.

I would guess the total weight of the meat and machine was about 450 pounds. Under normal circumstances there would be no way I could roll this much weight while laying on my back; it is amazing what adrenaline can do when you are pumping enough of it to last a year or two.

I pushed up with everything I had and let out a muffled

grunt. The three-wheeler rolled back upright and I scrambled out of the hole in a nano-second. I promptly unloaded the rest of the meat and packed it across the stream. Along with the wet and muddy meat, I was soaked in mud from my shoulder blades to my ankles.

My good buddies were not impressed when I related my story to them. They were just concerned that it had taken me so long to get back for the next load. They wanted to get back to camp and then head for Anchorage. It's nice to have friends who are sensitive and caring, but how would I know?

The rest of the meat-hauling trips and ferrying the meat to camp in the Super Cub went without incident. Reinhold could take off with only one piece of meat per trip due to the shortness of the lake. Finally, Reinhold took the last load and said he would return to fly Ed back to camp. Pete and I would drive the three-wheeler back.

Now, remember the informative comment that alders tend to grow down-slope? Well, Pete and I found ourselves standing on the bank of the creek looking 100 yards uphill at a sort of punji pit of flexible stakes. We didn't have any choice but to just point the three-wheeler uphill and go for it.

We went about three feet before we had alders jammed into the brake pedal, between the tire and the fenders, and under the handlebars. We cleared the alders out and tried again with the same result. It was becoming very clear that we had not given the situation enough thought before driving down into this canyon. In other words, we were using our standard M.O.

Pete and I were both in good shape physically, even though you could probably question our mental capacity. We spent the next three hours picking up a 150 pound three-wheeler, moving it forward three or four feet, and dropping it through the alders. Repeating this routine, we reached the top of the canyon soaked in sweat and bone-tired.

Ed and Reinhold flew over us a couple of times for moral support. That was nice of them, even though we didn't appreciate them at the time. When we got to the top of the slope and broke out into the tundra we were too tired to celebrate. We just saddled up and headed for the camp. All the meat was stacked up on the shore of the lake with a note from our former friends, saying they had left for Anchorage.

It was late in the day and the weather was starting to turn bad, giving us the choice of leaving right then or spending another night at the camp. There is a rule among most pilots to not make decisions or fly when you are very tired. I managed to violate both parts of the rule with one decision. We jumped into my plane and took off. The lake is at 1,400 feet in elevation. Anchorage is at 70 feet. When we took off we had a cloud ceiling of about a 500 feet. It was reasonable to assume as we traveled toward Anchorage that the terrain would drop lower and we would get more and more ceiling. It didn't work that way. By the time we were about one third of the way home the clouds had dropped right down to the trees. I opted to turn back.

That is when I discovered the clouds had dropped down behind us also. We were in deep kimchee. There was no place to land and I was not an IFR pilot, trained to fly in the clouds. The only place that looked open was the Lake Creek canyon, which is about a quarter-mile wide and 200 to 300 feet deep. It snakes along with many curves, and ends up in the Yentna Valley, which is on the route to Anchorage. Flying down that canyon would be like flying through a big long curving tube. This was not an option I liked, but I had really run out of other ideas.

I advised Pete that he would probably not age quite as much if he closed his eyes for the next 20 minutes. He didn't take the advice. That took 25 years off his life. I slowed the plane as much as possible and dropped under the clouds and into the canyon.

When I went into that canyon I had about 1,500 hours of flying time under my belt; when we came out, it felt like 3,000 hours. In some of the steep turns the wing tips were within feet of the trees on the sides of the canyon. When we came around each turn, we didn't know if we would find the canyon full of clouds or not. If that happened I would have no choice but to climb up into the clouds and fly blind with the instruments back toward Anchorage. This type of decision is often the last one that non-IFR pilots make in their lives.

We had to watch both wings and make sure we didn't get too low or too high. It was not a fun trip. When we came around the last bend and broke out into the wide flat Yentna Valley it was a tremendous relief. We still had very little ceiling, but we could follow the Yentna River without fear of running into a hillside.

It had been a hard day. We had packed meat, fought our way through the alders with the three-wheeler and completed a very harrowing flight. But when we came out of that canyon neither of us was tired. It's funny what a little excitement will do to pump you up.

The rest of the trip was stressful due to limited visibility, but at least it was not terrifying. By the time we got to Anchorage the ceiling was up to 1,500 feet and we had five miles of visibility. I landed on Campbell Lake and taxied to my house. We were a couple of used-up hombres when we crawled out of that airplane. I will admit, though, that I almost fell asleep during the 30-foot walk from the plane to my house. All of my systems were running on empty.

It was two days before the weather had cleared sufficiently for us to return for the moose meat. Of course, a grizzly had found the meat alongside the lake and had eaten the back straps and tenderloins and buried the rest. Like a bulldozer he had torn up an acre of tundra and piled it on his cache. This trip just kept getting better and better. We dug the meat back up, and because it was in meat sacks we managed to salvage most of it. It took two trips to fly it back to Anchorage where we had the meat cut and wrapped. Not having heard from our former friends, we debated if we should give them a share. Pete suggested we give them the part the bear took. They could go retrieve it themselves.

Ed and Reinhold showed up a few days later bearing gifts of alcoholic beverages showing sufficient remorse for not helping. We relented and gave them a share of the meat as well as the bill for processing it. They didn't argue.

KILUDA BAY AGAIN: ARE YOU NUTS?

I don't know why we keep going back to Kiluda Bay. Almost every time we go there we damned near get killed. It must be that it is just a real neat place to hunt or we're just plain stupid. Probably both. There have been several incidents of falling off mountainsides, getting stranded by surf, foul weather, unusually dumb caretakers, high seas and equipment failures. All these things happen, but we still go back. I can't explain why.

Kiluda Bay is located on the east side of Kodiak Island. It is a very remote location, many miles from the nearest road or airport. The closest community is the Alaska Native village of Old Harbor, which is 30 miles by sea from the lodge. The area is mostly steep, grass-covered mountains with some alder patches and small stands of cottonwood trees. The severe weather in this part of Alaska is notorious.

Kiluda Bay Lodge on departure day.

105

It was several years ago that Billy, Bear, and I were hunting on a point across from the lodge operated by an old friend, Rocky. I have hunted and fished with both of these guys on many occasions, and for this trip, we were joined by Stanley, a big friendly construction guy who loves the outdoors.

Relaxing at Dog Bay on the one nice day of the year.

Bear is always great to have along when you need excellent outboard mechanic skills. Billy was a special agent with the

FBI for 26 years. He spent almost his whole career in Alaska. Billy is a very friendly guy and tends to keep his head in stressful situations. He is married to Susan who obviously didn't marry nearly as well as Billy. Susan loves to fish, but has always had the good sense not to go hunting with us. I have been in tough spots with both of these guys and we always seem to survive. It is probably due to dumb luck and....well, just dumb luck.

The area we were hunting was open grassland located mostly on steep terrain directly across from the lodge. (With a good set of binoculars, you could easily observe us from the lodge.) There are two small beaches, but the rest of the shoreline is mostly rock cliffs.

It was overcast with occasional rain squalls. Late in the day, we had taken two or three deer and were ready to return to the lodge. We were using the decrepit, 14-foot aluminum open boat that was powered by one of Rocky's marginal motors that tended to sputter a lot and quit frequently. The boat was old and flimsy, but only leaked a little.

To get back home we had a couple of options. One was to run down the shoreline to the head of the bay and then along the other shore to the lodge. The other option was to just cut across the bay which was one quarter of the distance.

Of course we opted to cut across. Heck, the weather was not bad and in our minds we were able seamen. You would think, after all of our weather-related close calls in this place, we would learn. But we have proven over and over again that we don't learn or think well. That is why our trips have such high adventure.

It was about two miles across the bay; we had a 10-knot wind and maybe one-foot waves, easy going for this area. It was a typical set-up for Kodiak; lure you in with nice weather, then lower the boom!

We were about half way across when Kodiak decided to unleash the big wind on us. Before we knew it, we were in three to four foot waves. Suddenly, the nice day was a dim memory. The wind was coming from the direction of the lodge, so we just kept going straight ahead. Turning around would have resulted in the boat capsizing. Our route was really the only option we had that didn't involve swimming or being dead; we were not certain we would avoid either of those possibilities, but at least we had a chance. Alaska was squeezing the trigger.

As the boat crashed into the waves they would break over the bow. The spray would land right on us and the motor each time. When the water hit the motor it would start sputtering and so would my heart. Bear was running the motor, and each time it sputtered he would put in a little choke and get it running smoothly again. His outboard motor experience was really paying off.

Billy and I were in the bow with the paddles, ready to keep the bow into the waves if the motor quit. We were sure it would be a futile effort, but it made us feel better to be prepared for action. Later, Bear told me he wasn't scared, but I did notice he was not engaging in any idle conversation during the ride.

The water temperature this time of year in Kodiak is around 35 degrees. Cold water hitting us in the face and leaking through our rain gear was certainly keeping us awake. The boat slamming into the waves also kept our attention.

Rocky's boats were not in the best of shape so the structural integrity of the craft was suspect, particularly in this situation. We were also taking on a lot of water. Our extensive planning prior to the trip had not included obtaining a bail bucket or pump. In fact, we did not include any survival or communications gear. All we had were life jackets, so at least they would be able to find the bodies. I guess when you plan a trip while consuming mass quantities of beer you miss a few things.

We settled into a routine: hit the wave, fix the motor, take on more water and calculate the diminishing odds of survival. It took us 45 minutes and several lifetimes to reach the lodge. When we got there we were soaked to the skin, with the deer floating in the water that had accumulated in the bottom of the boat. Our rifles and packs were scattered around the boat, covered in water and deer blood. Everything was saturated, including us. It took 10 minutes to pry the paddle out of Billy's hands and I had to change underwear. Bear stopped hyperventilating about an hour later.

The caretaker guys at the lodge said they enjoyed watching the show through their binoculars. They did say they were perplexed that our hair stayed straight up on the backs of our heads with so much wind and rain. When we inquired why they didn't come out to help us, they said someone needed to be around to notify our next of kin and they took that responsibility very seriously. The fact is they didn't know we were having motor problems. They just assumed we were stupid and chose to make a crossing in high winds. These guys are strong believers in Darwin.

Normal people would have been deterred from going out in bad weather by such an experience, but we are neither normal, nor smart. Kodiak had a clean shot at us and missed, so obviously we were invincible. With this premise firmly in mind, the next morning we loaded up the flimsy boats and marginal motors and headed down the bay in heavy snow and minimum visibility. Stanley and I were in one boat; Billy and Bear were in the other. At this time, Stanley had limited experience surviving hunting adventures with me. He was about to get a crash course.

As we went around the point into Dog Bay we spotted several deer on a plateau surrounded by 150-foot cliffs with a very steep and high mountain on the back side. The plateau was mostly grass with a few alders in the gullies. A ridiculously lucky shot from the boat at 300 yards dropped one of the deer. We went to shore and found a way up to the top, which involved some rather sophisticated rock-climbing.

Once we got to the top we had little trouble finding the deer. In fact we spotted another buck, which I promptly shot. Once we had the deer dressed out we began contemplating our return to the boat. It seems that once you claw your way up these rocks it is very dangerous to climb back down the way you came. We began a search for a better route. There were several gullies cutting into the cliffs, but they didn't go all the way down and were very steep.

We finally found a small gully that seemed to have a reasonable grade, but we couldn't see all the way to the bottom. The last 20 or 30 yards were out of sight. I was sure that once I got part way down, the rest of the gully would be in sight and if there were any problems we would figure it out then. The ground was covered with ice, which meant that once we started down, there would be no turning back. I volunteered to be the second guy down. Having made this decision, we rolled both deer down the gully. They bounced down the chute and slid out of sight.

At this point, Stanley reopened negotiations over who

would go first. Seeing as how he was bigger than I and had a larger caliber gun, the original decision was reversed. I started down the gully.

There were two problems with this gully. One was that it was narrow, very steep, and covered with ice (with occasional clumps of grass sticking out of the ice.) The second problem was a small creek in the bottom of the gully that was frozen and, therefore, very slick. Part way down I was walking with one foot on either side of the creek ice and holding onto clumps of grass to keep my balance. One slip and it would be a luge ride with no sled and an uncertain finish line.

At about the halfway point I could see all the way down to the bottom. It was not a pretty sight. The gully ended at a 20-foot cliff with large boulders strewn around to break my fall and/or several body parts. Going back up was not an option; it was just too slick.

This was not a good deal and was actually getting worse. Having not heard from me, my genius friend had also started down and was already past the point of no return...at least I wouldn't die alone. I was concerned he would slip and knock me down the chute like a curling stone. Where I was standing, the gully was so steep I could touch the ground with my hand without bending over.

After studying the situation for some time I concluded there was only one way out. About 10 feet to my left were some alders growing on a steep slope. If I could get enough leverage to jump off of this slick, side hill and land with one foot on a six-inch square of flat ground five feet away and grab an alder branch before I lost my balance, I might be able to use the alders to side-hill over to more alders that went all the way down to the beach. The odds of this being successful were as long as the previous sentence.

Because we were both in the gully, the odds of someone finding another way down and going for help were slim. I therefore took the jump option under serious consideration. It was jump, or wait for spring.

You make several major decisions in your life--who to marry, what career to pursue, what moose gun to buy, etc.--but it is seldom that you make a decision that will result in your being dead or not. These are the really hard decisions. They are even harder when you are dumb enough to get yourself in a predicament like this in the first place.

In this case, it was hard but really pre-determined.

I studied that 6-inch square of flat dirt and ice for a long time and then just jumped. It seemed like I was airborne for a minute or two. My left foot came down a few inches above the flat spot and slid down to it. I swung my right foot out in front of me and lunged for the alder. I grabbed an alder branch and clung to it with both hands, which left me sprawled on my face on a very steep ice-covered slope, thanking God and his entire staff for getting me through that jump.

I grabbed the next branch over and started working my way to the main alder patch. My equally frightened and soon-to-be-religious companion followed suit. We lowered ourselves through the alders to the beach, picked up our deer and started back to the lodge.

On the boat ride back in it dawned on both of us that throughout this whole ordeal in never occurred to us to take our rifles off our backs. It is interesting that we never considered leaving the guns behind to make the jump less dangerous. The NRA would have been proud.

The rest of the deer hunt was conducted on relatively flat ground near the lodge. We didn't get as many deer, but we didn't say "Oh no, we're gonna die!" once. Life is full of trade-offs.

SOMETIMES PRINCE WILLIAM
HAS BAD MANNERS

Sam and I went hunting and fishing in Prince William Sound several times a year in his luxury cruiser. Back then, Sam was a partner in my firm and also owned one of the larger construction companies in Alaska. He had grown up hunting and fishing and thoroughly enjoyed the outdoors.

I always admired Sam's ability to cut through the details

and minutia of business and get to the heart of the issue. In contrast, I found him to be more of a "gentleman" hunter than a gut-it-out type of guy. This was reflected in his boat. It was a 45-foot Ocean with overstuffed furniture, twin marine 300 diesel engines, forced air heating, TV, a stateroom, and many other conveniences.

Going out with Sam was always a cushy experience. We would hunt Sitka black tail deer in the fall and winter and black bear in the spring. We even came across an occasional brown bear. Often we would spot bears from the boat and then plan a stalk.

I remember one trip in particular with Sam and Raymond, a retired hunting guide who now worked for Sam. We spotted a large black bear while we were anchored in Bainbridge Passage. He was on a snow slide right where it intersected the beach, next to a 15-foot drop-off where the tide had washed the snow away.

I decided to shoot from the boat because there was no way to go ashore without spooking him into the brush. Shooting from a boat even when it is anchored is very difficult. I figured this out after I had fired the 10th or 12th shot with little effect. The bear took off up the very steep snow slide, with me blowing holes in the snow all around him. I finally hit him and he came tumbling down the slope over the cliff and onto the rocks below. Sam commented that that should take care of him.

We were all astounded when the bear got up and started running down the beach. I shot him several more times before he went down. Sam commented that he was the toughest bear he had ever seen. As Raymond and I ran to the skiff to retrieve our trophy, Sam yelled, "Hey, he is back up again." I grabbed my rifle and gave him two or three more rounds.

Sam warned us that if that bear got in the water and started swimming toward the boat he would fire up the engines and leave. He wanted no part of an invincible bear. He had no more than made the statement when the bear got back up lurched into the water and started swimming. It only went 10 feet and returned to shore. Sam took his hand off the starter. I shot the bear again.

We then launched the skiff and went to shore. I started toward the bear and Raymond went in the other direction.

Experience guided Raymond's path; ignorance guided mine. As I walked up to the bear he got back to his feet. I finished him with one .300 Winchester Mag to the head. I am not sure what would have happened if I had missed, but I am sure Raymond would not have been hurt. He was far too smart to walk up to that bear before watching it for a while. When we skinned him we found 11 bullet holes in his hide, several of which should have killed him. He was a 6-foot, 8-inch boar and one tough puppy.

The Super Bear once he was finally subdued.

In addition to hunting, we fished for halibut, cod, salmon, shrimp and crab all year. Prince William Sound is one of the best places to fish in Alaska. It has relatively protected waters that literally teem with fish. We trolled for salmon, mooched for halibut and cod, and set crab and shrimp pots. There were a few minor problems over the years, but nothing to write home about. We consistently filled our freezers with fish and deer. We traveled to all corners of the sound looking for game and fish and just exploring.

There are hundreds of islands and passages as well as harbors and rivers. It would take you many years to get to all the places in the sound, but they would be very enjoyable years. I really grew to like good ol' Prince William and was pleased when Princess Diana named her oldest son after the Sound. I didn't even know she frequented the place.

Bob with a Prince William Sound halibut.

One spring, Sam and I decided to take his daughter and my youngest son with us on a spring bear hunt and fishing trip. The kids were six or seven years old at the time. We were bound for Evans Island in the western sound, about 90 miles from the quaint Alaska village of Whittier, where Sam kept his boat.

Getting to Evans Island is a two- to three-hour trip down Knight Island Passage. The scenery is spectacular, with snow-capped mountains on both sides, blue water and radiant green on the tree-covered slopes. We had calm seas and clear weather, so it was a very enjoyable cruise. We had great luck and caught halibut, lingcod, black cod and a few salmon. The kids were having a ball. We fixed them up with lightweight poles and let them catch two- to seven-pound black cod until they were tired. We saw sea lions, seals and whales. We had porpoises running alongside of the boat and the kids got some good pictures of them. We also had a pod of killer whales traveling alongside of us for a mile or so. The kids were getting quite a show and were truly enjoying it. We were pleased with our decision to bring them on this trip.

After loading up on fish, we just kicked back for the next day and kind of toured the western Sound. We went through Bainbridge Passage and out into the Gulf of Alaska where Sam and I caught some 100 to 200-pound halibut. Then we cruised the shore of Montague Island and then back to Evans Island. The weather was pleasant and we thoroughly enjoyed ourselves. We saw some black bears, but passed on trying for one. We were, therefore, relaxed and feeling good the next morning when we started back to the quaint Alaska village of Whittier.

The one consistent thing about Alaska weather is that it is not consistent or predictable. We called the weather-guessers first thing in the morning. They predicted 10 to 15-knot winds and two-foot seas, a piece of cake for a 45-foot boat. We set off along the shore of Knight Island intending to cross Knight Passage near Culross Island. Knight Passage is about 15 miles across at that point. Sam's boat cruses at 20 knots and can handle two-foot waves with no problem. We figured it would take us less than an hour to make the crossing.

The weather-guessers were right, but so is a broken clock twice a day. We had two-foot seas and some wind, but no big deal. The sky was now overcast and it was looking a little nasty, but still nothing to get us very concerned.

We reached our crossing point and headed across the passage. The conditions were not ideal, but certainly not threatening. We were about half way across when the wind began to kick up out of the north--about a 50-mile fetch at this point.

This allowed the waves to build quite a bit before they got to us. With the high mountains on either side of the passage there is a tendency to funnel the winds and increase their velocity. We soon found ourselves in 15 to 20-foot waves with spray breaking over the bow as we hit each wave. Sam was at the wheel and things were going okay, but a little tense. We had the boat oriented straight into the wind and she was handling the seas just fine. Due to the wind direction we had to change course slightly and were now headed toward Eshamy Bay instead of Culross Passage. Both kids were a little scared.

I was reassuring them that we were fine when I noticed that Sam was having some problems with the wheel. I went over to him and asked, "What's up?" He said that the steering had gone out and he had to turn the wheel four or five times before the boat reacted. This was not good.

Sam asked me to take over and sat down. I grabbed the wheel just as we started down the backside of a wave. The main problem was that when the boat got to the bottom of each wave and started up the next wave the bow would start to turn to one side or the other. You didn't know which way it was going to go until it started turning. You would then turn the wheel like crazy to get the bow back into the wave, before the boat turned sidewise and flipped over, which would result in a four-course, sit-down dinner for the crabs.

This was a real challenge because you had those four or five turns before anything happened. I also noticed that the steering problem was slowly getting worse, as were our odds for survival.

I started using the two props to help steer so I was a very busy guy--turn the wheel, then manipulate the throttles, then turn the wheel again. It didn't look good and the thought of killing those two little kids just kept hammering in my head. I had slowed the boat down to adjust for the rough seas, so we were only doing about 10 knots or less. Our one-hour crossing had turned into a two-hour ordeal.

To this day I don't know how we did it, but we made it to the other side. I think God was looking out for those kids. They already had been punished enough with the burden of us for dads....

We anchored in Eshamy Bay, fixed dinner, and discussed what to do. We could call for help and a tow, or if the weather settled down we could make temporary repairs and limp back to the quaint Alaska village of Whittier. We opted to attempt to figure out what had happened to the helm and see if we could fix it. You would think an engineer and a contractor could handle a little steering problem.

Sam and I tore into the steering system and finally discovered a leak in a hydraulic hose. We patched the leak and used the last of the hydraulic fluid to restore the system. We were good to go!

The next morning we set out for Culross Island. This meant crossing five mile-wide Port Nellie Juan, and we ran into similar seas on this crossing. Partway across, the wind came up and the seas were up to five or six feet. Once again, the steering went out and we had another wild ride. It was not as long or as dramatic as the first one, but still scary enough.

As you come around the corner into Culross Passage there are a lot of rocks in the water so it is best to steer a course well offshore. The problem was that the further offshore we went the bigger the waves were. We split the difference and plotted a course closer to the rocks than normal, but still enough offshore for a margin of comfort. With the faulty steering it was a gamble. We made it into the passage, but it was a tense few minutes.

It turned out we had two holes in the hydraulic hose and inadequate intelligence to test the system after repairs. We stopped in Culross Passage to do further repairs. Since there was no hydraulic fluid left, we used the last of our Jack Daniels as a substitute. Considering what we had been through, it was a major sacrifice. We made the rest of the trip to the quaint Alaska village of Whittier in relatively calm seas using the two props as the main steering device. My son has never asked to go back to Prince William Sound. Sam has moved his boat to Seattle, so I don't get to the Sound much anymore. I kind of miss ol' Willy.

You might ask why I refer to the quaint Alaska village of Whittier instead of just Whittier. Well, Whittier is a town of about 300 or 400 people in Prince William Sound. Until recently, the only access was by boat or railroad; there was no road to the town. There is a bar owner in Anchorage named Mr. Whitekeys. He says he owns the sleaziest bar in Spenard, the sleaziest part of Anchorage. Once, while addressing a Rotary Club, Whitekeys was asked to define sleazy. He thought a minute and then said, "Whittier."

During the 1990s, the State of Alaska spent $80 million building a 13-mile road to Whittier that shares the Alaska Railroad tunnel cutting through the mountains from Portage. That is about $200,000 per resident. Seeing as how only about half of them wanted the road, I guess that makes it about $500,000 per Whittier resident who wanted a road. If they'd had to pay for it, I wonder what the mortgage payment would be.

The State of Alaska paid for it and now collects a fee to use the tunnel/road. I inquired as to how that was doing in terms of paying off the debt. They told me the fees didn't even pay for the cost of the people collecting the fees. Another successful government project!! We refer to it as the longest cul-de-sac in Alaska; so we could refer to Whittier as the sleazy place at the end of the longest, most-expensive cul-de-sac in the world... or a quaint Alaska village. (I prefer not to hurt their feelings.)

FISH MUSHING AT THE KING HOLE

We once had a secret fishing spot we called the King Hole. It has since been discovered by some "guides" and is pretty well fished out. The King Hole had a small run of fish and just couldn't take the pressure of a professional operation. We seldom took more than 25 or 30 fish out of the hole each year. The guides took that many in a week. It was a good spot, in its prime, to catch king salmon without the crowds.

One of the reasons there were so few people at the King Hole was that it was a real challenge to land and take off in that small stream. The landing channel was about 500 feet long and then went around a 90-degree turn. It was also only 75 feet wide with brush and trees on both sides. That was enough room to land if you were skillful, but too short to take off.

The takeoff trick is to go around the 90-degree bend, get the plane on the step, and then make a step turn around the bend and take off in the 500-foot channel, all the while keeping your wings out of the trees and your passengers from having a heart attack. It is quite a sight to see a floatplane careening around that corner on one float with the trees whizzing by 5 feet off the wing tips. It was an exciting landing and takeoff that most pilots preferred to forego. It's amazing there aren't large piles of twisted aluminum all around the King Hole, but I don't recall even one accident there. We were very tight mouthed about the King Hole, so very few people even knew about it to begin with.

The King Hole is really a small, slow-moving stream that runs into a very large fast-moving river. The kings come up the river and into the stream to spawn. It is located about 70 miles north of Anchorage in a low-lying area in the Yentna River valley, 60 miles from the nearest road. It is surrounded mostly by tundra with trees and brush along the banks of the stream. The water is somewhat colored, but much clearer than the water in the river, which is glacial-fed and full of rock flour. The kings run in June, so the whole area is bright green with very lush flora.

One of the best fishing spots was a small spit right at the mouth of the stream. The trick with this spot was to keep the fish from running into the fast-moving river and breaking your line. Once you got a fish on, you would walk upstream and try to keep the fish in the slow water. My wife Candace, *aka* Ma Bell, and I were there with several of our friends from the Shell Lake crowd. The group included Scooter, the Shell Lake 'ranger." Scooter was a very outgoing fellow who had a way of enjoying himself under any circumstance. Scooter's wife, Champagne Ann, was also in attendance, another person who fully appreciated humor. The rest of the party was Kenny, the Shell Lake "marshal," and Dave the Torch, the Shell Lake "fire marshal." Both of these guys were what I would describe as lovable oddballs.

We were fishing with eggs at the mouth and were getting some nice kings. I wandered back into the woods to take care of nature calling. In doing so, I discovered a small canoe about five feet long and 18 inches wide. It was made out of canvas and small- diameter branches. It had obviously been there for several years, and its structural integrity was thus somewhat suspect. I carried it back to the group and announced that I would be taking the canoe out in the stream to catch a king. We should have realized this was a formula for disaster, but it seemed like a good idea if you didn't give it much thought.

Landing a king at the King Hole without the use of watercraft.

I got my paddle and anchor out of the plane, picked up my fishing rod and launched. I was surprised that the canoe didn't leak or turn over or create any other disaster that normally should have happened. Everyone was getting a kick out of me paddling around in this miniature boat. I was "the man." I stopped near the mouth and started fishing.

It wasn't long before I hooked a good-sized king. I was using 40-pound test line, so when the king took off up the stream, I just held on and off we went, with the king pulling me like a dog team pulls a sled.

I was yelling, "Mush fish, mush!" I had this guy right where I wanted him. Everyone was laughing so hard they could barely stand up. The way things were going the king would soon tire and I would have him. Things did not look good for Mr. King. I anticipated he would tow me a mile or so upstream and then tire out. I would paddle back downstream with my catch to the applause and admiration of my friends. This wasn't really a plan - it was just reacting to an uncontrolled series of events.

The king then made a strategic decision. He switched ends and started running downstream toward the river, with me in tow. Being at least as smart as the fish, I just threw out the anchor to stop the canoe; the problem was that I forgot to tie the rope to the canoe (which brings into question my comment about being as smart as the fish).

As the last of the rope disappeared over the side of the canoe my options narrowed: cut the line and let the fish go (which I believe is against the law in Alaska), or be dragged into the fast-moving river.

I reasoned that the first option would result in considerable ridicule from my friends. The second would result in an exciting ride part way down the river, ending with me pinned against a logjam with the other debris. With the speed at which the water was moving in the river, the odds of survival unscathed were akin to a P.E.T.A. member at an NRA convention.

In the meantime, the fish was accelerating and, consequently, so was I. As we approached the mouth of the stream and my group of friends, I began giving them instructions on how to save me. I don't think they could hear me over the laughter. I noted that no one was making preparations for my arrival or rescue. This was not the glorious return I had envisioned.

I had resigned myself to cutting the line as I sailed past the group. At the last minute, Ma Bell waded into the stream over the top of her hip boots and grabbed the canoe with a gaff hook and pulled me to shore.

She told me later that it suddenly dawned on her that if I went into the river I would probably lose the 40-pound fish, so she had to do something; besides, she needed me to fly the plane. I appreciated the fact that she had come up with two good reasons to save me. She did reflect on the fact that I was well insured and she would have become a wealthy widow, but concluded that the widow status was only a matter of time considering my exploits to date. My friends, on the other hand, were perfectly content to watch me go down the river in a very small boat.

Just wait until one of them is in a tight spot....

WHEN IT RAINS THE RIVERS GET DEEPER?

I have a friend named Vic who is a commercial fisherman in Cordova, a community known as "a small Alaskan drinking village with a fishing problem." Vic is also an avid deer hunter. Like most commercial fishermen, he is a big burly guy with lots of time on his hands when the fish are not running. This works out well for me because Vic also has a fishing boat to use on our deer hunts. We have gone on several trips to Hinchinbrook Island and other islands around Cordova. He is an excellent outdoorsman and sailor. This usually kept me out of trouble on these trips, but not always.

John and I went hunting with Vic in the late fall. John was one of my managers. He was also a surveyor and therefore comfortable in the woods, but didn't have a lot of experience hunting. He was an outgoing guy, but a little strange in some ways. He always kept you guessing as to what he was thinking. It made for an interesting trip with Vic being so straightforward and John being oblique.

In tends to rain in Cordova quite a bit. In fact, they say people in Cordova know it is winter when the rain turns to snow. Late fall is when they get most of the rain. We knew that, but went hunting anyway.

Cordova is located in Prince William Sound, so the area is heavily forested with a very rugged coastline. The mainland and almost all of the islands are also very rugged mountain terrain. It makes for some challenging hunting. Not only are you struggling up mountains through thick brush, you are usually dealing with some sort of precipitation.

Blacktail deer are very good at hiding in the bushes, which is another challenge to filling a freezer. One upside is that when the sun does shine, this part of Alaska has some of the most spectacular scenery in the world.

Vic's boat only cruises at five or six knots, so it took us most of a day to travel from Cordova to our hunting area. We left

Cordova early in the morning and cruised along the north shore of Hawkins Island until we came to Hinchinbrook Island. Then we traveled along Hinchinbrook's shore to Deer Cove. We had good visibility most of the way with high overcast and light winds. It is a beautiful trip if the weather will let you see the mountains and the tree-covered islands.

We arrived at Deer Cove late in the day and found a good sheltered anchorage. We had dinner, told a few lies and hit the sack. This was one of Vic's favorite hunting spots. It is relatively flat land near the coast, but quickly rises up into mountain terrain. There are a lot of clearings that make for good spotting locations. The weather was looking like rain, but nothing unusual for this area. Things were going well; we were off to a good start on this trip.

We had three-wheeler ATVs with us on the boat, so when we finished breakfast, we took them to shore, anticipating the big load of delicious deer we would soon have to haul. This task was somewhat of an ordeal. Our ATVs weighed about 300 pounds each, so we couldn't just pick them up to move them. We used the winch to lower them into Vic's 14-foot aluminum skiff. We took the skiff to shore and tipped it on its side and drove the 3-wheeler out of the boat. This sounds a lot easier than it was. It took us 30 minutes to get the first three-wheeler out of the boat without breaking something on the three-wheeler or tearing up the skiff. It was also a challenge to get the vehicle out of the boat without getting too much of the ocean into the boat.

After going through this routine three times we had used up half the morning. The long shoring done, we saddled up and headed for the hills. It had not rained for two days, so we were on a roll. The plan was to ride the vehicles as far as we could inland toward the higher terrain and then hoof it from there. Blacktail deer tend to stay in the high country until snow drives them down. There are lots of game trails and clearings, so we had good going most of the way.

After about five miles we came to a stream that was too deep to cross with the three-wheelers, so we parked them and waded across. The water was right to the top of our hip boots, but it wasn't moving very fast, so we had little trouble getting across. The stream was only 30 feet across because it was confined to the bottom of a steep gully. This gully widened out as it went up into the mountains, turning into a large drainage basin. We were aware of this fact, but just didn't put together the implications of a wide drainage basin and a rising creek. The high water mark, which was several feet above the creek surface, also would have been a clue for anyone paying attention. Putting all these facts together would have involved thinking, but we were on vacation, so we avoided this activity at all costs. Vic should have known better, though.

It seems it is always easier going out than coming back in the Alaska bush. We headed up the side of a mountain looking for deer. We split up so we could spook the deer toward us in a classic flanking maneuver. I had gone only a short distance when a buck came trotting down off a small brushy ridge. John was on the other side of the ridge, so I am sure he spooked him right into me. The buck stopped to look over his shoulder and that was the last thing he ever did. I dressed him out and pulled him up a tree to keep him away from bears and continued my hunt.

I remember thinking to myself that things were going too well. At noon, we got together and determined we had collected four deer. It had been raining for an hour at that point, so we decided to head back. The rain was becoming much more intense and we were getting wet even with the rain gear.

We arrived back at the stream to find it was now three feet deeper and had morphed into frothing whitewater. It dawned on us that the rain had something to do with that and it was getting more intense by the minute. We talked about building a shelter and waiting it out, but the rain could last for several days. We had stashed a survival suit on the way in and I recovered it and quickly put it on. Vic noted he was staying fairly dry, but John expressed some interest in the survival suit. I ignored him.

It was apparent that crossing the roaring torrent was out of the question. By now we were all wet and tired. Hypothermia and Darwin's theory were starting to set in on us. We debated several really dumb ideas on how to get across, but logic and common sense finally won out - one of the few times that has happened.

We resolved to walk downstream for five miles to where the river ran into the ocean. This was only a mile from the boat. We reasoned someone could swim across at the mouth where the current wasn't so strong. It was not a great plan, but the best we could come up with at the time.

On board Vic's boat with a buck.

In the meantime, hypothermia was taking more and more of a toll on us. We started downstream through heavy brush. It was going to be a long hard walk. As we walked, I berated Vic because he should have known better. He readily admitted that he had screwed up. This made me feel better because now I had someone to blame. Problem was, I was still cold, wet, tired and on the wrong side of the creek. John walked in silence, eyeing my survival suit. I made a point of not letting him get behind me. It was a solemn group of guys trudging through the wet brush with daylight starting to fade. The creek continued to rise and our spirits continued to sink.

Sometimes, I think the Big Guy upstairs looks down and thinks, "Look at those poor dumb doofusses. They have probably killed themselves this time and most of my entertainment is watching them screw up." So He decides to save us just one more time.

I am sure that is what happened in this case. All of a sudden, it quit raining and just as that happened, we came upon a large tree that had fallen across the stream. We quickly scrambled across and walked back upstream to the three-wheelers. We motored back to the boat where we dried off.

As we sat in the boat I noted that the river was about 100 yards wide at the mouth. With November water temperatures being about 38 degrees, I doubt a swim across the river would have gone well. We returned the next day to retrieve the deer. They were where we had left them. In bear country that is not always the case. We had our deer, we weren't dead or hurt, and the sun had come out. Things had turned out just fine.

I often wonder just how many times God will step in just for the laughs.

GRIZZLY BEARS 24-HOURS-A-DAY IS STRESSFUL

My brother John, Mom's favorite, agreed to go up to my moose camp to hunt with me and one of his friends named Gary. John was the most excitable of my brothers. He also was the least competent. I swear he could disable an anvil in a sand pit barehanded. John just coasts through life with no worries. He has never been successful at anything other than being a bad example, but he is a very likable guy with hundreds of friends. He has never been able to keep a job. There have been many times in my life where I really envied him for his worry-free lifestyle. Gary, on the other hand, was a hard-working fellow. Without much education, he was mostly a laborer and odd-job guy. He had a family, so he was always struggling to make it one way or the other. John and Gary had been good friends for many years.

The moose camp is in a small copse of trees next to a large clearing. The clearing is more than a mile wide with spruce and birch trees on all sides. The edge of the trees contains lots of willows and other brush; it is therefore ideal moose habitat.

Upon leaving the camp on the first morning, we spotted a bull just on the edge of the trees about 50 yards from the camp. There was no stalk. Someone just yelled, "Hey there's a bull!" and we all started blasting away.

The critter took off down the edge of the trees, growing heavier by the second from the lead intake. After a few hundred yards, he finally fell over. This was the shortest moose hunt I can recall. He was a nice 40-inch bull in good shape. We all congratulated ourselves and set about taking him apart. Within two hours we had all the meat hanging from the meat pole located 50 feet from our tents. The gut pile was only a few hundred yards from the tents. This was a bad thing because gut piles tend to attract unwelcome visitors and I am not talking about in-laws.

Bears have a sense of smell that is 10 times better than a dog. They can smell guts from a mile away. There were no bears on the gut pile the next day, so we resolved that there were no bears in the area. We came to this conclusion without any other facts or the use of any logic. (The combined IQ of the group was barely a positive number, so that precluded thinking things through.)

I had to leave for a few days and advised John and Gary I would be back as soon as I could. I took the plane and left them totally unsupervised. Between the two of them they had a total of two days and two nights of Alaska outdoor experience. The odds were firmly stacked against them. I am sure Alaska was counting them as easy pickings.

Bob, John and Gary with the moose before inviting the bears over.

The next day these two geniuses noticed that the gut pile had been buried. This sparked their curiosity, so they went over to investigate. What could possibly have dug up all that ground to bury those guts???? It was pure chance that they took their guns with them for this short walk. They poked around the area for a while before they noticed a very irate grizzly bear coming out of the woods. They began backing away, which is what you are supposed to do. They were doing fine until Gary spoke. The bear picked up on the sound and immediately charged Gary.

It had been raining and John said later that the wet bear accelerated so fast that he left a mist in the air behind him—an acute observation considering the circumstances. Gary was carrying a .264-caliber Magnum with 100-grain bullets, which is way too light for a bear gun. The odds were with the bear at this point. Gary had about two seconds, so he just fired without aiming. He hit the bear right under the chin, breaking its neck. The bear hit the ground about 30 feet away. This wasn't dumb luck; this was *extremely* dumb luck.

John was watching all this when he caught a movement out of the corner of his eye. He spun around to find a second bear charging him. They were now in round two with the score Bears-0, Dummies-1.

John was shooting a 30-06 with 200-grain bullets, so he was a little better equipped, but the bear was still too close. There was no time to use the scope, so he just pointed and fired. He hit the bear in the spine right behind the head. It went down less than 10 feet from John's feet (five feet from his eyeballs). Bears-0, Dummies-2. Alaska had launched two of her best offenses and failed. I am sure she was getting frustrated.

Both guys hyperventilated for the next few minutes and then skinned the bears. They were young bears, probably four-year-olds. I suspect it was their first fall without Mom. They still weighed over 400 pounds. Our boys now had two bear hides and a moose in the camp, which turned it into one big bear bait station.

Alaska had missed with the bears, so she decided to make them pay with weather. The wind and rain picked up, so the guys had to stay up every night in the rain keeping the bears out of camp. The camp was just two pop-up nylon tents and a meat pole. We had put the tents in the lowest available spot so all the water would run into them. This kept the sleeping bags nice and wet. They spent days and nights trying to keep the fire going. On the fourth day they ran out of cigarettes and beer. The situation was getting desperate.

John and Bob with one of the bears.

On the sixth day, the weather finally broke enough for me to get to them. Even then I had to come down through a glory hole in the clouds to get to the lake. (Glory holes are vertical holes in the clouds and are famous for suckering pilots into marginal weather. It is always a gamble to drop down through one because you don't know what kind of weather you will encounter once you have committed.) I found John and Gary soaked to the skin, tired, and grumpy. The tundra around the camp was worn flat by bear trails. I didn't ask how it was going.

The weather was not looking good, so I loaded John and the moose meat up and flew him to the lodge on nearby Shell Lake. This is only a 15-minute flight, so I would be able to get back and get Gary before it got too dark. I left the meat with John. I instructed him that, if I didn't get back, to get a boat ride over to my cabin and stay there. As I flew back to the moose camp, I had an uneasy feeling that John would somehow screw this up because that is what he does best.

I found Gary waiting for me on the shore of the lake with the camp gear and the bear hides. We loaded up and headed for Anchorage. By the time we got home and unloaded, it was too late too go back for John and the meat.

For the next two days the weather once again prevented

me from flying. That nagging feeling about John kept getting stronger. I couldn't imagine how he could screw up at Shell Lake. With my cabin and the lodge, he should be living well, but his strongest ability was to mess things up in almost any situation. When you know someone all your life, you learn to count on their strongest abilities. John didn't let me down.

I got to Shell Lake on the third day. I found John at the lodge. He had decided to stay at the lodge and run up a bill rather than stay at the cabin. He had paid his bill to Zoe, the lodge owner, with moose meat. He had also gone over to my cabin and shot up all my ammo just for fun. The weather was coming down, and I didn't have time to beat the hell out of him, so I just loaded him and what was left of the meat into the airplane and flew home.

Two days later, Delusional Dave, Joe and I went back to the moose camp to see if we could get another moose. John was reluctant to return to the camp and opted to stay home (one of the few good decisions I have ever seen him make).

Joe is a friend of mine who lives in Indiana. He is a taxidermist in his spare time. He uses all the money he makes with taxidermy to pay for hunting trips around the world. It is a real treat to listen to his hunting adventures while in camp. Delusional is an engineer who works for me and is so dedicated a hunter that he goes out on adventures with me year after year at the risk of life and limb.

It had quit raining and on the second day we were two miles south of the camp working on a bull we had spotted in the area the day before. Delusional was on a small ridge when he spotted a set of horns moving through the brush. He tried everything he could to get a look at the body, but could only see those horns. The bull finally picked up Delusional's scent and began exiting the area. He took off through the woods right at Joe. Joe said later that in all his years of hunting all over the world he had never seen a sight quite as awesome as a bull moose trotting through the woods. Joe dropped him with a couple of shots. He turned out to be a nice 60-inch bull. It took us most of the day to butcher him and haul him back to camp on a four-wheeler. We hung the meat in the camp 50 feet from the tent. It had been a long day, but we were feeling pretty good about things at that point. We didn't realize that John and his pal Gary had baited every bear within 10 miles of the camp into our area. This set the stage for an exciting and eventful night. Alaska was still trying to get even for failing to kill off John and Gary.

The meat pole at moose camp.

We had a nice dinner and turned in for the night without a worry in the world. The no-worries part changed dramatically when at about midnight we heard a crash near the meat rack. I got up and took the pen flashlight and shined it in the direction of the meat pole. Three sets of eyes were looking back at me. I sounded the alarm by yelling, "BEARS!!!!"

This activated Joe and Delusional. We rushed out into the darkness. The smell of bear hit us like a tidal wave. Joe loaded his gun and fired a shot in the air sending the bears on their way. It also sent me 10 feet into the air because he didn't notify me of this plan. Things had suddenly gone from calm and peaceful to extremely stressful. I was sure it would take months of counseling to get the bears' heads straight again. Joe, Dave and I could probably have used some counseling ourselves.

There was a light rain falling, so we went back in the tent and got dressed. It is not proper etiquette to chase grizzly bears around in the dark in your long johns. Upon inspecting the meat rack we discovered one hindquarter had been removed and buried nearby. After some discussion, we determined we would need to put the meat up in the tree, at least 20 feet off the ground, to avoid any further thievery. It took us an hour to dig up the quarter and get the meat up the tree. We tied tin cans around the tree to act as an alarm in case the bears planned further visits during the night.

We were convinced that the bears were too traumatized to return and were on the couch at their shrink's office. Just in case, we also decided one of us should stay awake in shifts to listen for the cans. Unfortunately, we only had the one pen flashlight, which didn't emit enough light to see anything; it would just light up their eyes in the dark. We also had a Coleman lantern, which put out lots of light, but was awkward to use for our purpose.

We were all awake when the cans went off the first time; we went out in the rain and saw two sets of eyes. We fired a shot and they took off. We lit up the Coleman lantern and walked over to the meat tree. The same hindquarter that had been buried had been pulled partly down. As we were moving it back up the tree, we heard a noise behind us. When we shined the light in that direction we spotted three bears between the tent and us. Then, just to keep things interesting, we noticed there were two more bears on the other side of the tree. We were standing at the meat tree with grizzly bears on both sides of us! One option was to go up the tree. Of course, that would make us just three more pieces of meat on the meat pile. The other option was to get back to the tent somehow.

Joe said later that you couldn't have driven a pin in his butt with a 12-pound sledgehammer at that point. We decided the best plan was to move around the three bears between the tent and us and attempt to access the rest of the guns which were conveniently located in the tent.

When we started moving we were startled by a noise from another direction. The pen flashlight revealed three more bears. We now realized there were at least eight bears in the camp. They had us outnumbered almost 2 to 1 and outweighed by 10-to-1. Of course, we were well prepared as we stood there in our socially unacceptable long johns with a pen flashlight, one gun with three rounds in it, and a combined IQ of 8.5.

This seemed to be one of those fight-or-flight options the head-shrinkers like to talk about. Trouble was, either of those choices would probably result in us ending up as bear scat. We had to go with our weakest asset.... we had to think our way out of this situation.

We had bears to our right and left front; the tent was straight ahead about 30 feet away. We figured if we fired a shot the bears would run away from us and we could make a run for the tent. The odds were that some of us would make it and get to the rest of the guns. We started walking toward the tent with Joe ready to fire as soon as any bear started for us. The bears made some noise and jumped around a little, but seemed more interested in each other than in us.

We made it to the tent. At first no one could talk because all of our hearts were in our throats; the situation had now gone from terrifying to just scary.

That was the longest 30 feet I have ever walked. We sat in the middle of the tent with our backs to each other, fully armed. During the rest of the night we listened to the bears growling at each other and the tin cans banging away. We stayed put. We all enjoy moose meat, but not enough to go toe to toe with eight grizzlies for a few steaks.

The next morning we observed that the same hindquarter that had been buried was gone, but the rest of the meat was still right where we put it. The bears had moved back into the brush, but we were not sure where. From the tracks, we deduced that our visitors had consisted of a sow with two young cubs, two adult bears, and another sow with two big cubs.

We also figured out where the hindquarter ended up when we spotted one of the big adult bears running across the clearing behind the camp--with 150 pounds of meat in his mouth like a dog with a stick. Delusional had a bear tag, but unfortunately the bear was into the brush before he could get a bead on him. Our one chance for revenge was forever lost. Bears-1, Us-0.

While Joe stood guard, Delusional and I got the meat down, loaded it into the plane, and I took off for Anchorage to deliver the meat to the locker. I returned three hours later to find Joe and Delusional still armed to the teeth and on full alert. I also noted that everything was packed and on the beach. I surmised the hunt was over. There had been no more bear sightings, but there was also not much enthusiasm for spending another night in the camp.

We left the bears to their counseling sessions and Alaska to licking her wounds after taking her best shot with two of her best weapons--weather and bears--and missing once again. I was sure they would both be waiting for us next year.

I KILLED 80124 – OR DID I?

In 1976 I bought my first Cessna 185. This is a four-seat, high-wing, single-engine airplane with a 300-horsepower engine. It is one of the more popular airplanes in Alaska. Her number was N80124.

I came across her while doing a survey job just east of Nome. It was a federal Bureau of Land Management (BLM) survey where we were setting section corners over several hundred square miles in very remote country. Most of the work was accomplished using helicopters, but we also needed a fixed-wing aircraft to move people and supplies between the various base camps.

I was told there was a Cessna 185 for sale in Kotzebue, so I flew over there to investigate. 80124 was parked on the landing strip with a "For Sale" sign in her window. It was love at first sight. I located the owner, reviewed the log books, and after a prolonged and intense negotiation of just over two minutes, purchased my new buddy. In the course of the next four months 80124 completely paid for herself on that job.

That fall I flew back to Anchorage in my new plane, feeling like I had Alaska by the tail. I had some exciting times in this plane, including learning to fly a high-performance tail dragger and earning a float rating. I recall one time when a friend of mine named Merrill, who was an airline pilot, was giving me a lesson in 80124. We had gone up to Birchwood strip to do some touch and goes.

Everything went well until we were headed back to Anchorage. We were at 2500 feet when the engine quit. Merrill simply said, "Go through the emergency procedure," so I did, and the engine started right back up. (It is common practice when giving instruction to pull the gas and kill the engine as a training procedure, so I wasn't all that concerned, and I was pleased that I had passed the re-start test.)

When we arrived back at Merrill Field in Anchorage (my friend Merrill is named after the same guy as the airfield) and got the plane tied down, Merrill said we should pull the cowling and see if we could figure out why the engine quit!!! It had been a real emergency, but I hadn't panicked in the " training exercise." This experience would help me in the future when we had emergencies because I had learned to stay calm when things happened.

80124 did this to me a couple of more times until I figured out that when the tip tanks were empty and the tip tank pump was on, it pumped air into the main tanks. When a bubble of air got sucked into the fuel line it would kill the engine. I duct-taped the tip tank switch closed - problem solved.

80124 was not ideal for a floatplane. She didn't have a short-takeoff-and-landing (STOL) kit or a longer bladed float prop. She also had some floats I had bought at an auction that were not the best performers available. They were Aqua floats and were built in such a way as to increase the drag much more than most other brands of floats. Because I had learned to fly floats in 80124, I didn't realize just how poor a performer she really was. I would go to places that my pilot friends would say were "no sweat" for most 185s and end up scraping treetops on takeoff. I just assumed it was my piloting skills and not the airplane.

After 200 or 300 hours of flying time, I had pretty much figured out what 80124 and I could or could not do. Over the next 1,000 flight hours we became close friends. We traveled throughout Alaska, picking our landing spots with care. We did have a few close calls, but 80124 always came through when I needed her. I think it was because she had more horsepower than I had IQ.

The one time I really let her down was on a cold November day. I was flying my family out to Shell Lake for Thanksgiving. I had delivered JJ and Christopher to the lake and was returning to get Candace and Gretchen. I was on straight skis and landing on Campbell Lake. The lake was glare ice with no snow. (When landing a plane on ice, you pull the nose up at the last minute to stall the plane just before it touches down. It is called flaring the plane.)

As I was approaching the lake I observed three kids playing along the shoreline. I was determined to keep an eye on them as I landed. Just as I flared, two of the kids decided to run across the lake right in front of the airplane. I hit the throttle and popped the plane back up into the air and went over the kids.

Then I made a mistake. Instead of going around and doing the landing over I just set her back down on the ice. Now I was sliding down the lake on very slick ice without enough lake remaining to stop before I hit the bank.

I was headed right at residential property that sloped up from the lake, so I assumed I would just end up in John's back yard. No harm there. Unfortunately, John had a one-foot-high brick wall at the edge of the lake. I hit that; broke both of the skis and both gearboxes, and the nose of the plane hit the ground, bending the prop. It took more than $23,000 to fix the damage. I also had to charter an air taxi to get the rest of us to Shell Lake and back. 80124 forgave me for that screw-up and performed just fine after she got out of surgery five months later.

In the fall of 1985, we were caribou hunting south of King Salmon with several friends, including Fritz, who had his 185 along as the second plane. Fritz's plane had all the good stuff. He had a STOL kit, EDO floats and a float prop.

I had forgotten my caribou tags, so I made a side trip to get them. I landed in the river at King Salmon to visit the state fish and game office to pick up the tags. This involved docking on the beach. We grounded on the gravel beach, tied the plane up and took care of my tag business. Then we returned to the plane, spun her around and loaded up.

As I taxied out into the river I noted that the right wing seemed to be lower than the left wing. After a minute, it was very much lower than the left. We quickly realized that the right float was sinking. This would cause the plane to turn over, which would ruin our whole day. I immediately turned back for shore and hit the throttle. We barely made it back. Upon examining the float, we discovered that a rock had punched a hole in the right front float compartment. 80124 had thrown a shoe. We now had a repair problem in a small remote town.

We needed to get the plane out of the water to patch the bottom of the float. After inquiring around town, we located a contractor who had a wheel-mounted crane and agreed to lift the plane for a couple hundred dollars. He drove the unit to the beach, deployed his outriggers and picked her right up. He then said he had some business to take care of and would be back later. We paid him the $200 and off he went. We completed repairs in two hours, but then couldn't find the contractor to lower us back down. After several hours, we finally found him in a local bar. He had been there with our $200 since he left us hours earlier. Even in his impaired condition we got the plane back in the water. I think 80124 was trying to hint that she didn't want to be on this trip.

When we got back to the caribou camp, the other guys pointed out that I was supposed to have picked up some beer. I had forgotten due to all the other problems. My popularity in the camp dropped considerably. "It's too bad you poked a hole in your float, it's good you didn't sink the plane in the river, and we're sorry it cost you $200 to get it fixed, but you forgot the beer! How could you be that insensitive?" I resolved to revise my friend-choosing program as soon as I got home.

After two days we hadn't seen any caribou, so Fritz and I took the planes up to look for the herd. We flew for three hours before finally locating the animals. By this time we were low on fuel, so we headed for Naknek to fuel up. At that time the gas dock was located on a lake at the airport. It is down in a hole so there are 30 to 50-foot banks around most of the lake, which coincidentally had a bad reputation for turning airplanes into wrinkled balls of aluminum along its shores. When I landed, the plane seemed to kind of drop out of the air the last few feet, giving me a long bounce upon landing. 80124 was hinting again. She didn't like this place or this air.

Fritz had a similar landing. I commented to Ken, my passenger, that the air seemed a little strange. He just shrugged. He was not a pilot, so it didn't mean anything to him. He was soon to find out just how important air characteristics really are. As we fueled I just kept watching the light wind on the water. Everything seemed normal but I had a bad feeling. Fritz also commented that the air felt funny when he landed. The warnings were there, but we didn't have the mental capacity to process them.

The plane was empty except for Ken and he only weighted about 150 pounds. There was plenty of lake, even for 80124, so it should be no sweat as far as taking off was concerned. Fritz was still fueling, so I opted to take off first. Everything went fine until we were about 50 feet in the air. All of a sudden 80124 just quit flying. The airspeed was over 50 knots and the nose was at the right attitude, but for some reason we were dropping right out of the air. There was nothing I could do but keep full throttle and hope the ground effect would catch us before we hit the water. Ground effect occurs when the air deflected down from the airplane hits the surface; the updraft sort of cushions the plane and helps it fly. But not this time.

We hit on the water about 50 feet from the end of the lake and bounced big-time! It was obvious that we were going to crash into the alders at the end of the lake. It seemed like everything slowed down considerably at that point. I swear it seemed like I had an hour to decide what to do next, but the problem with all this perceived extra time was that I still had no good options. We were going to crash; it was just a matter of picking the spot.

I opted for full power to keep the nose as high as possible and try to hit the alders floats first and then cut power. As we slid through the alders I thought we would be stopped by the branches and that maybe we could save the airplane, too. That hope was dashed when the right float hit a rock and the plane went over on its back. This also seemed to happen in slow motion. When we hit on our back, we broke off both wings, drove the left flap through the back seat, and bent the fuselage. The only part of the airplane that wasn't smashed was the front half of the cockpit. 80124 and I were not having a good day. One fuel tank was cracked and gas was running all over the place. Ken and I were left hanging from our seatbelts in the upside-down plane.

I have been bummed out on many occasions, but this had to be one of the top three. Ken advised me that he wasn't hurt, but suggested we get the hell out of there. I agreed and we let our seatbelts go. This is where we incurred the only injury of the incident. Ken forgot to brace himself and was almost knocked out when landed on his head. I got out my door and turned to see how Ken was doing. He started yelling he couldn't get his door open. I suggested he come out my door, which he did with much enthusiasm.

80124 critically injured in Naknek.

We then left the fatally wounded 80124 and walked back to the shore. Fritz was already taxiing down the lake to check on us. Boy did I feel bad, but also damned lucky that no one was hurt. I sat on a rock on the shoreline with my head in my hands mourning my good friend 80124 as we waited for Fritz. We rode back to the gas station with him.

The local cop was waiting to take our statements. As we discussed the event with him a woman ran up yelling that a plane had crashed. The cop said, "Yes, it's at the end of the lake."

She said, "No it was at the end of the airstrip." Sure enough, a Cherokee 6 had the same experience. They took off, got 50 feet in the air and then just fell to the ground. There were four people on board, but no injuries. Both planes were totaled. Naknek Airport was two for two on airplanes for the day. The other pilots decided to wait a few hours before taking off. It was a wise choice; I wasn't sure the lake had its 24-hour bag limit of airplanes.

Ken and I got a ride to King Salmon with the cop to get a flight home. On arrival, I called my wife and asked her to pick us up at the airport. She asked why we were flying home commercially. I replied, "I killed 80124." We both commiserated about the demise of 80124. She also had a good relationship with the plane after many hours of passenger time. Later that day Fritz went back to the caribou camp. He had to ferry my passengers back to King Salmon to catch a commercial flight.

80124 in better times taking off from Shell Lake.

The National Transportation Safety Board investigated both incidents and determined that a "microburst" had caused the accidents. This occurs when the wind is blowing straight down and literally shoves the airplane right into the ground. Neither crash was pilot error. But, I still felt really bad about good ol' 80124. She had been a good friend and it was not a good way for her to go, even if it wasn't my fault.

The only good thing was that I did have hull insurance. With that money I bought N4448R and have been flying her for over 15 years now. She is a 185 complete with all the good stuff like a float prop, STOL kit and EDO floats.

It was about three years later as Triple 4-8-Romeo and I were flying into the Cordova airport when the tower got a call asking for landing instructions from Cessna 80124! I followed her in and went right over to the plane and introduced myself to the owner. It turns out my insurance company had sold 80124 "as is, where is," and this guy had bought her. He'd had a fire that burned up the cockpit in his old 185, but he'd saved the rest of the plane. He just put the wings, etc. on 80124's cockpit and was good to go. Because the cockpit carries the aircraft's registered name with it, 80124 was resurrected in Cordova.

He let me hug her once more before we parted company.

Bob Bell

CHAPTER 3:
Lessons Learned at Work and Play

HEY, YOU'RE NOT DEAD!!!!

Most of my close calls have had to do with recreating in Alaska, but I have managed to sneak in a few while working, too. My firm does a lot of work on the North Slope of Alaska. Much of that work is surveying in remote areas in support of oil exploration.

It is difficult to describe the arctic coast of Alaska to someone who hasn't been there. First of all, it is a very flat place surrounded by more flat places. Once you get out of the foothills of the Brooks Range, a change of elevation of 25 feet is a big deal. I would guess that at least 40 percent of the surface area of the coastal plain is water. There are thousands of lakes and several rivers. The rivers are wide, shallow and very channeled. The lakes are shallow and are mostly oriented northwest to southeast. The orientation has to do with the prevailing wind.

In the summer the land is covered with tundra vegetation that seldom grows more than an inch or two above the surface. A predominant landform is the polygon-shaped indentations formed by ice lenses. These polygons have sides from two to 20 feet and are quite distinctive when viewed from the air. It kind of looks like a dried-out pond during a drought. In the brief summer the air is full of mosquitoes. In the winter it is just flat, white, dark and cold.

Typical polygon-shaped terrain.

There are only about four inches of annual precipitation on the North Slope. The snow is very fine grained and blows back and forth all winter. If there are any obstructions, they are soon drifted over. This creates a very flat, totally white, landscape.

A rare happy time at Camp Lonely.

Winter in the arctic is a dangerous time. When you walk out of a building you are immediately assaulted by wind driving these fine grains of snow into any exposed skin. Your visibility is minimal or none at all and subject to change by the minute. Chill factors can range down to 100 degrees below zero or more. If it is -20 degrees and the wind is blowing 20 mph, your exposed face will be frost-bitten in 15 seconds. It takes a very small mistake to wake up dead in the arctic. It is not a good vacation spot in either season.

One of our bigger jobs was in the National Petroleum Reserve Alaska (NPRA). This is an area the size of Indiana on the arctic coast between Barrow and Prudhoe Bay. NPRA is a very remote place in a very remote part of Alaska. We were engaged by Husky Oil Co. to provide surveying and construction inspection throughout the project area. This involved sending survey crews several miles from the base camp to set survey marks for future construction. We would also stake the trails for the Cat trains. These Cat trains were Alberta Trailer Company (ATCO) modules set on skis. The modules would be pulled across the frozen tundra by tracked Caterpillars, thus the name "Cat trains". We would move these trains for up to 100 miles to get to the drilling sites. A camp for up to 100 people could be transported in this manner.

Now, the name of the base camp was "Camp Lonely," and, trust me, it was appropriately named. It may not have been the end of the world, but you could easily see it from there! So when we sent crews out from Lonely they were really in the middle of nowhere, especially in the winter. Because of the flat topography, the darkness and everything being white, it is just very difficult to find anything or any place.

One of the project sites was called Harrison Bay and it was about 30 miles east of Lonely. Husky asked us to send a crew to the site to get some survey data. There was nothing there at the time because construction had not yet begun. They just wanted some topographic information so they could design the well pad. It was February, which meant the temperature was about −30 degrees with perhaps 10 knots of wind. This was not uncommon for the time of year. In fact, it would be considered a rather balmy winter day.

We sent out a three-person crew with Craig in charge. Craig had lived in Alaska for many years and had worked for me for several years. He was a very personable guy and everybody liked him. But, sometimes he was a little too happy-golucky for the arctic and it got him into some tight spots. This would be one of them. They were driving a Sno-Cat, which is a tracked vehicle the size of a station wagon, with a range of about 100 miles, and seating for three people and gear. It has some insulation, but without a heater it doesn't really provide any shelter from the cold. The plan was for them to travel to the site, do the topo and return. We assumed this could be completed in 10 hours. (On the North Slope the sun sets in late November and doesn't come up again until mid-January. It is dark 24 hours a day, so it doesn't really matter what time of day you are working, it's all dark and miserable.)

Prudhoe Bay oil field on the North Slope

Now, you need to keep in mind that I must recruit surveyors who are willing to work in these adverse conditions even though there's survey work available to them in much warmer and more hospitable areas. Therefore, I ended up with a hardy and personable crew --but one whose strong points were not exactly in planning ahead. This crew was made up of good, hard-working guys with lots of arctic experience -- experience they could ignore, and did, at will.

We loaded up the Sno-Cat with survey gear and some survival gear and sent them on their way. This was prior to global positioning systems (GPS), so they were to follow reflectors we had set at quarter mile intervals between the site and Camp Lonely. The last thing I told them was to monitor the radio, take a spare radio, and watch the weather. If it looked like the wind was picking up, get back to camp. They all nodded their heads and headed out into the darkness. These were macho surveyors with arctic experience, lots of gear, lots of confidence and not a lot of IQ. Besides it was just a little 30-mile jaunt to Harrison Bay and back. What could go wrong?

They had been gone about six hours when the weather-guessers warned us that a front was moving in and we could expect high winds and white-out conditions. In a whiteout all you see is white. You lose your depth perception, your sense of direction, and you can't see your hand in front of your face. We got right on the radio and started calling the crew. We got no reply. In the meantime, the wind was picking up. We learned later that the radio had quit working shortly after they reached Harrison Bay and they had forgotten the spare. See what I mean about planning...? Rather than considering this a problem, the crew had just gone on about their work. I refer you back to the IQ comment above.

Meanwhile, back at Lonely, we were going into major pucker mode. We knew the Sno-Cat had about 15 hours of fuel and then they would be out in minus 30-degree weather with minimal survival gear. If the storm lasted more than 24 hours they would most likely freeze to death. The weather was moving from us to them so there was no way we could get to them and back without being caught in the storm.

There was nothing we could do from our end because we were now in whiteout conditions and sending anybody else out to find them would be nothing short of suicide. Any rescue team would be lost within 50 feet, let alone 30 miles. The storm lasted three days. We spent the whole time sick to our stomachs with worry and then grief. We knew there was no way they could have survived this long in these kinds of conditions. Camp Lonely was a small camp with about 75 people in it at the time. Everybody knew each other and we all considered ourselves friends. The camp had the atmosphere of a funeral home.

When the storm did finally break, I led a group of three

Sno-Cats out to the site to recover the bodies. I can't describe how bad we all felt and how much we dreaded the task ahead of us. It was a very long trip in all of our minds.

Upon arriving at the site we couldn't find the Sno-Cat anywhere. Remember that it is dark all day long, so we started a search by circling out from the site. We assumed the cat would be drifted over by snow and would be very difficult to find. After about an hour one of the guys in my group spotted the Sno-Cat. It was parked next to a small Eskimo hunting shed about two miles from the site. There was smoke coming out of the smokestack. We rushed over and pulled open the door. There sat my crew, all nice and warm and with a whole stack of Playboy magazines!

I was so relieved that I just burst out, "Hey, you're not dead!" They all laughed and asked if they would get paid for the time they had been out there. Just to show how happy I was to see them, I readily agreed.

It turned out that one of the control points they needed for the survey was near this shed, so they knew where it was when the storm hit. They knew they couldn't make it back to Lonely, so they just headed for the shed instead. There was plenty of fuel for the stove, the aforementioned magazines, and food from the survival gear. They did complain bitterly about running out of cigarettes on the second day!

After this incident we put in place strict new safety rules for remote projects and have never had a similar incident since.

I JUST DON'T LIKE HELICOPTERS

I developed an aversion to helicopters as an army officer in Vietnam. With few exceptions, every time I went somewhere in a helicopter I ended up getting shot at by somebody. I also experienced some landings that would be classified as crashes in the civilian world. I recall once when I was trying to get the last of my guys in the last helicopter at a hot landing zone.

Bullets were flying everywhere when the warrant officer flying the helicopter stuck his head out the window and said, "Sir, can we get going? These guys are shooting up my aircraft."

I was too busy to enter into a detailed explanation at that moment, but once we were in the air I pointed out that I was much more worried about my men getting shot than his helicopter. He replied that we both have our priorities.

I concluded that you just can't trust helicopters, and the guys who fly them are somewhat suspect as well. That basic lack of trust has stuck with me all these years. Helicopters just shouldn't fly. When the power is off they have a 90-degree glide slope (straight down). They don't have wings and they are just plain ugly.

Therefore, I was somewhat dismayed when it became apparent that most of the summer transportation on a National Petroleum Reserve Alaska (NPRA) job we had would be by helicopter. As I mentioned earlier, NPRA is very remote, with only a few small villages and no connecting roads.

That surveying project lasted for 10 years, and we were flying around in these contraptions the whole time. No one got killed or even shot at, but we had three incidents of helicopters falling out of the sky with me or some of my employees on board.

I had two Yugoslavian immigrants working for me at NPRA. Their names were Bernie and Vinco. These two were always on the same crew. If we needed a third member of the crew it was Paul. This was one of my best crews. They had a very strong work ethic and were extremely loyal. I couldn't ask for a better crew. They had "escaped" from Yugoslavia and were delighted to be in America. They were also very appreciative of the work I gave them and made sure they did the best they could on every assignment. They had "Old-World" values of hard work and respect for those with whom you worked. Bernie was the Party Chief and was known for his accuracy and also for his practical thinking.

All three were aboard a helicopter returning from a job east of Camp Lonely. They were about five miles from camp flying in some marginal weather. The pilot, a Vietnam vet, had decided to follow the coastline because in the limited visibility he could at least see the beach line. They were flying 400 feet above the ground going about 100 knots. The pilot was looking down at the beach-line, and they were all caught off guard when another helicopter suddenly came into view going the other direction at their same elevation. It took a violent maneuver by both aircraft to avoid looking like two dragon-flies in a very compromising position. It happened so fast that everyone was left looking at each other with that "what just happened look" on their faces.

Bernie was in the co-pilot seat, so he noticed that immediately following this maneuver, all the gauges in the instrument panel dropped to zero. He was pretty sure this was a bad thing and, turning to the pilot, he asked what their situation was. The pilot replied that they had lost the engine and were auto-rotating down. He said he hoped to land on the beach and not in the water. Somehow this didn't relieve Bernie's fears. He asked if he should tell Vinco and Paul who were in the back seat and were not aware of the problem. The pilot said there was no point in worrying them. It became very quiet in the aircraft.

When a helicopter loses its engine, it only has one option-- straight down. As I said earlier, these things shouldn't fly and when they don't have power, they don't. Auto-rotation is a helicopter term for falling out of the sky with little or no control. I would call it crashing.

In a real airplane you can at least glide to a safe landing. So here these guys were, going straight down in the fog, five miles from safety, and hoping they didn't land in 30-degree water. I am sure Bernie and the pilot aged quite a bit in the next few seconds. Vinco and Paul thought they were landing at the airport so they were quite relaxed as they chatted about what was for dinner that night.

They got lucky and landed on the relatively level 50-foot wide gravel beach. They had put out a mayday on the way down so the camp dispatched another helicopter to pick them up. Having realized what had happened, Paul opted to walk back to camp along the beach. It took three of us to get him in the helicopter the next morning to go to work. It was just another day on the job for Bernie and Vinco.

Helicopter sitting safely on the beach a few feet from the Arctic Ocean.

✳ ✳ ✳ ✳ ✳ ✳

The second incident involved a fellow named John who was my Manager of Operations on the NPRA job. John was in a helicopter flying from a site 50 miles southwest of Lonely. It was just him and the pilot on board. Because it was late in the day, they were on a beeline for Lonely trying to make sure they got there before dark. The season was fall, so it wasn't uncommon for the temperature to drop below zero at night, which makes for uncomfortable, impromptu camping.

They had gone only about 10 miles when they lost the engine. The helicopter went into autorotation and down they went. They hit on the side of one of the few hills in the area and went bouncing down the slope, but didn't flip over. If they had, the main rotor would have torn the helicopter, and them, to shreds. It would have taken the ravens days to pick the edible parts out of the wreckage. They were very lucky.

John was one of those guys who led a charmed life. The troops used to say he could fall into an outhouse and come out smelling like roses. Well, with this incident the shine was coming off his charm.

They sent a mayday that was picked up by another helicopter nearby, but the second helicopter already had three people on board. We now had five people and four seats. Leaving someone behind was not really an option, so they just unloaded everything from the helicopter, including the survival gear, to make room for one more passenger. They only had about 45 minutes worth of gas.

It was getting dark by this time, but they figured they were only 30 minutes from Lonely. They could get close enough to see the lights before it got dark if everything worked out right. Of course in these situations it rarely does. With the odds pretty well stacked against them they took off for the camp. There was no GPS then, and Lonely didn't have much for homing radar. So our guys were flying by the seat of their pants. They took a compass reading and went for it, with everyone on board contemplating their mortality.

After 30 minutes it was dark and they still hadn't spotted the lights of Lonely. The pilot finally said they would have to set down and gut it out until morning. It would be the overnight camping trip from Hell. All the survival gear had been left behind to make room for the extra passenger. They had, maybe, 15 minutes of gas remaining, which would be needed when they knew where they were going. The pilot called the radio room at Lonely to advise them of their situation. The mood in the aircraft was somber at best. Lonely called back and said they could see the lights of the helicopter. If he would turn 45 degrees right, he would be headed straight for Lonely. The shine was back on John's charm. They landed with less than 5 minutes of fuel left. It was one of the few times everyone was glad to be arriving at Lonely.

****

I was a participant in the third incident. As I said, I don't like helicopters, but sometimes you just do what you have to do. I was a reluctant passenger in a flight to a place called Peard Bay, 50 miles southwest of Barrow. At that time Peard Bay was an abandoned Distant Early Warning (DEW) Line site. We were tasked with bringing the airstrip up to standard for use by Herc (C-130 Hercules) airplanes. When the previous occupants had left in the 1950s they didn't clean up after themselves. (I am sure they must have been teenagers.) There was debris of all kinds scattered all over the place.

There were a few abandoned buildings with the roofs blown off and a landfill that had not been covered, so all of that stuff was scattered around the site. It was a real mess.

I was flying in a Jet Ranger, which is a small to medium-sized helicopter. We landed and the pilot jumped out, leaving the motor and the blades running. I have never understood helicopter pilots. The ones I met in Vietnam were clearly crazy and most of these pilots were alumni of that group. You can't blame them for being about half nuts, but you can blame them for being so damned proud of it.

The pilots on this project were just as nuts, but in a different, more sophisticated way. I suppose that with age comes a little more control. So I was not surprised when, once we landed, this clown jumped out of a running helicopter and left me there in the back seat wondering what was going on. He ran about 100 feet and started giving hand signals to a Bell 212 helicopter. The signals were directions on where to land. The 212 ended up landing about 50 feet from the Jet Ranger I was sitting in.

Now, a 212 helicopter is much bigger than a Jet Ranger and creates quite a windstorm when it lands. As this 212 landed it started blowing all the debris around like a tornado going through a trailer park. A four-foot by eight-foot piece of corrugated sheetmetal was blown into the air and came down in the main rotor of my Jet Ranger.

The Jet Ranger reacted like a power floor-polisher running amok on a carpet with no operator. The thing was bouncing all over the pad; there were pieces of sheetmetal flying everywhere and I was tearing the inside of the helicopter all to hell trying to get out. I didn't have any Vietnam flashbacks, but various ways to kill the pilot flashed through my mind.

The whole episode lasted maybe 30 seconds--or two hours. I am not sure. Anyway, when things settled down I was still in the helicopter; the helicopter was still upright and my opinion of helicopters and their pilots had not changed - it was just reinforced.

The pilot ran over and immediately checked his bird for damage. Once he was satisfied the helicopter was not seriously damaged, he asked if I was O.K. I was not!!! I really needed to kill somebody at that point, but because I needed him to fly me back to Barrow it would have to wait until we got back. I had enough time to settle down by the time we got to Barrow, so I suppose he is still out there somewhere flying helicopters.

Helicopters, like sewage treatment plants, are a necessary evil but I will never enjoy being around them. I still have occasion to send my guys out in helicopters, but I haven't been in one since Peard Bay and that is fine with me.

TEENAGED GIRLS, DOGS AND BROWN BEARS DON'T MIX

I took one of my daughters (who was 13 at the time) and one of her friends fishing at a place called Big River Lake, about a one-hour flight west of Anchorage. You fly down the west side of Cook Inlet about 100 miles, on a very scenic route where moose, bear and even beluga whales can be seen. I have always enjoyed this trip.

Big River is a large lake nestled in the mountains at the opening of Lake Clark Pass. It is surrounded on three sides by very steep terrain covered in spruce trees and alders. The fourth side is open tundra and the shoreline is mostly water grasses and lily pads. It is a glacial lake, so it is very gray due to the rock flour in the water.

Wolverine Creek flows into the lake at the northeast corner. It is a small clear creek that travels through some very steep terrain before emptying into the lake. Depending on the level of the lake, the clear water can extend out into the lake up to 50 feet in a 20 to 30 foot-wide stream. The red salmon school up in this area, preparing for their run up the creek. The water is only about two feet deep at this point, so the fish are very visible. It's not uncommon to see 500 to 600 fish at a time.

Regulations require fly-fishing only at the mouth of the creek, so the trick is to cast your fly among the fish and then watch the fish closely. Red salmon tend not to strike, so when your line floats into a fish's mouth it will raise up its head and shake it side to side. When you see a fish doing this, you give a jerk and hook him in the side of the mouth. It is somewhat unorthodox, but it works like a charm.

The bears also have a field day with these fish, but they don't require fishing poles and hooks. They just jump in the water and grab the fish. It seems that when there is an abundance of fish, there is also a corresponding abundance of bears.

My daughter, Gretchen, was born and raised in Alaska and had some exposure to bears; her friend had not. They were typical teenaged girls, somewhat excitable, but always up for a new adventure.

When Gretchen was much younger, she was the family fish-whacker. Every time someone would catch a fish, Gretchen would give the fish a name and then whack it in the head with a stick. We would come home with a fish stringer containing Joe, Ed, Mary, etc. Her friend, on the other hand, was new to Alaska and this was her first trip into the wilds of the back country. She was a little nervous about flying in a float plane, but seemed comfortable when we arrived at the lake. It was a nice sunny, summer day and things were very peaceful. Unfortunately, that was about to change.

A small brown bear at Big River Lake fishing with Bob.

On this trip we also took along our German shepherd dog, Kiska. Of course, I didn't anticipate any problems, but I took along my .44-caliber Magnum pistol just in case. This was just an afternoon fishing trip like many others we had done. So why worry?

We parked the airplane about 100 feet from where we would be fishing to avoid the rocks in the water. The two girls, the dog and I walked over to Wolverine Creek, and the red salmon were there in good numbers. It is an ideal situation to catch fish. We crossed the stream and set up on the rocks. The fish were thick and we were almost immediately into them.

We had eight salmon on the stringer, each with a name and a dent in its head, when Gretchen's friend let out a shriek. I looked up and noticed a very large brown bear boar walking along the beach between the airplane and us. Both girls were now making a lot of noise and the dog was going nuts.

I pulled the .44 Magnum out of my shoulder holster and promptly dropped it among the rocks at my feet. I got down on my hands and knees and fished the gun out of the rocks. While doing this I yelled at the girls to get over to me and grab the dog on their way. They both managed to get behind me in record time while still screaming. They missed the part about the dog. Gretchen's friend was in a total panic. Gretchen was more concerned about her friend's state of mind than the bear. Typical Alaskan kid....

Dogs can be handy in bear country because they can alert you to the presence of the bears. There is a downside, however. Dogs have a tendency to charge a bear. Once they get close enough to realize that they have made a huge mistake, they tend to run back to their master, usually bringing a very angry bear with them. This leaves you with some unpleasant alternatives. You can shoot the dog so it doesn't come back to you and gives the bear something to deal with as you depart the area. Another scenario is to shoot the bear and hope you don't end up with a really mad, wounded bear. One other plan is to try getting the bear to give up by firing shots over his head.

Our dog was definitely in the "charge the bear" mode. I was looking at a 900- pound bear, my 100-pound dog, and what now appeared to be a very *puny* .44-Mag pistol. It was clear the girls were not going to be much help, so I advised them if the bear came at us they should jump into the water and attempt to make it to the plane.

I was now screaming at the dog to come back. The bear, meanwhile, was observing us with some disdain, but was not particularly upset. The three alternatives were running through my head as Kiska moved toward the bear. I really didn't want to shoot my dog. After a lot of yelling and pleading, I finally got the dog to return to me and got hold of her collar. The bear gave us a dirty look and slowly lumbered off into the brush. Suddenly, all seemed very quiet. It was probably because all of us were holding our breath.

We never saw that bear again, but we didn't wait around, either. To get to the plane, we had to walk right past the point he disappeared into the brush. If we didn't walk along the beach we would have to go into heavy brush on steep terrain. There was no other way to get to the plane short of swimming. I had the girls walk just ahead of me with the dog. I had the fish so that if the bear came back I could toss it the fish to occupy him while we made our escape. We left just as quickly as we could get ourselves to that plane! Gretchen's friend never asked to go fishing with us again. I can't imagine why.

A few years later I was back at Big River Lake fly-fishing for red salmon. I took my .300-caliber Winchester Magnum rifle loaded with 250-grain Barnes cartridges this time. If there was going to be a bear problem, I would be ready. When I got to the stream I leaned the rifle against a tree and walked 100 feet to the water and started fishing. There were five people fishing on the rocks across from me. They were typical Alaskans, armed to the teeth with guns and fishing gear.

I had been there just a few minutes when one of the guys on the other bank advised me that I might have a problem. He suggested that I look behind me. I turned to find a young brown bear with my rifle in his mouth. There I was with a fishing pole in my hand, facing a brown bear with a gun. This had to be one of the more unique positions in which I ever found myself.

Adolescent bears are a real problem. They are teenagers and therefore very unpredictable. Four hundred pounds of unpredictability with four-inch claws and teeth is not a good thing, so this situation, although somewhat humorous, was also very dangerous. The guys on the other side of the stream found some humor in it, but they still had their guns. I contemplated several options, none of which was good. So I just decided to go with stupidity.

I asked my "friends" if they would cover me while I threw a rock at the bear to startle him, hoping he would drop the gun. This is not a tried and true method of dealing with bears. Once they got done taking pictures and regained their composure, they agreed, so I picked up a rock about the size of a softball and pitched it at the bear. Contrary to my intent, the rock hit the bear right between the ears with a loud "thunk." He dropped the rifle and ran about 100 feet and then turned to face me. He was snapping his jaws together and jumping around on stiff legs. The bear was not a happy camper. Neither was I. My new "friends" were still enjoying the show, but now had their guns to their shoulders. It was becoming an OK Corral scenario.

The situation seemed to be deteriorating rather than improving. My choices were to attempt a retreat or move toward him and retrieve the gun. I was concerned a retreat would encourage a charge, which would be a further deterioration. I had no idea how good of a shot my friends were. I started walking toward the gun thereby closing the distance between the bear and myself. As I got closer he became more agitated, as did I, but he held his ground. I picked up the rifle and backed away. In fact, I backed up all the way to my airplane and departed the area. The guys on the other side of the stream continued to fish and chuckle. The bear wandered off into the brush.

Just to show that I am not gender-biased when it comes to the risk of turning my kids into bear scat, I did return to Big River Lake several years later with my 10-year-old son who goes by his initials, F. T.

We were fishing for reds with fly rods and having good luck fishing off the rocks on the far side of the creek. F. T. hooked a red and it took off down the shoreline like a rocket. The fish had almost all of the fly line out before the kid got him turned around. It was flopping on the surface about 10 feet from shore when a brown bear rushed out of the alders, grabbed the fish and took off down the beach.

I suppose proper etiquette would have been to yell, "BEAR ON!!" But all I could do was yell, "Drop the pole!"

The kid probably couldn't hear me over the sound of his own heartbeat and the adrenaline rush. He just held onto that pole and played the bear. When the critter hit the end of the line, the 10-pound leader was just a little too light and the bear broke off. F. T. might have turned him with a 20-pound leader. We decided we were close enough to our limit of fish and called it a day. Once again, it was the long walk back to the airplane with the gun in one hand and the fish in the other.

F.T. BELL

In recent years, the fish and game department has put several new rules into place for fishing Wolverine Creek. For instance, you must have a boat or fish off your floats. You are not allowed to stand in the water. You must have a "bear-proof" container for your fish, and there are a bunch of other rules to avoid bear/people conflicts. It kind of takes the fun out of the place. They also have "bear viewing" guides with boats full of animal-rights types who want to look at the bears.

We have had a few conflicts between animal-rights activists and Alaskans. In fact, on the trip with F. T., when I was getting our gear out of the plane, a woman in a nearby guide boat wanted to know why I had a gun with me. I replied that we would be fishing near the bears and if it got down to me, my kid or the bear I would prefer it be the bear. She exploded in anger, started calling me names, said she was going to turn us in to Fish and Game, and spoke ill of my ancestry.

My first inclination was to blow a hole in the bottom of their boat. But my kinder, gentler side prevailed, so I just smiled and went on about my business. Sometimes the bears are the better company. The fishing at Big River Lake is good, but I am not sure it is good enough to justify these kinds of extracurricular activities. I guess I need to find a new red hole.

LOOKS GOOD TO ME,
GO AHEAD AND LAND

Before I had my pilot's license, I went hunting and fishing with a good friend named Fred. Fred was of slight stature, but he was a tough little guy who was also an excellent pilot. At the time of this adventure, he was a student at the University of Alaska Anchorage (UAA) and had a full-time job. Consequently, Fred didn't have much money or time for recreation.

I also had a full-time job, but only took one course per semester at UAA. Therefore, it was usually me who initiated most of the outdoor adventures. Fred had a Taylorcraft airplane, which is a very small, two-person plane. I doubt the whole plane weighted 1,000 pounds empty. I think it ran on a Norelco motor he had removed from his electric razor. The electrical system, including the radio, was powered by a car battery located between the two seats. When you unbuckled your seat belt, you had to be careful that the buckle didn't hit the battery and short out the electrical system.

One Saturday in March Fred called me and asked if I would fly with him to his father's cabin to repair the roof. I readily agreed and we set off for the cabin on a remote lake about 90 miles from Anchorage. The trip was across Knik Arm and up the Susitna

Valley. In Fred's plane it would take about one and a half hours. This is all low country covered in spruce and birch with no hills over 200 feet.

It was a clear winter day and the plane was equipped with skis. In Fred's case the skis were wooden and small even for this little airplane. It was a pleasant flight with smooth air. We observed several moose and a few other critters along the way. It was a good day so far; we planned to be there for just a few hours to fix the roof.

The lake we were going to was a long and thin affair with steep topography on all sides. This caused snow to gather on the lake. When we arrived we noted that there was quite a bit of new snow. We were concerned that the snow might be too light and we didn't want to sink in when we landed. We were also concerned with overflow. ("Overflow" occurs when snow builds up on the ice and its weight causes the ice to buckle and sag. This forces the water to seep up through cracks in the ice and into the snow. You think you are landing on snow, but you end up in two or three feet of water with a little snow on top. Landing in overflow can ruin your whole day.)

Fred made a pass letting the skis touch down, but keeping up the air speed. By doing this most of the weight of the plane is carried by the wings. It takes a very light touch for a pilot to successfully complete this maneuver. Then we climbed back up and came around to observe our tracks. If the tracks turned black that meant there was overflow. If they stayed white, you had to judge if they were very deep or not. This is a little trickier. They didn't appear to be very deep. I said, "Looks good to me. Go ahead and land."

Fred made the mistake of listening to me and put her down. By the time we realized we had made a mistake, it was too late. Snow was blowing through the prop and over the airplane. We must have looked like some high-speed snow-tunneling machine. We were in way too deep to get enough airspeed to start flying again. Fred had no choice but to shut her down and let the chips fall where they may.

When the plane quit moving we had to open the window to dig enough snow away from the door to get it open. The plane was four feet deep in the snow, almost up to the wings. Our quick trip to the cabin was going to take quite a bit longer. When we got clear of the plane, we were waist-deep in snow. Fred was now questioning my advice, using considerable profanity. Standing on a remote Alaska lake with your plane buried in snow is not a good feeling.

We broke a trail to the cabin and found two sets of snowshoes. Breaking trail for 100 yards in four feet of snow is totally exhausting. I broke most of the trail with Fred following along bemoaning his choice of friends. I didn't complain. We returned to the plane with the snowshoes and then began stomping out a runway in front of the airplane. This was slow and exhausting work. By nightfall we were about one third of the way done.

We spent the night in the cabin wondering if anyone was looking for us yet. (I made it a point to always be between Fred and the gun rack.) There was no phone or radio in the cabin and the plane's radio was not working. We were on our own. The next morning we were up early stomping away.

By late afternoon we figured we had a long enough runway, so we dug the plane out and built a ramp up to the runway. Fred fired her up and taxied up the ramp. I jumped in and away we went-almost! Building that runway was hard work and we just were too optimistic about how much we would need. Needless to say, we ended up in four feet of snow at the other end of the runway. This was really getting old.

We went back to the cabin for the night. We were both exhausted and Fred's mood was not improving. The next day we dug the plane out again and got it turned around. This meant digging out a large area so the plane could turn. We then stomped runway until late afternoon. (Keep in mind this involved covering each square foot of the runway two or three times to get it solid.) Lifting those 5-foot-long snowshoes all day long was a real killer.

Now, we were sure we had plenty of runway. We hadn't made a good decision yet on this trip, so I was still apprehensive. We also needed to avoid the hole from the first burial, so we had put a dogleg in the runway. I was sure Fred could maneuver around that problem. When we took off this time we succeeded in avoiding the hole and getting airborne. It was a long and silent trip. When we got home, we found out everyone had just assumed we had decided to spend the weekend at the cabin, so they were not even concerned. Boy, it's nice to have family to look out for you.

AIRPLANES HAVE BACK-UP SYSTEMS FOR EVERYTHING - BUT GAS

Small planes have redundant systems for almost every vital function. They have two sparkplugs for each cylinder, they have vacuum and electric instruments, and they even have two sets of controls in the cockpit. The designers want to make sure that if something fails, there is a back-up.

The one big exception is gas. When you are out of gas, you are out of luck. That is why most of us pilots are very focused on fuel management. I guess pilot intelligence is another system with no back-up.

The fuel gauges in my 185 are just not that accurate. I can be showing dead empty on both tanks and still have up to 20 gallons on board. I don't like carrying around the extra weight, but I am still not willing to try outguessing the gauges.

A wrong guess can have a very unfavorable impact on your aging process. In fact it could end the process altogether. I also keep track of the hours flown vs. the gallons per hour in order to estimate remaining fuel. Even with these precautions, I still have had some fuel shortage problems, none of which were fun experiences.

Laid Back Lee was the chief of surveys for my company and an Alaska Native, born and raised here. He is an easy-going guy and quite familiar with flying around the state in small planes. It took a lot to get Laid Back excited about anything.

Several years ago Laid Back and I flew over to the Dillingham area to look at a survey project we were preparing a proposal to complete. The trip over was pleasant - with clear skies and no turbulence. The flight plan took us over the Chigmit Mountains, across the Mulchatna and Nushagak River valleys and then to the Tikchik Lakes where the project was located. I spotted several moose, a few bears and even some Dall sheep in the mountains. Laid Back saw nothing because he was asleep - some of the most spectacular scenery in the world and Laid Back sleeps away.

N4448R in ski mode at Lake Hood.

The Tikchik Lakes are a chain of large lakes connected by short rivers. They are world famous for their fishing that includes all salmon species as well as rainbows, grayling, and arctic char. We inspected the project and then decided to stop at the outlet of one of the lakes to see if we could pick up a salmon or two. As I was setting up to land, we noted a group of five fishermen working a school of red salmon with one guy sitting on the beach not fishing. We also noted that the red salmon were in fact very red and therefore of very little value as table fare. Laid Back, who was now awake, inquired as to why people would be fishing for "ripe" salmon. I had no idea. Once we landed I walked up the beach to chat with the guy sitting on a rock. Turned out he was a guide and his clients were a bunch of Germans who wanted to catch the reds so they could be mounted in their fine spawning colors. Oh well, to each his own.

Laid Back and I walked down below the reds and managed to pick up several large rainbows and two silver salmon. With the salmon in the float we departed for Dillingham to refuel and head for home. So far it had been a very pleasant day. When we got to Dillingham, I bought only enough fuel to get us home. Because the lake there is quite short, I wanted to be as light as possible, and the cost of fuel was much higher there than in Anchorage.

The cost difference can quickly become insignificant if you don't have enough gas to finish the trip ... but I wasn't thinking that way at the time. When I look back on this, I am not sure I was thinking at all and Laid Back was...well, laid back.

There are no places to get fuel between Iliamna and Anchorage. You see the signs on the road "no more gas for 100 miles." Well in this case, it is no more gas for one and a half hours or 25 gallons of fuel consumed. When we flew over Iliamna, I determined we were in good shape fuel-wise and kept on going--fat, happy, and over-confident. Laid Back was asleep.

Because it was a clear day, I decided to fly over the mountains instead of through the pass. This required that we climb to 9,000 feet to clear the mountaintops. What I didn't realize was that I was also climbing into a strong head wind. I didn't have a GPS in those days, so I wasn't aware of my diminished ground speed due to the head-wind. We were well past the halfway point before I realized that it was taking far too long to get over the mountains and into Cook Inlet. Our nice, uneventful trip was going to hell in a handbasket. Going back was not an option because it would take longer than going ahead. It was time to get focused. I woke up Laid Back who pondered our predicament and went back to sleep.

I "leaned out" the engine and dropped as low as I could into the mountain peaks. This put us into some turbulence, but less head-wind. Once we cleared the mountains, I dropped down to 1,000 feet and started along the coastline. There are several lakes and rivers along the path but, few of them were near any habitation. To land on them would involve a long walk or another plane bringing you some gas. Both gauges were showing empty. They were not even bouncing.

Laid Back was now awake and becoming concerned. If he was concerned, then I should have been on the edge of total panic. We were still 45 minutes from Anchorage.

This was now what we pilots call a "two-quarter" flight. This is when you are so puckered up that the only part of your butt touching the seat is the size of two quarters. Laid Back and I were both looking ahead to the next lake or river to determine if we could get there if the engine quit. You could cut the tension in that airplane with an ulu. Laid Back later told me as we flew along he was reflecting back a few years one winter when he was in the back seat of a 172, piloted by a friend of ours. They had run out of gas and were dropping through the clouds with a dead engine. They had no idea what was below them. It was completely silent in the airplane when Laid Back turned to the other guy in the back seat and asked if he would convert to Catholic if Laid Back had five gallons of gas. The guy didn't answer. They managed to land in a frozen clearing with minor damage. In our case, we were both Catholic, so the option of converting to save us wasn't there.

The last few miles along the mud flats from the mouth of the Little Susitna River to Lake Hood is low flat country with one or two landable lakes. There is also the very undesirable option of landing in the inlet with its treacherous waters. Laid Back was totally alert now. When I was on final approach to Lake Hood I was still expecting the engine to quit. It didn't. The fuel god was with us. When I refueled the plane we realized that there were two gallons left. That is about eight minutes of fuel. Laid Back commented that he had never seen anyone manage fuel so precisely and that he had not used that much adrenaline in years. He then went home to take a nap. I sat on the float and hyperventilated for a few minutes and then went to get a beer.

It was about two years later that I took off for moose camp from Lake Hood to pick up some friends. I had full tanks and was in good shape for the one-hour trip. As I cleared Lake Hood, the tower called me and said it appeared I had fuel spraying out behind my plane. There is no way this could be a good thing....

I couldn't see anything from the cockpit, so I said I would land on a lake across the inlet to check it out. The fuel tanks in a Cessna 185 are located in the wings. The gas caps are, therefore, on the top of the wing near where the wing attaches to the cockpit so they can't be observed from inside the plane. Upon landing, I discovered the gas cap on one of my tanks had come off and all the fuel in that tank was gone (the air moving over the wing sucks the gas out). I replaced the gas cap and returned to Anchorage to fill the tank again. That was about a $300 per hour flight just in fuel cost.

I resumed my flight to the moose camp to pick up Mark and his dad who was visiting from Wisconsin. At the time, Mark was an Air Force sergeant stationed at Elmendorf Air Force Base in Anchorage. He was not a great outdoorsman and tended to get lost quite a bit. Therefore he was somewhat nervous about being out in the woods, but he loved hunting and fishing, so he managed to overcome his apprehension. His father was on his first trip to Alaska and on his first moose hunt. Dad was a bit overweight and not in good physical condition, so he was struggling some with the rigors of the moose hunt. They had been at the camp by themselves for a week, so I was not sure what I would find when I showed up. I was quite sure I would find two guys ready to go home. I went through my checklist before landing and noted that both tanks were showing a little over half full. Since I fly with my fuel selector on both tanks it made sense that both tanks would be down, but half gone was more than I would have expected. I just assumed it was the gauges. I landed and loaded the guys up. As I had expected, they were both ready to go home. While taxiing out onto the lake to take off, I noticed that the fuel gauges were showing empty. This didn't make sense so I cut the engine and climbed up to inspect the gas caps. Sure enough, the same cap had come off and the tank was empty. The other tank was almost empty because the fuel selector being on both had allowed gas to migrate to the empty tank and then out the top. Also, all the gas used on the trip up came out of the remaining tank. This could be considered a design defect or a pilot defect depending on your point of view. (Interestingly enough, the gas tanks in a 1976 Cessna 185 are rubber. When the cap is off the wind over the wing not only sucks out all the gas, it also sucks up the bottom of the tank, making the gauges read half full when it is really completely empty. This really is a design defect that Cessna corrected in later models.)

We returned to shore where I had some fuel stashed. I put in 15 gallons. It should take 10 to get home, so we had some insurance. The way this day was going I needed all the insurance I could get. I then replaced the gas cap and in typical Alaskan fashion duct-taped it down. (In Alaska, if you can't fix it with duct tape, it is broken beyond repair.) By this time Mark's dad was giving him one of those "what the hell have you got us into" looks. Mark wasn't looking all that comfortable, either. I assured them both that I had the situation under control. They were very tired, so they actually believed me. Of course, I have now used 105 gallons of gas to fly one hour, which would normally require 15 gallons. The economics of this was soon to be an insignificant footnote to this ordeal.

As we took off and started back to town I watched the gauges closely. They were showing a quarter tank on both tanks, which was about right. It was an hour flight, so after I was satisfied that we were in the good hands of duct tape, I settled back and started talking with Mark and his dad.

We were 15 minutes from Lake Hood when I noticed both tanks were again reading one half full. (This was not good because I knew we had not taken on any gas during the flight.) I correctly concluded that the cap had somehow come loose again and my fuel situation was now undetermined. I opted to keep going because we were at 4,000 feet and I could dead stick into a number of lakes if I had to. I didn't bother to fill in Mark and his dad on the situation. No sense in all of us flying in fear!

The biggest problem was crossing Knik Arm. It is two miles across and if the engine quit half way we would probably end up in the inlet in some real nasty water with very strong currents. This would not be good. I personally know three pilots who landed in the inlet and were never seen again. I didn't want to join that unfortunate fraternity. The engine sputtered once just as we reached the far shore of the Arm. I rocked the wings and she started humming along just fine. (By rocking the wings you roll the gas to the outlet and fill the fuel line to the engine. It gives you another minute or so of fuel.) I now knew I was down to very little gas, but I had Lake Hood made even if she did quit. We landed without incident and made it to my slip. I doubt if I had a gallon of gas left. I checked and sure enough the cap had come off again. It turned out the locking pin was broken, so the cap showed it was locked but it really was not. I don't think I have ever revealed the whole story to Mark.

This is also the only time duct tape had failed me. Another legend debunked.

****

I frequently donate a weekend at my cabin on Shell Lake to the Rotary auction. One year, the weekend trip was purchased by a local doctor who was the son of one of our ex-governors. He brought three kids ages 7 to 13 and his wife, so it took two trips to get them all out to the cabin. Of course, it also took two trips to get them back. This is a straightforward flight of about 45 minutes over the Susitna Valley. I have made this trip hundreds of times and knew how much gas I would need. With full loads I wanted to have the minimum amount of fuel to reduce weight for take off. I calculated the fuel I would need to make the two trips and kept track when I delivered them to the cabin. Therefore, when it was time to go get them I ordered the proper amount of fuel, which was delivered by the fuel truck. I wasn't there when he delivered the fuel and I didn't check to make sure he had put as much fuel into the plane as I had ordered. I won't make that mistake again.... It is bad enough to kill yourself, but when you kill the governor's son and two of his grandsons along with you, that makes the papers.

On the first trip, I picked up the wife and the daughter and returned them to town. The gauges were showing less gas than they should, but their accuracy was subject to question. Just in case, I put in five more gallons and took off for the lake. When I got to Shell Lake again the gauges looked low, but I was sure I had plenty of gas. There are few things more dangerous than overconfidence combined with stupidity!

I loaded up the guys with the doc in the co-pilot seat and the two boys in the back, and we headed for home. We were over Cook Inlet when the engine suddenly quit. It is amazing how quiet it is in a small plane when the engine quits. You could easily hear four sets of butt cheeks tighten right up.

I went through the emergency procedure and it restarted. I had no idea what had happened so, I just kept going. Again I was looking at the option of going into the inlet. There was a large container ship churning along, so if landing in the inlet was the choice I planned to land in his wake and hope someone got to us before the currents sunk the plane. I didn't share this idea with my passengers. It is interesting to note that no one asked what happened. There was zero conversation in that airplane. The engine quit again while we were on final approach for the lake. Again, no conversation, just the sound of buns tightening up. I landed without power.

Once we were on the water I got her going again and we taxied to my slip. As I was taxiing the tower called me and asked what was going on. I lied to them and said I had accidentally pulled the mixture instead of the prop and killed the engine. I didn't want to have a long and unpleasant conversation with some FAA guy. The governor's son was a good sport and said he admired my calm under those circumstances. I noted that he had remained calm also. The boys had no comment.

I did run into him while buying new underwear the next day. When he asked what I was buying, I said, "socks" as I hid the package of shorts behind my back.

The next day I grabbed my mechanic and we set about figuring what had happened. It turned out to be two things. First, I had told the gas guy to put 15 gallons in each tank. He had only put in 15 gallons total. I was an hour short on fuel to begin with. The second problem was that the valve to check for water in the gas on the right tank was stuck, so I hadn't been draining water out of that tank for sometime. Consequently, there was a pint of water in that tank. With the low fuel situation, the water was sloshing around in the tank and some of it got into the fuel line and shut down the engine.

These three incidents occurred in the course of 1,500 hours of flying time. They were all preventable and were all potential killers. A big part of being a pilot is to anticipate these problems before they occur and prevent them from happening. I know incidents such as these have definitely made me a much more cautious pilot.

I also have developed very strong buns....

ALASKANS ARE A SPECIAL BREED OF PEOPLE

I have been all over the United States and several countries. This has allowed me to meet a large variety of people from many different cultures. In all my travels, I believe Alaskans are the most unique of all the people I have met. They are not only hardy and inventive, but they are the most friendly and helpful people I know. Of course, there are exceptions, but they are usually Cheechakos (newcomers). Let me give you some examples.

Some friends and I were moose hunting near McGrath. This is a small town on the Kuskokwim River in interior Alaska. It is the hub for the region. It became the hub of interior Alaska in 1907 when gold was discovered at Ganes Creek, and it still has an active mining industry.

McGrath is a little different than most remote Alaskan communities. It is more of a town than a village. That is probably because the town has a high percentage of non-native citizens, so there are not as many family connections as you see in most villages. It is located about 200 miles northwest of Anchorage. There are 500 or so hardy souls there year round. This number increases considerably during the Iditarod Sled Dog Race as McGrath is one of the main checkpoints in the 1,049-mile race. There are no roads to McGrath; therefore, the airstrip is the "main street" of the town.

We were hunting out of an FAA facility named Farewell about 75 miles south-west of McGrath. We had landed on the strip there and planned to camp out in our tents along side the strip. It was November and quite cold but we were prepared. The FAA flight service station guy and his family were the only residents of Farewell. When they saw us putting up tents, they came out and offered us one of the unoccupied buildings. It even had a stove to warm it up. That night they invited us over to watch a movie. Their hospitality was unexpected but greatly appreciated.

We had used most of our fuel flying over from Anchorage and scouting for moose, so the next day we headed to McGrath for fuel. When we left Farewell the weather was good with 25 to 30 miles of visibility. The weather deteriorated as we flew west and was marginal when we arrived at our destination. There was a light fog right over the town. As we flew over we could look down through the fog and see the airstrip, but when I dropped down into the fog to land, I couldn't see ahead through the fog to line up on the strip. We made several passes with the McGrath radio operator trying to help guide us. I didn't have enough gas to get anywhere else, so I had to get down one way or the other. After about the fifth try one of the guys asked if we were going to be able to get the airplane down. I replied that no one had ever left one up here! It didn't seem to put him at ease.

I finally got a little break in the fog and landed. What I didn't know was that they were working on the runway. There was a six-inch vertical break in the pavement partway down the strip and we hit it right after landing. The bump bent my tail wheel yoke and flattened the tire. I was not a happy camper.

It was Sunday morning and most of the town was closed. We did luck out because the Northern Commercial store was open. The NC stores in rural Alaska are general stores that sell everything from food to hammers. In McGrath, the NC store is located on the runway along with the FAA building and the local bar. We parked the airplane in front, went in and explained our predicament to the manager and only employee. He reflected that most of the local pilots go over that bump slowly so they don't break things. I could see this was going to be a long conversation....

It appeared we were his only customers so far that day and he just was glad to have someone to talk to. After a long talk on the state of world affairs and our current governor, he allowed that we should probably get that wheel fixed before it got too dark to take off. He showed us to the store's shop, which was equipped with a full set of tools, a welder, and tire patching supplies.

It took us a couple of hours to complete repairs. We had to heat up the yoke and pound it straight and then replace the axle with a bolt we modified. We also patched the tube and then we had to get everything back on the airplane. None of us were mechanics or welders, but you know what they say about monkeys, typewriters and major works of literature. What we ended up with was not pretty, but it was functional.

When we were done we inquired as to what we owed him. He charged us $.25 for the tire patch. I couldn't believe it. I told him if he ever got to Anchorage and needed a favor to call me and gave him my business card. I never expected to see him again.

I got the call three years later. The NC store manager had just landed at Lake Hood and found that his truck wouldn't start. He was en route to the Pioneer Grocery (a bulk sales store that was here prior to Costco) to load up on supplies and needed a truck. I loaned him my survey rig. He called me when he was done and said thanks and was on his way back to McGrath. We were even until next time.

****

On the way home from caribou hunting along the Mulchatna River, we stopped for gas at King Salmon. This is a small town located on the Naknek River about 300 miles southwest of Anchorage. There is an Air Force base there and it is also the main hub for the Bristol Bay red salmon fishing fleet. The facility that sells avgas to float planes is located on the bank of the river with a small dock to tie to while refueling. We landed on the river and tied up to the fuel dock. As I got out of the airplane my foot hooked my headset and it fell in the river and sank. This was a real bad deal. I now had no way to talk to the control towers or anyone else. We were stuck.

When I explained the problem to my companions, they had several comments about my heritage and IQ. I was at a loss for a counter-argument. This unpleasant conversation continued as we entered the store that sold the fuel. The clerk could not help but overhear what we were saying. During a short break in the diatribe, he asked if I would like to borrow his headset. I said sure, but we were going all the way to Anchorage, and I would have to mail it back to him in King Salmon. He said that would be fine. His plane was being worked on, so he didn't need the headset for a week.

Now here we have a guy loaning a $200 headset to someone he doesn't even know, trusting that he will mail it back to him. I asked why he would trust me to do that. He said I looked like an honest person. This sent my friends into convulsions of laughter. (He also noted that he had the tail number of my airplane, so if he had to find me he could.) I mailed the headset back to him along with a couple of movies.

****

I was flying back from halibut fishing in Homer with my wife and another couple. Homer is located about an hour's flight south of Anchorage near the end of the Kenai Peninsula. It is on the road system and, in fact, is the end of the road. It is a very tourist-oriented town with sightseeing tours and excellent fishing.

We typically land on Beluga Lake and then bum a ride to the fishing boat. It is a several hour trip out to the fishing grounds and back. Once there, pulling 100 pound plus halibut up from 300 feet of water tends to wear you out.

So it had been a long day and the plane was loaded with four people and several hundred pounds of halibut. I didn't want any more weight, so I didn't put any more gas in the plane. I had calculated what it would take to get to Homer and back and was confident we were OK. We took off without incident. It was just getting dusk as we were flying over Kenai about 20 minutes from Anchorage when I noticed that the gas gauges were showing empty. I was fairly sure I had enough gas, but those gauges were really worrying me. I opted to land on Arness Lake and try to figure out what to do, rather that take a chance crossing Turnagain Arm with marginal fuel supplies. When I announced this decision the vote was three-to-one against landing. I pointed to a small bumper sticker on the dash of the plane. It reads as follows, "This airplane is flown from the left front seat only. Anyone wishing to dispute this fact will please note the mistletoe attached to the pilot's coat tail."

By the time we landed it was fairly dark. I taxied to the nearest house that had lights on, tied up to his dock, knocked on the door and explained why we were there. I asked if I could use his phone to call someone to bring us some gas. He invited me in, saying he didn't have any gas, but he was sure his neighbor did and he would give him a call. Sure enough, the neighbor had 10 gallons and he would bring it right over. The guy showed up five minutes later with two, five-gallon cans of fuel. The cans had State of Alaska painted on the sides. We put the fuel in the plane and I asked how much I owed him. He said nothing; he had swiped the gas from Fish & Game. Nobody in that area likes Fish & Game, so taking their gas was just fine with these guys. They also insisted that I take the cans with me. We shook hands and I loaded up and took off.

The rest of the trip was uneventful (other than the night landing at Lake Hood which is always an adventure.) The next summer I was planning a trip to Homer. I still had the gas cans except they were now painted a different color. I filled them with fuel and stopped at Arness Lake and dropped them off with the neighbor. He was pleased to get the cans back, but seemed disappointed that they had been repainted. He said the gas would be available the next time a plane needs fuel. Typical Alaskan.

****

I have been sailing out of the quaint Alaska village of Whittier for over 30 years. I have been on 50-foot yachts and 16-foot skiffs and everything in between. There have been lots of adventures in Prince William Sound (some recounted in this book.) In all that time I have never encountered anyone who wasn't willing to help if another boat was in trouble.

One fall we had been out to Green Island hunting deer. We had gotten a few animals and were rushing back to the quaint Alaska village of Whittier so we could catch the last tunnel opening of the day. If you miss the last opening, then you get to spend the night on the boat. It was already dark, but we could see the lights of town. It looked like we would make it with 30 minutes to spare when we noticed a light being shined at us from the middle of Passage Cannel. We cut the power and idled over to the boat.

It was two guys in an open 18-foot skiff. Their motor was on the fritz and they needed a tow. We brought them on board, tied their skiff off to our boat, and headed for the harbor.

While we missed the last closing and spent the night, we didn't begrudge these guys for making us late. They were in trouble and we did what was necessary to take care of them. We could have left them to the next boat that came along, but that would not have been right. Besides, they bought our dinner that night.

The very next summer we were on our way back to Whittier again in Passage Cannel when the u-joint on our drive line blew apart. We were dead in the water with no way to repair the damage, so we called the harbormaster and asked for help. A longliner came on the air and said they were 30 minutes away and they would come and get us. They lashed us to their boat and delivered us to the harbor. I asked what we owed them for the help. They replied "If we are ever in trouble, you will help us." What goes around, comes around.

I could give many more examples of people in trouble in the bush and finding people willing to help in any way they can. This is also true in urban Alaska. This is just a special place and it is a real privilege to be able to live here.

SWIMMING IN ALASKA
CAN BE PROBLEMATIC

I was sitting in the Kit Kat Bar in the Lonely DEW line facility. This is a bar that has never been featured in Sunset Magazine. This DEW line site is about half way between Prudhoe Bay and Barrow on the arctic coast of Alaska. The nearest road connected to the world is 100 miles away. The bar is one of the main tourist attractions in Camp Lonely, which is occupied only by construction workers.

It was Sunday afternoon and I had been sitting there drinking with two other engineers for several hours and several drinks. My companions were Scary Gary and Plano John. Scary was a high-energy guy who was always coming up with some sort of scheme to make money or goon someone. At the time he was working for me as a construction engineer and I had to keep an eye on him all the time so that he didn't cause too much disruption on the job site. He was an incorrigible practical joker and he constantly pushed the envelope.

Plano, on the other hand, was all business. He was a contract engineer with the client and worked at a daily rate. He hailed from Plano, Texas, hence the nickname. His sense of humor was miniscule at best, but he did like his liquor. Once he had a few, he would actually lighten up a bit and even smile at a joke or two.

As the number of drinks piled up, our conversation turned to things we had not done in the arctic. There were several mundane things but Scary came up with one of the more interesting ideas, which was to swim in the Arctic Ocean. All three of us had not had that pleasure. Scary concluded that since the ice was out at this time, we should remedy this gap in our collective experience. Plano was not so sure. We all concluded that we needed to have a swim in the ocean on our resumes if we wanted to be taken seriously as arctic engineers.

So we adjourned to the beach with Scary leading the way and Plano reluctantly following along. It was only a 100-yard walk from the bar, but it seemed to take us a long time to get there. Walking on tundra while impaired is difficult. The beach at Lonely is about 25 feet wide and made up of gray pea-gravel. The road from the DEW line facility to Camp Lonely runs by 50 feet from the beach. It is about a mile to the camp from our beach party location. The Arctic Ocean is quite shallow here, so even though we had only a light breeze, we still had a one-foot surf.

We stripped down to our birthday suits. After a short and somewhat incoherent discussion, we decided that I would count to three and then we would all just run as far as we could into the water and plunge head-first into the surf. This was a good plan for a bunch of drunks and it went off without a hitch.

I was instantly aware that we had made a huge mistake. The water temperature in the summer is between 28 and 35 degrees. I would imagine that a casual observer on the beach that day would have been reminded of one of our nuclear submarines firing three missiles from under the water. We ran to shore more than we swam. I suspect our total time in the water was less than 3 seconds. I also observed that as we jumped into our clothes and rushed back to Lonely for hot showers, everyone was quite sober. It's funny how you can drink so much booze and not remain pretty well loaded after a brisk swim.

Looking back on this decision, I think the several drinks we had consumed may have clouded our judgment. I am sure glad I don't have to do that again.... now that it is on my resume.

****

My next swimming adventure was also in the arctic. We were collecting data on the depth of the water in the Colville River. The 400-mile-long river flows into the Arctic Ocean about 80 miles west of Prudhoe Bay. We wanted to take a construction barge up the river to Umiat and we needed to know if the river was deep enough to accommodate the barge.

I was collecting this data by standing on the floats of a helicopter with a survey rod in one hand and holding onto the helicopter with the other hand. The helicopter would hover a few feet above the river and I would lower the rod until it hit bottom. We could then determine the depth.

This was a low-tech plan for a low-IQ crew.

We had been doing this for several hours when we came to Ocean Point where there is a large pool in the river. Up to this point the water depth had never been much more than four feet.

I had gotten into the habit of kind of leaning on the pole as I lowered it and catching my balance when it hit bottom. I didn't realize this pool was much deeper. The river is also several hundred feet wide at this location. The trap was set. All Mr. Colville needed was a victim and I was available.

The helicopter was hovering about three feet over the water when I lowered the rod. Instead of hitting bottom it just kept going --and so did I. Suddenly, I found myself being swept downstream in some very cold water. The current in the pool was not that fast, but a short distance downstream its velocity increased dramatically as the river narrowed. There was no way to get hold of the wet, slippery 'copter floats. I realized I was in some serious trouble. The thought that the river was plenty deep for a barge at this point shot through my mind. I don't know why.

The crew in the helicopter tried to maneuver the craft so they could grab me, but only succeeded in almost landing on me a couple of times. I refer back to the IQ assessment noted above. My situation was not improving.

I was wearing hiking boots, jeans, a wool shirt, and a down parka. None of these were helpful for swimming. The guys in the chopper were trying to find a rope to throw to me, but were not having much luck. I opted to shed the parka and swim like crazy for a gravel bar near the outlet of the pool to avoid being swept into the fast current. This was a successful strategy.

As I sat on the beach thanking my lucky stars, I noticed my parka and the survey rod floating past. I waded in and retrieved them. Other than my pride this was a no-loss accident. The helicopter landed on the gravel bar and picked me up. I had a short but intense discussion with the crew about trying to land on me. I was a wet, cold and thoroughly embarrassed guy.

We went back to Lonely where several people offered to give me swimming lessons. There was also a life vest with my name stenciled across it on my desk. I was touched by their concern.

****

Our oldest son had a swimming adventure at our cabin at Shell Lake, 90 miles northwest of Anchorage. It is two miles wide and six miles long. The Iditarod Trail runs right by the lake. Our cabin is a 20 by 30-foot affair that sits up on the bank 20 feet above the water. This affords a nice view of the lake and the surrounding mountains.

We like to catch fish, so in winter we cut holes in the ice and put pop-ups in the holes. With our nice view of the lake we can just sit in the cabin and watch for the flag to go up and then run down and pull up the fish. The whole family was there for Iditarod weekend.

We had drilled a hole in the ice to get water and to fish. The hole was about eight inches in diameter, cut through six feet of ice. I noted when I drilled it that water was coming up through the hole to the top of the ice and flowing into the snow. There were several feet of new snow on the lake, so I didn't worry about the snow soaking up the water. With that much snow I figured it would only impact the bottom foot of the snow.

What I didn't realize was that the water would continue to flow out of that hole all night long. There is a thing called "cold water thawing." If water runs over ice, it will thaw the ice. Consequently, the ice hole was getting bigger and bigger throughout the night. By morning the hole was 3-feet in diameter, but you couldn't tell because the snow was bridged over the hole. The pop up was still perched on the snow bridge. Everything looked the same. Old man winter had set his trap.

Christopher, who was a teenager at the time, walked out to check the fish line we had left overnight. When he got there, the snow under his feet gave way and down he went into the hole up to his armpits in water. He couldn't get out because his clothes were soaked and heavy and there was nothing to grab but wet snow.

We heard him holler and rushed to pull him out of the hole. We also pulled up the fishing line and found a nice burbot on the hook. We took the kid and the fish back to the cabin to warm up the kid and to cook the fish. Christopher was advised that we didn't encourage swimming at Shell Lake until June and we would appreciate him following our advice for a change. He assured us he would keep that in mind.

Left to right: Nancy, Ruth, Candace and F.T. at Shell Lake.

CHAPTER 4:
I'm Not the Only Idiot in Alaska

The previous chapters have all involved misadventures of yours truly. I would like to document the misadventures of some of my fellow Alaskans to show you it's not just my gene pool that tends to run a little shallow.

HOW MUCH DEER MEAT IS NEEDED TO FEED THREE BROWN BEARS?

My good buddy Billy was hunting deer on Kodiak Island. He was hunting with several friends, but had wandered off by himself. Being an FBI special agent deluded him into thinking he could take care of himself. There are several problems with hunting alone on Kodiak Island. One of the problems is that the brown bears on that island have learned that the sound of a rifle shot means a deer is down! They tend to investigate every shot they hear. In fact they are nicknamed "dinner-bell bears," the dinner bell being the sound of the rifle. The area he was hunting was well forested with large spruce and many alder patches. There were lots of places for critters, big and small, to hide.

Billy had just shot a nice buck in a small clearing surrounded by alders, spruce trees and steep terrain. He was in the process of gutting the deer when he heard some bears approaching through the thick brush. Everything on his body puckered right up. He yelled at them, but that only caused them to speed up enroute to his location.

Billy and me with one of my moose.

The old fight-or-flight instinct kicked in and seeing as how the bears had obviously chosen *fight*, that left Billy with the only other choice: *flight*. He was at the edge of a steep bank that went down about 20 feet. At the bottom of the bank was a large spruce tree. Billy ran down the bank, left his gun on the ground, and scrambled up the tree. As he was scrabbling up through the limbs, a sow bear with two third-year cubs came into the clearing. The cubs were probably 400-pound bears, the sow around 700 pounds. I am sure they seemed much bigger at the time. They went right for the deer.

This is when Billy realized that he had climbed up a tree that was right next to the bank. This put him 20 feet up the tree, but eyeball-to-eyeball with the bears from 10 feet away. A little more planning probably should have taken place. As he hung there in the tree trying not to make eye contact, he reflected on the wisdom of choosing this tree. His FBI training had not covered this particular situation.

The bears tore into the deer. Three brown bears on the same kill is not a polite situation even if they are related. Being in a position to observe this up close and personal is also not something you strive to do. In this case, the situation quickly deteriorated. They were soon fighting over various parts of the deer as it was ripped apart. Billy, in the meantime, was contemplating his options of getting out of the tree or just staying still and hoping the bears would be satisfied with just the deer. The deer weighed about 150 pounds, so that would be 50 pounds for each bear. That should be enough, Billy thought. If it wasn't, there was another 185 pounds of meat hanging in the tree just a short leap away.

Before Billy could make up his mind the bears picked up the deer pieces and took off. So did Billy. He declined to shoot several more deer while enroute to the camp.

YOU CAN'T FLOAT A FROZEN RIVER

Sam and two of his employees were floating the Innoko River one September in search of moose. Sam owned a construction company and was a partner in my firm at the time. Sam is a big guy, but he has a tendency to let the other guys do the work whenever he can. He loves the outdoors, but does all he can to make it as comfortable as possible when he is afield.

Sam is a real take-charge guy, so one of the first things that happens in camp is that Sam takes charge and has everybody working hard to see that he is comfortable. Raymond, on the other hand, was a very accomplished outdoorsman and had been a guide for many years in Alaska. He has a very dry sense of humor and is a delight to have on any trip. Raymond had retired from guiding and was now working for Sam.

Sam and Raymond had flown to Ophir for a float and hunting trip with a third guy. It is about a five-day float from Ophir to the pick-up point. Ophir, located five miles northwest of

McGrath, was the site of a gold rush in 1886 and its population peaked out in 1908 at about 1,000 sourdoughs. It is now
an abandoned town with just a few old buildings still standing. It is near the half-way point on the Iditarod Trail Sled
Dog race, where the first Iditarod musher to arrive is reward-
ed with $3,000 in gold nuggets.

The plan was to launch at Ophir and then float down river
just past Cripple where the river is wide and slow enough to
land a floatplane for pick-up. This is all relatively low, forested country with lots of clearings. There is thick brush along
the banks so you have to stop and crawl up the bank to glass
for moose. Sam's group was using some top-quality inflatable
rafts, tents and gear right out of the L.L. Bean catalog. They
planned to be comfortable, but Alaska's weather had other
plans.

The first day was a pleasant float and that night as they sat
around the camp, a bull ran right into the camp. Sam grabbed
his gun and dropped him. They had their first moose with no
packing involved. The second day was also pleasant weather
but no moose. That night they were surprised to see the temperature drop below zero. The next day, it never got above
10 degrees as they continued their float. They already had
one moose and were looking for number two. Luckily, they
didn't get an opportunity to get a moose that day. In the late
afternoon, they set up camp on the bank of the river. Due
to the cold, it took extra effort on everyone's part to get Sam
comfortable.

That night the temperature dropped below zero again.
When they got up the next morning, they noticed there were
bits of ice and slush in the river, so they had breakfast, packed
up and launched the rafts. The temperature remained very
low; therefore, as the day wore on the river developed more
and more ice and less and less water. They finally pulled out
on a gravel bar when they had reached a point there was too
much ice to continue down stream without risking a hole in
the rafts. They set up camp to wait it out--without a radio or
any other way to call for help. It would take at least two or
three days to walk to the airstrip at Cripple and even if they
made it, there was no one there to help. A pleasant hunting
trip was now taking on a much more sinister complexion.

Meanwhile, the air taxi outfit that was to pick them up received word that the river had frozen. They called Sam's wife and advised her that they wouldn't be able to get Sam and his guys out. They told her they couldn't land on floats due to the ice and there were no wheel strips in the area. When she asked them what she should do, they said they had no idea - it was her problem now - and hung up.

That is when she called me.

After conferring with the weather-guessers, I concluded my floatplane was not an option. It also appeared that the river was going to stay frozen for the year. We would have to devise a rescue plan!

I called the Fish & Game guy in McGrath and explained the situation. He agreed that we couldn't get to them by wheels or floats, but that Fish & Game had issued an emergency order allowing helicopters to transport hunters and their gear. Normally this is illegal.

I called everyone who had a helicopter within 100 miles of the Innoko River. They were all busy rescuing hunters stranded on frozen rivers and lakes. I had no choice left but to charter a helicopter out of Anchorage. I think the total bill was over $2,000. (I'm not sure because Sam paid for the ride.)

It turned out they were on a gravel bar that was 800 feet long. We could have easily picked them up with a Super Cub from McGrath and saved about $1,500, but we had no way of knowing that.

Anyway, it was Sam's first trip in a helicopter, so he, at least, enjoyed the experience. He doesn't have the same disdain for those contraptions as I do.

IF YOU THROW STUFF IN A GRIZZLY BEAR DEN, IT CAN TURN UGLY FAST

Macho Jim and his two sons were spring bear hunting on Mount Yenlo. Macho is a rough and tumble guy who has been in Alaska for many years. He has a cabin on Shit Lake located right at the base of Mount Yenlo. I like Macho because of his no-nonsense attitude and his ability to just get the job done. His boys are also outdoor types.

Their family cabin is about 90 miles north of Anchorage just south of Denali National Park. It is a very remote location with the nearest road being 50 miles away. The lower flank of Mount Yenlo is spruce and birch forest with the middle part mostly alder patches with large clearings. The top third of the mountain is rock and tundra. In the winter the snow covers the alders so the mountain basically is just a very tall pile of snow.

The two boys, both in their 20s, were on one snowmachine; Macho was on the second machine. They were looking for grizzly dens near the top of the mountain. Their dad was about 800 feet below the boys as they drove around the steep slopes. You spot bear dens by the mud and debris scattered around the mouth of the den. It is deposited there when the bear comes out in the spring.

About mid-day the boys came upon a den. There were a lot of tracks around the area, which is usually an indication that the bear had completed his hibernation and moved on. It is not a sure thing; sometimes they go back in for another nap, so you should exercise some caution when approaching such a den. A grizzly bear that has just awoken after a five-month nap can be very unpleasant up close and personal.

Macho's boys weren't aware of this rule, so they just drove up to the den and looked in to see what was there. Not seeing anything, they threw some sticks in the den just for kicks. I am sure they got a kick out of the 10-foot grizzly boar that came boiling out of the den! I am sure every hair on their heads was sticking straight up.

This bear was in a real bad mood and quickly decided to terminate his tormentors. The boys chose not to buy into this plan and elected to vacate the area quickly. The bear was between them and the snowmachine, where they had conveniently left their guns, so they had no choice but to run like hell. They spun on their heels and took the obvious route away from the den, which was down the slope. The slope was very steep and covered with deep snow.

Macho was, meanwhile, 800 feet below sitting on his snowmachine with his .300 Winchester Mag, observing the mayhem above with a sense of impending disaster. The boys were running and sliding down the slope with the bear in hot pursuit. There was no doubt that the bear had the advantage and would soon overtake the boys. The fact is they were breaking trail for him.

This left Macho with the option of watching his boys turned into bear scat or shooting the bear. He was looking at a 200-yard shot at a running bear that was quickly closing the gap between two scrambling boys.

The thought of accidentally shooting a son instead of the bear crossed his mind. The situation was rapidly getting critical as the bear was within 15 feet of the boys. Macho fired his first shot and hit the bear. The bullet knocked him off his feet and the boys gained some ground. But then the bear got right back up and continued his pursuit. Now he was really pissed. Macho, the bear, and the boys repeated this exercise several times until the bear finally rolled over dead.

The boys were well past Macho before they collapsed. Macho was hyperventilating, the boys were exhausted, and the bear was dead. This was a reasonable solution considering the circumstances. They composed themselves, skinned the bear, and headed back to the cabin. They'd had enough bear adventures for a while.

When they got back to Anchorage Macho, made the mistake of calling the local newspaper and relating the story to a reporter. The paper published the story on the front page of the local Metro section. In the weeks that followed, there were several letters to the editor criticizing Macho and his boys for shooting the bear. (Even in Alaska we have a few animal rights folks, even though they don't enjoy the same status they do in Los Angeles or New York.)

Macho also received some irate phone calls. One caller asked him how he would like it if he came over and threw sticks at his house and then started shooting at him. Macho said he would be glad to give him his address if he wanted to give it a try. He also reminded the caller that he had hit the bear every shot, so he should make sure his life insurance was paid up. The caller hung up.

SHOOT THE BEARS, NOT THE BOAT

We had a real problem one fall with a grizzly sow and her three-year-old cubs at Shell Lake. The lake is six miles long and is heavily forested with spruce, birch, and alder. Lots of places for critters to hide. The cabins on the lake are generally spread out with 100 yards to a half mile between them. The nearest road is 60 miles away, so the lake is surrounded by wilderness. The bears were breaking into cabins almost every night. I suspect they spent the day lying in a brush pile digesting what they had stolen. They had a bird nest on the ground in the bear world. The damage was considerable.

Our cabin at Shell Lake before the bear remodeled it.

They went through the wall of my cabin and tore all the cabinets off the walls and turned the cabin into a garbage pit. We took a snow shovel and shoveled everything out the front door and burned it. We restocked the cabin and replaced the cabinets. Two weeks later they were back and trashed everything again. They came in through the same wall but decided to exit by another wall. This way they could double the damage. This was really getting old.

It wasn't just my cabin; similar incidents were occurring all around the lake. I think every cabin on the lake was hit at least once except for the lodge where Zoe lived full time. She is the quintessential Alaskan woman and I am sure the bears didn't want to mess with Zoe and her 30-06.

We formed a bear committee and came up with a plan. We would divide into groups of three persons and take turns sitting on the roofs of various cabins with shotguns loaded with 00 buckshot. The guns had flashlights tied to the barrels. The vigilantes of the old west were better organized than we were, but at least we were doing something.

There are about 35 cabins on Shell Lake, so the odds of us being on the cabin the bears chose were slim. We spent several nights to no avail. We would be sitting on one roof while the bears were dining at another location most likely chuckling at us.

Dandy Danny had a cabin near mid-lake. He owns a bar in Anchorage and is accustomed to dealing with rough customers, but this was different. He is a very outgoing guy but was somewhat intolerant of bears. He had spent several nights on cabin roofs to no avail, his disdain for bears growing each night. His cabin was a two-story affair with the top story being the bedroom. There was a window on the front of the bedroom facing toward the lake and the front porch. This window opened from the side and only opened half way. This would prove to be a major issue. Dandy's airplane was parked in front of the cabin 50 feet away, with his boat alongside.

During the night Dandy was awakened by a noise on his front porch. He looked out the window and there were the bears. They were trying to rip through the front wall of his cabin. He grabbed his shotgun with the 00 buckshot and stuck it out the window. They heard him and ran off the porch and took off along the shoreline. Dandy was having trouble following them with the gun due to the window only opening part way. Just as he was pulling the trigger he noted his airplane was in the line of fire. This caused him to hold his fire until the bears cleared the airplane. Now they were past the window opening. This required him to take the gun off his shoulder in order to stick it past the window. He was now firing the gun without being able to aim properly. He took his best shot and missed the bears. The shot wasn't totally wasted; he did manage to put nine .32-caliber pellets through the bottom of his metal canoe.

That was as close as our vigilante committee came to getting the bears. The Fish & Game Department finally showed up with a helicopter and hunted them down. The committee was dissolved and Dandy bought a new boat.

DON'T SHOOT THE BEAR *IN* THE CABIN!

We were having a problem with a black bear breaking into the cabins at Shell Lake, and it seemed to have a preference for Ann and Scooter's cabin for some reason. Scooter is a local surveyor and the official Shell Lake game "ranger." He is a fun guy and often would do some very off-the-wall activities such as water skiing down the lake in a tuxedo on his birthday. Champagne Ann was also a lot of fun. They were married at Shell Lake. We flew in more than 50 wedding guests for the ceremony, only one of whom died at the reception, but that is another story.

We were all at the lodge when someone thought they saw the bear near Scooter's cabin across the lake. Scooter and Ann had not arrived for the weekend yet, so we took it upon ourselves to deal with the situation.

Gordy and I grabbed a gun and motored right over to do this guy in. Gordy was raised on the lake and his mom, Zoe, owns the lodge. At the time Gordy was only about 16, but he was very well trained in outdoor survival. He should have known better than to get involved in a bear situation with me in charge.

We got to the shore and stalked up to the cabin. The front window was pushed open and we could hear something moving around inside. I told Gordy to stay at the front of the cabin and I would take the gun and go around to the back. He was then to make some noise and I would blast the bear when he came out the back window, which was still broken from his last visit. These spur of the moment plans always seem so fool-proof when you first come up with them --but hardly ever turn out that way.

I moved to where I could see both the back window and Gordy, so I gave him the nod. Gordy threw a rock at the cabin. Nothing! He yelled at the bear. Still nothing! So he jumped up on the porch and beat on the wall. That did it.

A Boone and Crockett-sized squirrel shot out of the window and went up the nearest tree. I was too surprised to shoot, so he got away. However, the bear that had obviously left prior to our arrival had still trashed the inside of the cabin. We returned to the lodge to report the damage but neglected to mention the squirrel.

Boundry dispute with black bear.

Later that day Champagne Ann and Scooter arrived at the lake. He was disappointed to find his cabin trashed again and not at all impressed with our bear control program. After giving the situation considerable thought, he decided that the best plan would to put a snare in the back window and just wait for the bear to make a mistake. So the snare was nailed to the header over the window. We all agreed that this was a good plan (as if we would recognize a good plan if we saw one), but we would continue to watch for the bear with our guns ready. Champagne Ann and Scooter spent the night in Junk Food John's cabin located next door to their cabin.

It was the next morning when Scooter noticed considerable commotion coming from his cabin. He quickly grabbed his shotgun and headed over. He found a black bear caught by one paw in the snare. It had torn the hell out of everything within its reach. So far the damage was confined to a five-foot circle, which was the reach of the snare.

Now I am sure Scooter was a little excited at this point, so he wasn't thinking real clear. (This has never happened to me, so I'm just guessing.) He had quickly grabbed a handful of shotgun shells as he headed out the door and had loaded three in the gun on the way over to the cabin. What he didn't realize was that he had loaded a 7 ½ birdshot and then two oo buck.

The second thing he didn't think about was that because he had approached from the back of the cabin, the bear was *inside* the cabin. If he had just approached from the front, the bear would have jumped out of the cabin through the window. He could have then been dispatched outside the cabin with little mess involved.

Without much thought, Scooter pointed the gun through the broken window and proceeded to let the bear have it with the birdshot from about 20 feet. This inflicted a large, but somewhat superficial wound, which produced considerable blood and tremendous activity on the part of the bear. The next two shots put the critter out of its misery, as well as ventilating the cabin in several places.

Scooter now had a dead bear lying in the middle of his cabin, bear blood splattered all over everything, and several new holes in the structure...far more damage than the bear had ever done.

Having heard the shots, the rest of us arrived on the scene a short time later. We commented on the total devastation and complimented Scooter on the thoroughness of his work. Champagne Ann didn't seem to be as impressed as the rest of us. I don't think I have ever seen a grislier scene in my life.

Scooter had to replace all of the carpeting, the bedding, and the curtains. The walls are still stained.

A short time later Scooter built a new cabin and converted the old one into a storage shed. I guess you could say the bear lost, but he sure made Scooter pay a price for the victory.

FISH CAN BE DANGEROUS TOO

My wife Candace used to go fishing with me quite a bit. You can probably guess Candace is a woman of tremendous fortitude since she has managed not to kill me in the many years we have been married. I know she has been sorely tempted on several occasions. My friends tell me that I married much better than she did. She is also a good sport and does like to get out in the woods on occasion. Our first date was a fishing trip to Lake Creek where she caught two kings and I caught none. She doesn't go much anymore; I think she either just got smart, or scared. I'm not sure which. Over the years she has caught a lot of fish, but two in particular got even!

The first incident occurred on Shell Creek several years ago. We were fishing for red salmon at what we call "the falls." This is where the creek is only 10 feet wide and drops about 20 feet in 25 yards. It is all rocks with the water rushing by at great speed. There are a few small pools in this area and they would be full of salmon as they rested on their trip up the falls.

The footing is precarious and there is very little room to stand near these pools because the creek has cut itself down into the rock, so there are very steep walls on both sides. A fall in the water here would result in a very unpleasant trip down the rocky falls to the stream below.

I was on one side of the falls and Candace was on the other. The only way to cross was either to go upstream or downstream 100 feet; there was no way to cross where we were standing.

I had caught a fish and was looking for a stick to put it on when I noticed that Candace also had one on. I didn't pay a lot of attention because I was occupied with my own fish. When I had the job done, I looked back across the creek just as Candace reached down and grabbed the fish by the gills. As she straightened up the fish started flopping around like crazy. I'm not quite sure how the fish ended up tail up and head down while Candace was hugging it to her chest with both arms, but that is what happened. She was now standing on slippery rocks next to a torrent of water with this fish slapping her in the face with its tail. The fishing line was wrapped around one arm and the pole lay at her feet. It's hard to imagine a more humorous sight in the outdoors.

Candace herding salmon on Shell Creek.

I was yelling at her to drop the fish, but she couldn't hear me over the roar of the water. I was also having trouble choking back the laughter, which greatly impaired my yelling ability. She finally turned her back to the water and dropped the fish on the rocks and beat the hell out of it. Meanwhile I climbed up the bank and into the woods and fell to the ground in hysterics. Once I composed myself, I resumed fishing but couldn't make eye contact with her for fear of bursting out laughing, which would not have been a good thing for my general health.

The second incident occurred at Donkey Creek Lake while

we were fishing for pike. This lake is about 20 miles east of Shell Lake. It is a medium-sized lake with a creek flowing from it to Donkey Creek Slough, which then empties into the Yentna River. The shoreline is mostly swampy with a lot of lily pads. It is ideal pike habitat and it had produced some very large pike. It was not uncommon to catch several in the 20-pound range each trip.

Shell Creek falls.

The thing about pike is that a 20-pound pike has 15 pounds of teeth, some of which are longer than those of my German Shepherd dog. You have to be very careful when unhooking a pike and I had so cautioned Candace.

She was standing in a weed bed almost to the top of her hip-boots, fishing the edge of the weeds. I was fishing off the airplane floats about 50 yards away. We were both catching small pike and letting them go. I noticed that she had hooked a larger fish and was having a little trouble getting him landed. I would guess it was a 10 or 15-pounder. The next thing I knew she was yelling at the top of her lungs at the fish, using language I had learned in junior high. I looked over and could see the fish had her by the hand. A tremendous struggle was taking place, with the winner in doubt.

In the meantime, I was paddling the airplane like crazy to get to her and the fish. I arrived on the scene a few minutes later to find the water full of blood. Not knowing if it was fish blood or Candace blood, I inquired as to how things were going.

Donkey Creek Lake pike after messing with Ma Bell.

At that point the odds of the water filling up with my blood went up dramatically. The fish was dead from multiple blows to the head, Candace's thumb was cut open from the first knuckle to the second and bleeding profusely, and my good standing was dropping rapidly.

I retrieved the first aid kit and got the wound cleaned and bandaged. I then inquired if she wanted to go home or keep fishing, compassionately noting that it appeared the big ones were starting to bite. After a long cold stare, she informed me she wanted to go home.

With this kind of fun, I don't know why she doesn't want to go fishing with me as much as she used to. We still have these kinds of adventures and she is missing out on them!

BULLS AND BEARS

It was a beautiful Alaska autumn day as I taxied down Campbell Lake piloting my float plane. Bob, Curt and I were leaving Anchorage on our way to Captain Curt's very first moose hunt. I was really looking forward to a pleasant few days at the moose camp, but even though conditions seemed almost perfect, there was still a feeling of anxiety.

Anxiety. That is Alaska to me. Even though I've been flying for over 20 years, I still get that knot in the stomach, a split-second of anxiety each and every time the airplane's floats break free of the water. Any float plane pilot understands what I'm talking about. There's a tendency for these planes to slip around just a little before taking to the air. It leaves you with a feeling of never being quite sure they're really going to fly properly once you're free.

Whatever the explanation that single moment of suspense is still always with me even after all these years. It's part of the adventure of flying that all pilots enjoy.

It's exactly the same sensation you get the moment you realize that the bull moose you have been diligently stalking is suddenly, and unbelievably, right there before you – and well within your range.

There is nothing quite so awesome as a full-grown bull moose plowing its way through the woods! Your heart stops. And a million worries flash through your mind – you might actually miss; or something – anything – is bound to happen before you can take that long-awaited shot.

That's a big part of hunting, you know, the anxiety. All the traveling to the site, the camping out, the hiking through the tundra, and the actual stalk of your prey all lead up to that one single moment when it's time to take aim. Of course, we all enjoy the many aspects of hunting, but that moment is an indescribable adrenaline rush. Even more so when it's your very first moose.

In my many years of Alaskan hunting, I have had the very good fortune to be along with four people as they took their first moose. The most memorable of these sportsmen went by the nickname of Captain Curt. He is a most likable guy who has spent most of his 30-something years in Alaska delivering the mail. He was a champion wrestler in college and participated in the Collegiate National Championship some years ago. Captain Curt is one of those people who always enjoys himself and manages to keep everyone around him in a good humor too. He is a physically strong fellow and well-suited to participate in the business of hunting and fishing, but he had never before had the opportunity to hunt moose. Since I never refuse the chance for a new adventure, when I met the captain through his uncle (who owns a cabin on the lake near mine), I agreed to take him for his first moose.

The other participant in our outing was my friend, Bob. He had been a bartender and beverage manager at the Captain Cook Hotel in Anchorage for over 20 years and had been my hunting and fishing companion for that same period. He was one of those rare people who can tell jokes for hours on end and never repeat himself.

Just to show the kind of person Bob was, I remember once he bought a very expensive Labrador retriever and hired a professional trainer to get her ready for hunting ducks. Bob entered that dog in field trials and worked and trained with her almost every day. On the opening day of duck season, Bob and I loaded the dog in my float plane and off we went.

As we dropped the first duck of our morning hunt in the lake, the dog's big moment was at hand....

Bob yelled, "Mark!"

The dog immediately spotted the duck, so Bob ordered "Fetch!"

She ran and plunged into the water all the way up to her belly – and then stopped. She looked, first at the duck, then at us, and proceeded to come straight back to shore.

Bob and that dog must have repeated this sequence at least three or four more times. Each time, as soon as the dog got belly-deep in water, back she would turn. I finally suggested to Bob that perhaps this highly-trained retriever *could not swim*.

When we got back to town I made sure all of our friends heard about the dog. For the whole next week people brought in a constant string of items to Bob's bar; things such as "water wings" for dogs, books on "How to Swim," etc., etc. Fortunately, the dog did manage to swim the next weekend (perhaps she read the book?), and Bob was a good sport and took it all in good humor.

It is difficult to find the words to describe what it's like when you first step out of your tent during a September dawn in Alaska. The air carries the fresh scent of trees and grass; the birds are waking up and chattering; and Mts. McKinley and Foraker loom up before you, their east flanks gleaming red with the first rays of the sun, their west faces white with snow. It is impossible at that moment not to be awestruck by the incredible size, utter wildness and sheer beauty of Alaska. The fall colors are everywhere – reds, yellows, greens, and so many more. The grayling are splashing in the lake. I just can't imagine a better place to be.

I was standing outside my tent drinking in all this beauty with my two friends, Bob and Captain Curt. We had finished breakfast and loaded our packs and were heading out for the first day of hunting. We had spotted two bulls the previous day only about five miles off the other end of the lake. One was a big bull, probably about 60 inches; the other was smaller, but still of good size.

Our plan was simple: try to get Captain Curt into position to take the larger bull. We decided to taxi the float plane down to that end of the lake; from there, Bob would go with Captain Curt to stalk his bull. My role would be to climb a ridge near the area where we last saw the two moose, and from my vantage point I could monitor their progress with binoculars.

Of course, as we all know, the best laid plans....

Captain Curt at the moose camp.

You can plan a stalk to such great detail – but then, somehow, it never turns out quite the way you thought. This is especially true in the wilds of Alaska, and our case was no exception.

At the other end of the lake, there was a 50-foot-wide stretch of floating tundra lining the shore. While taxiing down the lake, Bob rode the float on one side and Captain Curt on the other. Approaching the end of the lake, I killed the engine and both men walked to the front of the floats and waited as the plane worked its way to shore. I could hear Bob (the experienced hunter) as he explained to Captain Curt about "floating" tundra and how careful he would need to be as he stepped off the plane (so as not to break through to the water beneath). Captain Curt listened attentively. Upon reaching the aforementioned tundra, Bob immediately stepped off the float, broke through the tundra, and went into the ice cold water all the way up to his nose – gun, pack and all! It was several minutes before Captain Curt and I could stop howling long enough to rescue him.

This incident, of course, resulted in the first revision to our careful plan. It was now decided that Captain Curt and *I* should start out toward the area where the moose were (Plan B). Wet and cold, Bob, would make his way back to camp where he could change into dry things and then catch up with us later.

Captain Curt and I set out and stealthily approached the area where we had last spotted our quarry. It was decided that I should go up on a bald hill overlooking a cottonwood patch. Curt would work his way around the edge of the thicket, staying in the open so I would be able to signal him if I saw the moose.

When I reached the top of the hill, I had a great view. The tundra spread before me like an autumn carpet of auburn, russet, orange and green. The cottonwood and spruce trees stood out like green and yellow sentinels. As a backdrop, the Alaska Range's white snow and black rock covered the horizon to the north and west. There was also a stream running along the backside of the cottonwoods and it was full of silver salmon. I could see them lunging and splashing as they worked their way upstream. I also became immediately aware that there were several partially eaten salmon lying along the shore. That split-second of anxiety I spoke of earlier now returned.

As I watched, Captain Curt was slowly working his way around the edge of the cottonwoods. Suddenly he stopped in mid-stride. I focused the binoculars on him, but did not see a thing. Next, I searched the alders close by, but saw nothing. Captain Curt took another step. Then I saw a flash of antlers and almost instantly a second set of antlers. Both bulls were lying down in some willows just on the other side of an alder patch only about 75 feet from Captain Curt! (He told me later he heard and smelled them, but could see nothing.)

I kept hoping he would look toward me so I could signal him to move right. That way he could see around the alders and get a perfect shot when they stood up. I was holding my breath, but he never looked my way and I was relegated to the position of spectator.

Somehow, Captain Curt luckily chose to walk right straight toward those two moose. In his path was a fallen birch tree, and he stood up on the root ball in order to see over the alders.

Of course, the bulls heard him and immediately stood up. At that point, Captain Curt could only see glimpses of two sets of horns, but could not tell which was the bigger animal. All he could see was patches of horns and hide through gaps in the alders. Captain Curt said later that this was an adrenaline moment for him – even more so than winning one of his championship wrestling matches.

From my vantage point, I could see the two animals clearly. Both sets of radar-like ears pointed right at Captain Curt; the bulls were in full alert. The bigger was on Captain Curt's left. His immense rack had wide palms with three or four brow tines on each side. The spread must've been well over 60 inches.

The other bull was definitely a trophy, but still small compared to the huge fellow. They were a beautiful sight; their black and gray coats stood out in sharp contrast against the green alders and yellow willows.

As I watched, frozen, Captain Curt brought his gun up to his shoulders several times, but never shot. He later told me he just couldn't get a clear enough view. In that moment, all the years of waiting to finally get a shot at a moose went flashing though his mind. Would this be a lost opportunity just for lack of a clear shot?

The temptation was strong to just fire at any piece of visible hide, but he wouldn't know where he was really aiming and knew he might just end up wounding the animal. His adrenaline was really pumping now, but even though he was an amateur, Captain Curt kept his head and did not panic.

After about a minute (which seemed like an hour at the time) he got a clear view of a shoulder and did take his shot. I watched and waited anxiously, but both bulls bolted from the willows and took off in the direction of the lake, their great horns plowing through the thicket with seemingly no effort. There is nothing so impressive as a bull moose plowing his way through the woods, let alone two of them. It appeared that Captain Curt had missed his chance.

The bulls trotted over a small hill and were no longer in Captain Curt's view. Then they broke into the open tundra. As the big bull headed down the edge of the trees toward the lake, the other followed for about 100 yards. And then lay down. Captain Curt had his moose after all.

I walked down to the woods where a dejected Captain Curt was sitting on the birch root ball looking down forlornly. What a change when I told him the moose was down! He didn't care one bit that it was the smaller one. I informed him that we would need to get to work immediately on his moose because the bigger bull was heading right toward the lake – and would probably run into Bob as he was making his way toward us. I didn't relish having to butcher two bull moose in a single day. It was now getting late and we needed to get a move on.

Those of us who hunt have tremendous respect for the animals we pursue. I always approach a downed animal with mixed emotions. There is a certain sadness because an animal has been killed, mixed with the elation that your hunt was a success and you have a trophy and meat for another year. You also have to approach with caution because sometimes a bull will suddenly jump up just as you reach him and ruin your whole day by doing a tap dance on your chest.

As it turned out, Captain Curt's bull was 52 inches, not a bad first bull at all. He was lying on the tundra only about 100 feet from the alders. By now, the sun was just about to set and the no see'ums were out in force. We decided to gut him and prop him open to cool out. We would return the next morning with the three-wheeler to skin and quarter him.

On the walk back to camp there was no sign of Bob. By the time we got to camp, it was dark and Bob was already there. He hadn't seen the other bull, so we only had one to deal with the next day. We celebrated that night with a big meal of moose heart and a few beers and went to bed early, anticipating a big day of butchering and hauling moose meat.

The next morning we woke to another clear and pristine Alaska day. We went down to the lake and caught some grayling for breakfast and enjoyed a leisurely meal. We then loaded the three-wheeler with rope, knives, game bags and chain saw and headed out. We were feeling pretty good.

We had had a successful hunt; Captain Curt had gotten his first moose; it was a beautiful day and there were other bulls in the area. What could possibly go wrong now? It wasn't long before we found out.

When we got to the clearing where we had left Curt's moose, it was <u>GONE!</u>

Not only was the moose gone, but the gut pile, too. Upon closer examination we could clearly trace where this 1000-pound moose had been dragged. The trail proceeded about 100 feet across the tundra and into an alder thicket.

Captain Curt's moose after we uncovered its remains at the spruce tree.

At this point, the old split-second anxiety pretty much became constant. All three of us, guns ready, approached the alders. About 50 feet inside the alder patch was a small clearing where a lone spruce tree stood, and there was Captain Curt's moose. It had been wrapped around the base of the spruce and then buried, no doubt by a very large bear.

As if this weren't bad enough, we then noticed something that gave us a chill all the way down our spines. There, atop the pile of dirt covering the moose, sat a Pepsi can. Curt had left that can sitting on top of the moose the night before. It was as if the bear was warning us off.

After considerable discussion, we decided to salvage as much of the meat as possible. While two of us stood guard, the third cut the alders back with a chain saw. We then took turns digging out the moose. Most of the nose and the guts had been eaten. One hindquarter was raggedly ripped apart and was ruined, but we managed to salvage the rest of the meat.

I have to admit I have never, ever skinned and quartered a moose that fast in all my life – before or since. We briskly hauled our moose meat back to the lake and stashed it safely aboard the airplane. As I took off with our prize for the return trip to Anchorage, I couldn't quite resist flying over the alder patch one more time.

In the short time it had taken us to travel back to the lake, load the meat, and take off, the bear had reburied what was left of our moose and there he was – *lying right on top of the pile.* He was definitely one of the biggest boar grizzlies I have ever seen – and I have seen a lot of bears over the years in Alaska.

Alaskans have a variety of reasons for choosing to be here-- the beauty, the wilderness, the solitude, the people, the hunting or the fishing. But in the end, for me, it all boils down to the adventure. From the split-second of anxiety when the plane first breaks free of the water, to the major trepidation when you realize that a big boar grizzly has claimed the right to your kill.

The suspense of Captain Curt's first moose hunt sums it all up. It was an adventure we will long remember. That is what Alaska is all about.

CHUMMING FOR BEARS

A friend of mine named Raunchy Rick had an interesting bear encounter in King Salmon. Raunchy is a local radio talk show host. To say he is conservative is an understatement. He considers the John Birch Society a bunch of liberals. Besides running his mouth off from 5:30 a.m. to 9:00 a.m. on the radio five days a week, he also has a real job working construction. I filled in for Raunchy on the show one week.

Getting up at 4:30 a.m. to do the show and then going to work for the rest of the day would make anyone a little weird after a while. I am sure that is what happened to him. Raunchy is also an avid outdoorsman. He served on the regional game board for a few years. Even with all his experience, he still found himself in a real pickle one night on King Salmon Creek.

Raunchy and his pals John and Byron had made the same trip just two nights before. Same boat, same creek, same driver, same guns and the same people. But, that's where the similarity ended. The first trip didn't include dead moose, hypothermia, engine problems, sleep deprivation or a plethora of voracious brown bears at close range.

They didn't expect to see a moose. The "big moose hunt" was planned for the next day. This was a Saturday-night-just-for-the-hell-of-it trip. Oh, yes, Raunchy took his rifle, but that was just out of habit. When you spend a lot of time beating around Bush Alaska you learn to always take your gun. People who don't, pretty much qualify for wearing a badge marked "Damned Fool." He was sure he wouldn't need it, but safe is safe.

(Funny how two rounds fired from one rifle can change the ambiance of an after-work boat ride and turn a beautiful wilderness creek into a pretty spooky place, but I am getting ahead of myself.)

Raunchy was working on an environmental construction crew in King Salmon. This is a small remote town near Bristol Bay located on the Naknek River. They were cleaning and rebuilding an old Air Force dump site called South Barrel Bluff. It didn't bother them that the Bluff just happened to be next to King Salmon Creek.

This creek became their personal fishing grounds for the summer. It was full of kings, chum, pinks and silvers, not to mention rainbows, dolly varden and grayling. The creek empties into the Naknek River a short distance downstream from King Salmon. This is all low-lying ground with sparse trees but lots of brush. There are numerous moose, caribou, wolves and other critters throughout the area. The Naknek River and Naknek Lake are world famous for the fishing. Rainbows of 20 pounds are not uncommon in these waters.

Fishing slowed down by September. The bite of fall was in

the air and they wanted to go on a boat ride to enjoy the season. The plan was simple; get off work at 6:00 p.m., step into the skiff at 6:03 p.m. You can call it a skiff, but the locals referred to it as the aluminum barge. It was a 22-foot, flat-bottomed construction boat with a landing craft front end and an electric boom and winch on board. This metallic monstrosity was powered by a 460 HP V-8 engine that launched it out of the hole in just under a nano-second. It was a macho boat plus!

OK, maybe I've exaggerated a bit, but when guys talk about over-powered toys like the rocket sled, it's difficult to not want to scratch yourself, shotgun a beer and see who can belch the loudest. These guys had doubled their already overflowing shot of testosterone by packing two Ruger Super Redhawk .44 Mag, a .300 Winchester Mag, a .338 Winchester Mag and enough hunting and skinning knives to sink any lesser watercraft. They were men of the wilderness and ready for anything. Well, almost anything.

They left the dock, donned in rain-gear and hip boots, and headed down stream on the Naknek River. It was cloudy with light winds and occasional rain, but overall a nice fall day for this part of Alaska. John was the construction site superintendent; Byron and Raunchy operated heavy equipment. John and Raunchy each had valid moose tags and planned on using them the next day during the big hunt.

They hit the confluence of King Salmon Creek and the Naknek River at exactly 6:15 p.m. Raunchy knew it was 6:15 p.m. when they entered the creek because John, who was driving, turned to him and said, "Remember the time, 6:15 exactly." Raunchy remembered.

King Salmon Creek is generally only a foot in depth, with a few deeper spots when it bends. Like most creeks in the region, King Salmon Creek twists and turns like mad. Streams in this area tend to meander quite a bit due to the flat terrain. They also have low banks with spruce, alders and willows growing in profusion near the water.

The guys were on step to avoid hitting any shallow spots. You could change that to "try to" avoid hitting any shallow spots. It's tough when you're fighting a major bout of motion sickness from the tossing and turning of the boat, not unlike the motion of the "Zipper" ride at the state fair.

After an hour and 15 minutes of the nearly nauseating high-speed zigzagging, they stopped at least 20 miles upstream. The stream was narrowing down fast.

They decided (since most of the creek now was not as wide as the boat was long) that it was probably a good time to turn around. They found a wide spot and changed direction. Heading back seemed to be a bit more relaxing, mainly, I think, because they had somewhat of a recollection of where the sweepers (overhanging trees) and boat-sinking rocks were because they had run into and bounced off of every single one on the way up. These guys are not quick studies in safety or survival.

Traveling downstream always feels a bit slower than traveling upstream, because the water is flowing in the same direction you are. After traveling about five minutes downstream, they began to enter a bend in the creek and Byron began pointing dramatically to the right.

Three moose climbed majestically out of the water. As the boat came to rest against the far shore, Raunchy dove for his rifle and pulled it from the case as the three moose had all stopped and were just staring at our guys. I'm sure the moose were confused on just what this gargantuan silver aquatic animal was. Raunchy raised his .338 Mag. It was a long shot, maybe as far as 40 feet. In the 3x9 Leupold, set on 3x, he found the biggest set of antlers, set the cross hairs and squeezed the trigger. BOOM!! The 44-inch bull with three brow tines on the left and four on the right goes down.

Instinctively, he jacked another 250-grain slug into the chamber as he lowered the rifle from his shoulder. As he looked toward the downed bull, there was one of his buddies standing broadside! Raunchy glanced at John. He was fumbling around the bottom of the boat for his rifle. Raunchy yelled "here" as he tossed his Winchester in his direction. John caught it and drew it to his shoulder in one fluid motion. BOOM!! His 32-inch bull went down just as the third animal decided to show them its heels. Two shots, two downed moose, not bad for a joyride. Out of the boat they climbed to finish them off with matching .44s. They paused for a couple of choice pictures then gutted the animals and prepared them for transport.

They had shot the animals in a big, horseshoe bend and

they had fallen across the frog (the inside of the horseshoe) only 20 feet from the water. What great luck! They didn't have to haul them out on their backs. John moved the boat into position while Byron lowered the bow of the boat. Using the boom and winch they yarded-em into the boat whole. Being a construction stiff has some advantages. By 8:30 they had both bulls gutted and aboard. Things could not be going better. In less than two hours they had two moose down and in the boat and had not had to lift anything heavy. This is unheard of in moose hunting. Things were going too well.

They started downstream totally convinced that they were absolutely, unequivocally the greatest hunters that ever graced the face of the earth, quite possibly the universe. They were "bad" and they knew it. Oddly enough they didn't feel as confidently skilled as sailors, because now with an extra 2,000 pounds of weight, they couldn't get the boat up on step. The 460 HP V-8 super-engine was not as macho as they had believed. Just maybe, neither were they.

About five minutes later they had clogged the motor jet intake with grass. First they tried reverse to blow it out. Then they tried the scrape method, but it did no good. Finally, they shut the engine off to stop the suction. John reached down and pulled out enough grass to keep an entire herd of Angus beef cows happy.

Now with the jet-intake cleared of any and all obstruction, they were ready to cruise back to camp to claim their rightful title as Heroes! Such would not be the case, however, as John tried to start the engine. NOTHING. Apparently, when they used the winch and boom, it drained the battery. (I said these guys were "bad," not smart.) So much for cruising back to camp, they were obviously in for a long night, though none of them knew just how long or exciting it was to be.

It was now 9:15 p.m., Raunchy knew it was exactly 9:15 because John looked at his watch and said, "We're dead in the water at 9:15. Remember the time." Raunchy remembered.

Boats draw a lot more water drifting than when they're traveling at a high rate of speed, so they figured they stood a much better chance of actually floating out of there if they stayed in the channel. Byron grabbed a two-by-four and took up position on the bow and John placed himself at the stern.

For awhile, Raunchy fancied them to be gondoliers as he

floated along the waterways of Venice, sitting on the neck of a moose. Of course, never having been to Venice or in a gondola, he had no idea what he was dreaming about.

The thoughts of Venice quickly dissipated as darkness enveloped them at 9:30. Raunchy thought it was about 10:10 p.m. when the first brown bear began walking the shore next to them. John was in no mood to note the time.

I'm sure that to the bear and all his sharp-fanged, long-clawed carnivorous cousins that gave a social call to the boat that night, the boat seemed like a floating all-you-can-eat buffet with two entrees: moose and long pig.

Sometimes Raunchy and the guys could actually smell the bears, with the stench of dead, rotten, carrion. Sometimes they could see their beady little red eyes looking at them from the bank. Sometimes they could hear the grass rustling four feet away, as something large was moving through it, shadowing their every turn. There were times when there were bears walking with them on both sides of the creek.

You have to experience 1,000-pound brown bears walking nearby in the dark and in almost complete silence to fully appreciate just how tense these guys were at this time. To say things were a little tense would be like saying a 700 Nitro Express kicks a little. Nobody was breathing more than once a minute. The only sound was the gentle pad of bear feet on the soft ground and the occasional sound of a bear licking his lips in anticipation of a good meal.

I'd really like to emphasize the word "creek." It is not an ocean, lake, river or even small stream. It is a creek. Webster defines creek as follows: "creek" \ krek, krik\ *noun* (1) trickle of water, barely a trickle, (2) not enough damn water to keep a hungry brown bear from chewing your ass off." (2) is only in the Alaska version of Webster's.

At one point, Raunchy was in the front of the boat with Byron and they saw something black moving in the creek about 60 yards downstream. Raunchy told John, who was in the stern, to look, too. John had a hard time seeing it until "Yogi" turned to look at them. That's when his eyes gathered enough light to shine red, like blood.

They all felt a chill run down their backs. They drifted directly at him until they were about 20 yards away when he ran out of the water and into the bushes. The guys let out their breath in unison.

The fact is if a bear wanted to walk to the boat, he'd need to take just two steps from shore. He probably wouldn't get wet above the knees. The creek was just not that deep, but they were up it without a paddle, only two-by-fours! The situation could have been more precarious, but I don't see how.

Did I mention the boat was sinking, too? At the rear of the boat, slightly above the waterline, was a scupper on either side. (A scupper is a hole in the freeboard that is usually just above the water level so that water can flow off the deck.) With a ton of fresh raw meat on board these scuppers were now below the waterline, letting water in the boat. Since John and Byron were busy with their navigation and bear-control responsibilities, Raunchy took it upon himself to try to deal with the growing aquifer in the bottom of the boat. He plugged the holes as best as he could and began bailing with a bucket. While he couldn't plug the holes fully, it did seem to make it possible for him to stay a bit ahead of the incoming water.

As he bailed he noticed the water that was coming in was washing onto the fresh moose carcasses. As he poured bucket load after bucket load back into the creek, he realized this water was black with blood and let off *eau de moose*, a bear's favorite scent. It dawned on him that they were now chumming for brownies. The moose blood was flowing downstream to entice more bears to the creek, so they could greet the boat as it bounced along with the buffet on board. Funny how minutes seem like hours when you're drifting through the savage wilderness in absolute blackness followed by ravenous bruins of mammoth proportions.

The sweepers and brush were part of the unexpected fun too. I say unexpected because during the day, or even in periods of lower light, you can see them coming. But for these guys, as the darkness intensified, they had become something of a Russian roulette game when they sat anywhere near the side rail. At one point John quickly bowed his head toward Raunchy. Raunchy's eldest son was taking karate, so he saw it as a sign of respect. He began to smile until he realized John had bowed to escape a total facial reconstruction by the tree that apparently just barely missed Raunchy's head. There are some advantages of being only 5'10". It also helps to have a really hard head. Raunchy covers both of these bases very well.

A sweeper decided to attach itself to the port side where it dragged along with them for about an hour. They came to terms with it being there by convincing themselves that they might need the firewood. Without this justification they would have had to try to dislodge the sweeper while other sweepers were trying to dislodge them. The creek is fully lined with trees and logs are everywhere. Just ask any one of the hundreds of thousands of beavers who make this aqueduct their home.

Oh yeah, the beavers! Did they ever add a bit of color to the trip! Let me explain a cute little personality trait beavers have, for those of you who don't spend a lot of time around them. When a beaver is in the water (which is most of the time) and they get alarmed, they slap the water with their wide, flat tail and dive. While this slap is very interesting and even fun for most humans to hear during the day when the sun is shining and the birds are singing, it's more like the blast of a shotgun for drifters on a stream in dead silence late at night in the wilderness and in the company of several brown bears.

Couple the piercing decibels shattering the stillness with the anxiety built up from all the big, old, fat, hairy grizzly bears stalking them down the stream and I think you can see the entertainment value of a few dozen beavers. Let it suffice to say more than one of the rodents were put off by their presence and blasted them with their particular brand of shotgun, and it made for a less than enjoyable experience. In fact, though they didn't check, Byron, who was always in the front of the boat and therefore closest to the "slap," probably was in dire need of new underwear. As the night wore on he became more and more stressed. Raunchy and John were just verging on total panic. Other than that, things were going as well as could be expected under the circumstances.

It is doubtful that this creek could be drifted without running aground at least once. They did the best they could to exceed that and Raunchy was proud to say they were successful. They bounced off at least 10 rocks, high-centered on one for about 20 minutes, and ran up on gravel bars three times. All this in the company of several brown bears who planned to dine out that evening and invite the guys and the moose to the meal.

Raunchy thought it was about 12:30 a.m. when they were pushing the boat off a gravel bar and finally, after a good half-hour of rocking, the front end he was pulling began to swing into deeper water.

With his keen observational skills, he recognized that the cold sensation slowly climbing his leg was actually water rising inside his hip-waders. He took this as a sign to leap into the now-freed boat.

As he jumped, his rain gear snagged on a wing nut, leaving him hanging over the side, clutching the side rail like a desperate man who is about to be swept under a dead boat floating down a wilderness creek in the middle of Alaska. This, of course, pretty much describes his situation. Raunchy's partners had presence of mind enough to grab him and pull his wet body into the boat. They didn't want to do the lengthy report on what happened to him. It was easier to just save him.

Raunchy could have been fighting hypothermia for the rest of the trip but thanks to the amount of water that had entered the boat in the last 40 minutes, he had plenty of bailing exercise ahead to keep warm and keep the bears focused.

They finally returned to their job site at 2:15 a.m. Raunchy knew the exact time for the same reason as before. When John said it, Raunchy remembered. By this time the bears had given up and wandered away. Raunchy hopped out of the boat as the other two tied it off. Up on top of the bluff was the Kobelco excavator he had been operating most of the summer. He walked it down the slope until it was next to the creek and lowered the bucket down to the boat. The guys tied the moose to it and he lifted both of them out of the boat. They let them hang with the bottoms of their hooves about 10 feet off the ground so the bears couldn't use them as a piñata. The only things that had gone right on this outing were the ease of dealing with the moose and keeping track of time.

It was 4 a.m. before they finished their celebratory beverage, a beer, and headed off to la-la-land to dream something boring and mundane.